HER FATHER'S EYES

A novel

*Danielle —
Your beautiful
in your Father's
Eyes!
Kathleen
Kurlin
Ps: 37-4*

By

KATHLEEN KURLIN

xulon PRESS

ACKNOWLEDGMENTS

I'd be remiss if I didn't acknowledge first and foremost, my gratitude to my Lord and Savior for giving me words to say even when I felt like I had nothing to say. I am so blessed to have a relationship with my Lord Jesus and truly appreciate the gift of creativity in spite of the fact there are times when there is no explanation for why I think the way I think, other than because that's simply the way God made me.

Thank you to my husband, Robert, who's the best person I've ever known, who by his own admission is not a reader, but because he loves me, read every word of this novel and declared, "It's good. Really, really good!"

Thank you to my children, Lindsay, Jordan and Kelsey, who I love beyond reason, who gave me my space when I needed it and who ate their fair share of peanut butter sandwiches and microwave dinners so I could lock myself away in the solitude of my office to work.

Thank you to my grandson, Gage, whose very presence in my life adds joy and happiness beyond compare. I'm so glad you came into our lives. I am grateful for the pleasure of loving you so thoroughly. You have given me balance when I felt completely off kilter.

A HUGE thank you to my gal pals in my Tuesday morning writer's group who read and re-read, critiqued, commented, suggested and nagged me month after month to write the best story possible. Thank you to Elizabeth Blake, Ana Stine, Marsha Cleaveland,

Glynnis Whitwer, Michele Al-Bayati and Nola Kuester. You're all amazing women, equally gifted and the best support system a girl could hope for.

And of course – to my very own, "Gertrude," Debbie Clark who knows me better than most and loves me even though I'm a bit of an emotional retard.

And thank you to my many friends along the way who read this work of fiction (I hope you ALL know who you are) and offered feedback and praise, encouragement and support and occasionally sugarcoated your comments in order to save my feelings. I appreciate you all!

This book is dedicated in loving memory to my parents,
Jerry and Lee who have both passed on — who are gone
but never forgotten.
I miss you and love you so much more than I ever
shared with you.
If life had "mulligans" I'd be sure to tell you
Exactly how much you were loved!

PROLOGUE

Present Day

"Hurry! We're losing her! Get outta the way!" The chief resident in charge grabbed the paddles shoving the intern aside. The young man stumbled but gave the doctor a wide berth.

"Starting compressions. Charge paddles to 200! Clear!"

The trained medical personnel functioned like a well-oiled machine. All were busy with specific life-saving tasks in the over-crowded emergency room. In spite of their tireless efforts, the machine's monotone bleeps remained unchanged. All eyes darted back and forth from the doctor to the woman's lifeless body.

* * * * *

"Lord, is that really necessary? She's so young. She just had a birthday a few weeks ago. A 43-year-old woman doesn't usually have heart problems. It's such a drastic maneuver. Don't you think the bump on the head and the sucker jammed in her throat is enough?"

"Clearly not. This is all absolutely necessary, Grace. It's going to take more than a little mishap and a bump on the head to get her attention. I've been trying for so long to get through to her. She won't heed my words. She won't let me have control of this. She's a mature woman and it's past time for her to grow up. I've been patient with her far too long. Enough is enough!"

"But, Lord ... I'm sure she wasn't serious when she uttered those words. You know how people are. Sometimes they just blurt things out without thinking before they speak. It was just emotional desperation. And it means nothing. You created them to be emotional creatures."

"I know, Grace. But I have already given her so much, yet she remains unchanged in this area. She refuses to let me help her. No. This is the ONLY way she'll ever learn to trust me totally and completely. She needs to know that the power of the tongue contains life ... and death."

"All right, Lord ... if you're sure. I trust you. I just hope that she does, as well."

"We shall see, Grace. We shall see."

* * * * *

ONE

"For we must all stand before Christ to be judged.
We will receive whatever we each deserve for
the good or evil we have done in our bodies."
2 Corinthians 5:10 (NLT)

"That's not fair! You *never* let me do anything! Why don't you ever want me to have any fun? Sometimes I HATE living here!"

Housewife, Kitty O'Connell watched her daughter retreat in a huff — a whirlwind of angry teenage angst and hip-hugging tight denim.

"Yeah, well guess what? Sometimes I hate living here too!" Kitty countered out of breath. She was instantly awash in guilt as her mind turned to thoughts of desertion. Oh, how easy and tempting it would be to just get in the car and drive away from all these pressures. Sometimes being a mother was the hardest job in the world.

The slam of the front door a few seconds later punctuated her daughter's departure — the rattle of the windowpanes signaled the *all clear*.

"Dear Lord, I'm getting too freaking old for this! Forgive me for thinking about running away, but oh my gosh, that child makes me so crazy I can't think straight!" she complained to the empty room.

She stopped the treadmill resting her feet on the side panels to catch her breath. Grabbing a towel she wiped her face and then draped it over the back of her neck. Pulling the ends back and forth, she kneaded her tight muscles. Rolling her stiff neck from side to side, she reached towards the window to open the wooden blinds. Dust motes danced in the early morning rays casting prisms of color on the plush carpet. She dashed away the sweat dangling from her perfectly manicured eyebrow. Pausing to bury her face in the downy softness of the terrycloth, the urge to scream overwhelmed her. It wasn't even eight o'clock yet and already she'd fought with half the household.

She forced herself to resume her run. Nothing killed a workout more than a shouting match. Ten minutes of easy jogging and Kitty felt her tensions ease. Somehow the combination of sweat and steady breathing calmed her, erasing most of her earlier frustrations. Exercise was like that for her — a magic elixir.

The entire neighborhood envied her state-of-the-art home gym, as well they should. It was nothing short of spectacular. This room was fashioned for a tough endorphin seeking workout junkie. Kitty's obsession to combat the natural aging progression consumed her worse than any addiction to drugs ever could.

The latest in exercise technology was strategically scattered throughout the large space. A monstrous weight machine monopolized one whole corner of the room. A LifeCycle and elliptical machine stood at attention like twin soldiers in another corner; while a brand new top-of-the-line treadmill dominated yet another.

The treadmill, a birthday gift last month from her husband, Luke, replaced its predecessor, a recent disastrous equipment casualty. Cause of death — overuse. Kitty's reputation as a serial killer of exercise apparatus was the stuff legendary neighborhood folklore was made of.

Here in this room, Kitty reigned as the queen of her domain and all she surveyed. Inspecting her kingdom from atop her fast moving perch Kitty caught a good whiff of body odor being blown back in her face. She could dress it up and make it look nice, but it was still a workout room, and no amount of potpourri could disguise the smell of sweat when she was in the middle of her daily routine. This room was her sanctuary — her holy ground, and no one dared enter without permission. Although Kitty suspected the smell was reason enough to keep most at arms length beyond the circle of safety.

Kitty's 16-year-old son, Matthew knocked timidly on the door-frame and poked his head in. "Hey, Mom ..." the shaggy haired, lanky teen stopped mid-sentence and dramatically grabbed his nose. "Eeeww, gross! It smells worse in here than the boy's locker room after a football game in the mud with wet dogs! I need to ask you something but the smell is nasty. I need smelling salts – or a haz-mat suit."

Her son, the wise cracker. Parenting him proved to be extremely frustrating at times. How does one deal with a stand-up comedian in training?

"Thanks, Bud!" Kitty smirked at him. "I'm almost done. Whaddya want, mister? It's late. What're you still doing here?" Kitty grabbed her water bottle and took a swig, wiping her mouth with the back of her hand when she finished.

He covered his mouth and nose with both hands and made a tiny opening to talk through. "Two words, Mom. P.U.! The stink's so bad I think my eyeballs have been fried. I forgot what I came in here for."

Kitty gave him *the look*. Matthew appeared to catch the meaning immediately. He removed his hands and grinned his endearing smile and turned on the charm that he'd inherited from his father.

"I'm leaving in a couple of minutes. Did you forget that I didn't have first hour this morning?" Kitty nodded the affirmative in sudden remembrance. "Can I have $5.00 for lunch today, please? A bunch of us are gonna *walk* to the pizza place. Hint. Hint. The operative word being *w-a-l-k*. Gee, imagine if I only had a car to drive myself there then you wouldn't have to worry about me ending up as pedestrian road kill somewhere."

Kitty rolled her eyes, ignoring his gibe.

A fidgeter by nature, Matthew took a step closer and grabbed a handrail. He bounced up and down on his heels mimicking his mother's jogging motion. Kitty tried to be irritated, but with her only son, it was impossible. He was so darn cute, she simply laughed. Much to his credit, Matthew always seemed to know exactly how far he could go with her before she got angry. He made a couple of silly faces at her hoping to make her smile. It took a minute, but she gave in and returned his smile

"What happened to the money I gave you yesterday?"

"I dunno. I bought breath mints and junk and stuff at the book-store, I think."

"Junk and stuff?"

Matthew shrugged.

"I told you yesterday I was low on cash. I didn't make it to the bank yet. Did you check with your Dad?" Her fiercely swinging arms grew tired and she grabbed a handrail on either side for support.

"Can't. He left already."

Kitty's brow creased in concern. In all their years together Luke had never left the house without telling her he loved her and a good-bye kiss. Their morning argument must have upset him more than she realized. Distracted with uneasiness, she dismissed Matthew. "I think there's some cash in the side pocket of my purse. Help your-self, but don't take it all, please."

He stopped before he cleared the door and grabbed the doorjamb for a parting, "luv ya, Mom."

Her irritation momentarily forgotten, her heart swelled with the knowledge that Matthew wasn't too old for sentiment.

Within seconds worry snuck back up on her as she thought back to her earlier fight with Luke. So deep were her thoughts, they distracted her rhythm. She frowned, chewing on her bottom lip. Instinct told her she shouldn't have yelled at Luke this morning, but once she'd crossed the line — the argument momentum had sucked her in like a giant Hoover sucking baseboards.

* * * * *

"Good Lord, why are you so freaking stubborn on this issue, Luke? She's our daughter and she wants to move back home! She needs our help for gosh sakes!"

"She hasn't learned anything yet, Kitty! She's pregnant and still shacking up with that loser boyfriend of hers. He's leading her straight to Hell! How is God going to teach her anything if we step in and fix all her problems for her? How do we explain that to the other two children we have living here? How do we justify their sister's inappropriate behavior?"

"What about forgiveness, Luke? Why are you being so self-righteous! She's only 19! Maybe God's not trying to teach her anything this time. Maybe she's just needed time to grow up. You're confusing God with life! God doesn't have to fix everything!"

* * * * *

Even though she was a head shorter, the urge to poke her towering husband in the chest tempted to the point of distraction. She probably shouldn't have poked him like that. He really hated that. That's probably what made him leave the house so angry – well that, and the verbal lambasting she'd given him after the finger poking. There were times when marriage was way too much work. Now she'd have to apologize to him. The idea of giving in first made her nauseous. She grabbed the remote for the CD changer and cranked up the music. A healthy dose of classic rock-n-roll would take her mind off Luke. She'd deal with him later.

Running to keep time to the fast tempo, she studied her reflection in the floor-to-ceiling mirrors facing her. The words *plain Jane* and *mousy freckled frump* were just a few of the words that came to mind as she stared at herself. Shaking her head in disgust, Kitty tried not to zero in on the cellulite on her thighs, but her eyes automatically traveled downward. The jiggle of that stubborn extra ten pounds of body fat hypnotized her causing her gait to hitch slightly off-step. Wishing for longer legs on her barely average frame proved to be an exercise in futility, but one she practiced with regularity.

Seeing herself as others saw her proved nigh too impossible. She was incapable of accepting a compliment no matter how cleverly it was disguised. She could easily pass for 10 years her junior and her husband told her daily she was the most beautiful woman alive. But still, she was powerless against the low self-esteem battle raging within her. She pushed herself to workout harder to tighten her glutes and achieve those unrealistic buns of steel as seen on T.V. She rationalized that if she looked perfect on the outside, eventually – maybe she'd feel perfect on the inside. But then that was another whole issue altogether, too complicated to even think about.

Turning her face from side-to-side she examined her profile. The longer she looked at it, the more depressed she got. Her face was anything but perfect. The tiny crows feet were a daily reminder that she wasn't a young girl anymore. At 43, who was she kidding? As if the crows' feet and the cellulite weren't bad enough, the morning sunlight streaming through the window bounced off a gray hair playing peek-a-boo in the thick knot of waves atop her head reminding her she needed a salon appointment. The race against Father Time and the endless pursuit of beauty leaned toward exhausting, not to mention, pricey.

Stealing another drink of water, she swished the icy coldness in her parched mouth dislodging something from her back molar. Kitty tested it with her tongue, grimacing at the taste. It didn't resemble anything from her meager boring breakfast. Then she remembered her walnut brownie meltdown *after* breakfast. The brownie binge translated to at least an extra mile on the treadmill. Kitty exhaled her self-loathing.

Wiping her sweaty brow once more, she tossed the damp towel on the window ledge. Swinging her arms down by her side, the crinkle of a candy wrapper in her pocket distracted her. Plunging her hand in the pocket of her spandex leggings, she pulled out a sour apple lollipop. The superhero sucker had her name written all over it.

"Ah ... what the heck. I'm already walking an extra brownie mile, might as well add in the stupid sucker," she grumbled unwrapping the candy.

Being a quintessential multi-tasker, Kitty glanced at her open notebook on the shelf next to the treadmill. It was open to "Prayer Requests." Combining workouts with prayer time effectively killed two birds with one stone. Plus dwelling on the needs of others distracted her from the physical pain of exercise.

Good Lord. Where should I start, she thought. *I'm sure Luke would have me pray to be a more submissive wife. Yeah! Like that's gonna happen! How about if you help Luke not to be so stubborn and completely pigheaded!* Her throat constricted nearly choking her as she remembered her earlier debate with her husband. She took a long pull on her water bottle forcing the knot of emotion to slide down her throat where it immediately took up lodging in her stomach instead.

The annoying trill of the phone startled her from her reverie. She reached for the cordless phone and pressed the mute button on the stereo, silencing the noise. Kitty heard the unmistakable voice of her best friend funneling through the wires alerting her to the likelihood that Dani had her on the speakerphone. The clattering of a keyboard confirmed Kitty's suspicions. Not only was she on speaker, but Dani herself was multi-tasking.

"Hey, Gladys, it's me, Gertrude. Whatcha doin?"

Gertrude, a.k.a. Dani Clarkson and Kitty's best friend for 30 years, always spoke with such a slow easy drawl; most would suspect she had absolutely nothing else to do. The truth was completely opposite. Dani barely had two minutes to call her own since she and her husband of 16 years (her second) had started a small business two years ago.

Kitty and Dani met while in junior high school and had vowed life long friendship and devotion to one another no matter where their lives took them. With a certainty that only comes from youth and immaturity, they mapped out their lives and careers leaving little or no wiggle room for reality. Positive they would remain friends until they were 90, they decided they needed appropriate "old lady" names while they were still young. Their old lady names of Gertrude and Gladys became their secret code names in school so no one else would know whom they were talking about when they passed notes in class. For the past 30 years they still referred to one another by their old lady names rather than their given names. Even their children and husbands had trouble remembering which one was Gertrude and which one was Gladys.

"The usual. I'm in the middle of my morning workout," Kitty answered. "I've got about 15 more minutes to go or another mile; whichever comes first." Kitty shifted the lollipop in her mouth she'd been nursing for the last few minutes making conversation easier.

As expected, Dani responded with encouragement. They were each other's strongest supporter when it came to their never-ending pursuit of weight loss and the "perfect body." As Mother Nature and Mr. Gravity took over, however, the perfect body was becoming more elusive to both women. The realization that their 25-year high school reunion was nearly upon them had driven them both to unrelenting exercise routines and stringent diet restrictions.

Dani responded with her usual chipper voice, "Well, you go, girl. You're looking better than ever. No one would ever believe that you were about to become a grandmother. I'll bet when we go to the reunion people are gonna freak cause you haven't changed a bit."

Wanting desperately to believe her friend's encouraging words, Kitty increased her speed one more degree. "I don't know, Gertrude. Some days it feels like I'm never going to get there. I've been chasing this last 10 pounds for so long. Three pregnancies and my passion for pasta have wreaked havoc on my thighs. I think after the reunion, I'm going to quit worrying about it and eat whatever I want and get as big as a house. I'm sick of always obsessing about my weight. My legs are always going to look like tree stumps. I can thank my daddy for these charging rhino thighs. No matter how hard I try, I can't seem to change the way my body looks. Some days it doesn't seem worth all this trouble."

The click, click, clicking noise of Dani's sculptured synthetic nails beat out a steady staccato rhythm on her computer keyboard. "Trust me, sweetie ... after $5,000.00 worth of lipo, your thighs look better than a 20-year-olds. And you know you'd be miserable if you let yourself go and porked up. You're an exercise junkie and you won't allow yourself to give up. That's not you and we both know it. What's with the little pity party this morning, anyway?" Dani stopped typing and Kitty could hear the click of the phone as she took her off the speakerphone and picked up the receiver. "What's up, Gladys? Why so blue this morning?"

Kitty grabbed the bottom of her U.C.L.A. tee shirt and wiped the sweat from her forehead. "Aaahhhh, I wish I knew. Just woke up on the wrong side of the bed, I guess. Maybe it's P.M.S. I don't know."

Kitty couldn't see her on the other end of the phone, but guessed that Dani was sitting at her desk either doodling on a pad of paper, or twirling the ends of her shoulder length brown hair around her finger. "P.M.S. *and* ...? Spill it. What else is up?"

Kitty exhaled loudly. "Stop it! I hate it when you get like this, Miss Know-Everything." Kitty laughed in spite of her frustration. "Well, if you must know … I had a big fight with Luke last night and then again before he left this morning. And then, as if that wasn't bad enough, when I weighed myself this morning my weight was up a pound-and-a-half, so I finished breakfast with a brownie ball chaser. Luke was so angry when he left for work he didn't even kiss me good-bye or tell me he loved me. And he's *never* done that before. So, rather than finish the entire pan of brownies like I wanted to, I'm in here running my big buffalo butt off."

Dani snorted in laughter. "Kitty, Kitty, Kitty. What am I going to do with you? We'll get back to all that other stuff in a minute. But first, will you *please* stop beating yourself up! You look fine. You look better than fine, and you don't have a buffalo butt! Why can't you accept the fact that you're a beautiful woman and stop talking so negatively about yourself? I positively HATE it when you do that!"

"You know … bad habit. Old dog … new tricks. That sort of thing. Some things are just hard to change. I'll work on it. I'll feel better once I finish my workout and go cry in the shower. Maybe I'll yell at God for a while. Sometimes I think God's mad at me and he's punishing me."

"Why in the world would you think that?"

"Cause … Oh, never mind. I'm just frustrated in general, that's all. I'm probably more upset about this stupid fight with Luke than anything. I can't stand it when we fight." Kitty stepped on the side rails of the treadmill to fix the wedgie that was working its way to an uncomfortable level.

"You two hardly ever fight. You have the sweetest husband in the whole world. It must have been a doozie if he left for work angry with you. Wanna tell me about it or should I mind my own business?"

In all their years as friends, Kitty and Dani had one hard and fast rule they lived by. They never took sides when it came to marital discord. They vowed total neutrality and offered only support and encouragement. They were never allowed to voice negative comments about each other's spouse. Since both Kitty and Dani were now on their second marriages, that rule applied to previous spouses as well.

"We're having some major disagreements over the kids. We're butting heads over issues with all three of them right now."

"Whew! All three at once? It kinda makes me glad I only have two kids. One less child to fight over." Dani laughed hoping to ease her friend's tension. "So give me the *Reader's Digest* condensed version."

"Well, for starters, Luke thinks we should let Matthew get his drivers license. I say, no way — Matty's not ready. He barely turned 16. You've heard all the statistics about teenage drivers. What if something happened to him? I'd end up resenting Luke and blame him if Matthew got hurt in an accident."

"Yikes!" Dani said.

"There was a bunch of other stuff about Matthew's level of responsibility, and then that conversation flowed right into the ongoing battle about cell phones for the kids. You know the one?"

"Yep. Been there, done that." Dani answered.

"Somehow, that snowballed into our disagreement over letting Sarah wear make-up to school because he thinks she's too young. I say, she's a freshman, so it's okay."

"Ouch! I hear you on that one. We're having the same argument with Tiffany and she's a year younger."

"And of course we touched on the whole boyfriend issue. Can she have one, or not?"

"Hey, when you solve that one let me know so I'll know what to do about Tiffany." Dani said.

"Hah! I don't think Luke and I will ever agree on that one! And lastly ... and this is the biggie. He wants to continue administering that tough love stuff to Rebecca. He refuses to let her move back home with us, even though she's hinted she's ready. Luke is adamant about not wanting her to marry her boyfriend, even though he hates that she's living *in sin* with him. He won't let her come home until she breaks up with the guy. He doesn't want this guy to be any part of Rebecca's life or the baby once it's born. He thinks the guy is a total loser and he'll ruin Rebecca's life." Her walking pace increased as her agitation mounted.

"Well, Luke's right on the money with that one, Kitty. The guy *is* a loser. We *all* agree on that. He's 29 years old and still lives at home with his parents and spends all day playing video games.

"I know. It's just that it's so humiliating to go to church every week and have everyone asking questions about Rebecca and how much longer until the baby is born and stuff. I'm so embarrassed that she's pregnant and not married."

"She may have made a mistake by getting pregnant," Dani popped her gum annoyingly as she talked, "but, isn't it better that she have the baby and raise it on her own, rather than making an even bigger mistake by marrying that deadbeat? Two wrongs don't make a right, you know?"

"I know. I know. That's exactly what Luke said. I just hate being so embarrassed by the situation."

"So, you're more worried about what people at church think of you, rather than what's best for Rebecca and this baby. Is that right?" Dani drilled her. "You know, she could have had an abortion like the loser boyfriend begged her to do. How would that have made you feel?"

"Okay, Okay. I get it. You're as bad as Luke, Smarty Pants." Kitty's pace had increased so severely that she was gasping for air between sentences. "Enough of my problems, already. What did you call me for, anyway?" Kitty asked.

"Oh, yeah. I almost forgot. I won't keep you long. I'm going to email you this new diet I found on the Internet. It's very restrictive but it lets you take one day a week off. This girl in my aerobics class tried it and says she's already lost six pounds in 10 days. It sounds promising."

Kitty shifted her thought process at the same time she shifted the phone to her other ear cradling the receiver more comfortably under her chin. "That sounds somewhat encouraging. But, just how *restrictive* are those other six days?"

Dani, who chewed gum non-stop to stave off hunger pains, popped a bubble loudly. "It's pretty strict. Mostly tuna, chicken and salads, plain. No dressing. No red meat. No fruit, except grapefruit. Oh yeah, no breads or dairy, of course."

"Of course," Kitty interjected sarcastically. "Isn't no bread or dairy one of the Ten Commandments of dieting?"

"Well, duh," Dani snorted.

"You know me ... always looking for the next greatest diet out there. Send it on to me." Kitty sucked noisily on her lollipop, careful not to drool down her chin.

Dani's voice perked up. "What's that noise? What're you eating?"

Kitty adjusted the phone and the sucker once more as she grabbed for a handrail. She slowed her speed to allow her to converse more naturally. "Well, if you must know, I'm sucking on a superhero sucker. Sarah had a party at school yesterday and brought home a goodie bag. I did my best to stay out of it all night. But then this morning when I was in the kitchen, this sucker somehow found its way into my pocket, and then finally to my mouth."

"Gladys ..." Dani drew out the name and managed to make it sound like a disciplinary warning.

"Aw, c'mon. It's just a sucker! At least I didn't take the chocolate Kisses like I really wanted. And besides, I'm doing an extra ten minutes to make up for it. How much can just one little sucker hurt?"

"Ah, ah, ah! Remember our goal! Twenty pounds by reunion time," Dani reprimanded. Dani had always been the stronger of the two when it came to positive attitudes and staying on task. "You know it's that line of thinking that has kept you from losing those last few pounds. Not to mention, what was it you said you had this morning? I think you called it a *brownie chaser*. It's always something with you. You can't let suckers and brownie balls throw you off course. What's our scripture for the duration of these diets to see us through to the reunion?"

Kitty rolled her eyes and sing-songed her response, *"Set a guard over my mouth, O Lord; keep watch over the door of my lips."*

Dani oozed praise through the airwaves, "Good girl. Now let's not forget that, shall we?"

"Oh right! Like you're one to talk. How about your parent's anniversary party last week with the all-you-can-eat barbecue buffet and Died-and-Gone-to-Heaven chocolate cake? And did you forget about the church potluck you had - when was that? Oh yeah ... two days ago? Where was your focus and your scripture verse when you were snorfing down chocolate cake and pigs in a blanket then, *Missy*?" Kitty enunciated carefully to drive her point home.

They both laughed good naturedly, knowing intimately each other's weaknesses when it came to food.

"Okay, okay, you got me! But I can't help it. I'm a sap when it comes to those little weenie wrapped thingies. And these were no ordinary weenie wrapped thingies. They had sausage links in them. Absolutely irresistible! Now seriously, Gladys. You made me promise that I would ride you like a dog with a bone when it came to this diet. You said you were going to be a perfect size 8 by reunion time."

"I know, I know. I'm weak. What can I say? Actually, I think what I really said is that I am going to lose this last 10 pounds if it kills me! And by God – I am!"

Unaware that her shoelace had come untied, Kitty barely finished her sentence when she stepped on the errant lace. She tripped; landing so hard on the fast-moving belt the impact jarred the phone from her hand. It flew across the room, spinning a couple of times, but never disconnecting.

Sixty miles away, Dani listened frantically to the commotion on the other end of the line. Unable to see what was happening to her friend, the loud noises were a sure sign something was terribly wrong.

Dani screamed, "Gladys! Oh my God! Kitty! What's happening? Talk to me!"

The speed of the treadmill belt threw Kitty backwards where she sprawled in a rather unladylike fashion, arms and legs akimbo. The force slammed her head on a 10-lb. dumbbell on the weight rack behind her. Resembling something from a Three Stooges movie, she buckled; bouncing with such force she fell face down jamming the superhero sucker in the back of her throat. She lay helpless, choking and unconscious on the floor while the still operating treadmill wore a rough burned spot on her forehead.

Dani panicked realizing she couldn't call for help on her phone since she and Kitty were still connected.

"KITTY!" She screamed louder with still no response. Hysteria overwhelmed Dani. Her limbs shook with fear. She thought she was going to throw up not knowing what was happening to Kitty or how to help her.

"My God! My God! I need my cell phone! Where's my cell phone?" Dani yelled for her husband or children. No one answered her. "What a time for everyone to be gone!" She raced to the kitchen and found her purse. She upended everything on the floor in a scattered mess. Her belongings rolled around the tiled floor. Dani dropped to her knees shoving items all about, but couldn't locate the one thing she needed.

"OH MY GOD! IT'S NOT HERE, IT'S NOT HERE! WHERE'S MY CELL PHONE? WHO BORROWED MY PHONE AND DIDN'T PUT IT BACK!" Tears streamed from her eyes making black stripes down her cheeks from her mascara. Her long hair fell in her face, hampering her search.

Pushing herself up from the floor, she stumbled and fell against the table. She flew through kitchen towards the stairs. Taking the steps two at a time, Dani tripped over her own feet sending her right shoe tumbling down the stairs behind her. Racing to her 13-year-old daughter, Tiffany's room, she plowed through clothes piled on the bed. Dani kicked stuffed animals and personal belongings clearing a path, all to no avail. Her phone wasn't anywhere to be found.

With hope dwindling, Dani screamed at the top of her lungs, cursing whoever borrowed her cell phone last. "PLEASE GOD … HELP ME! KITTY NEEDS HELP!" Charging into Tiffany's bathroom, Dani screamed her relief spying her cell phone partially hidden under a washcloth lying next to the sink. She cried great gulping sobs. She was so distraught - she could barely make her fingers cooperate. With trembling fingers, she punched out 9-1-1.

Dani wailed out her emergency, but tragically help was too late in coming. Kitty's last words became an eerie self-fulfilled prophecy: *trying to lose those last 10 pounds did in fact kill her …*

TWO

The bright light nearly blinded Kitty as she slowly opened her eyes. She paused, blinked and rubbed her eyes as if waking from a long nap. Trying to get her bearings, it took her a moment to realize she was no longer in familiar surroundings.

She recognized her husband, Luke, standing silently huddled in a corner. Looking shaken and pale, he practically hugged the door to keep from being trampled as some sort of portable machine on wheels whizzed past him. Voices, muffled at first, now rang out loud and clear. What looked like dozens of arms and hands quickly went about the business of positioning the equipment and setting things in order. The machine hummed to life and added to the clamor in the cramped room.

"Hurry up! We're losing her! Get outta the way! Starting compressions! Charging paddles to 200! Clear!" The voices of hospital emergency room personnel all yelled at once to be heard. The incessant bleeping of machines combined with the yelling voices produced an earsplitting cacophonous noise in the small room.

Kitty searched for the sound of the chaos. Looking all around, it took a moment before she discovered the source of the pandemonium. Lying some 10 feet *below* her she saw her cold lifeless body stretched out on a hospital gurney. There were several people hovering about *her*, all busy with needles and blood pressure cuffs and tubes and instruments. The ministrations of this team of experts appeared to be producing no positive results.

"Hey!" Kitty yelled from her floating perch up high in the corner of the room. "Hey, somebody down there … do something! For the love of God, please listen to me. Luke! Can't you hear me, honey? Oh, Baby. Why are you crying? Don't cry, Sweetheart, I'm sure this is all nothing."

From where Kitty was suspended in the air she tried moving about. She started flapping her arms up and down like a frantic chicken to see if that would produce movement in her body below. When she looked down upon herself and saw that the flapping of her arms had no change in her immobile body, she tried kicking her legs as if she were sprinting in a relay race. Despite all her efforts, her body below remained motionless. Staring transfixed high in the corner, Kitty felt immobilized, held prisoner by an invisible puppeteer's strings.

"Can't anybody hear me?" Kitty yelled. "Why can't you see me? Oh for goodness sakes, just look up here! I'm fine. I'm sure you're all overreacting! Luke, Baby, tell them I'm okay! Tell them I want to wake up now! LUKE, PLEASE LISTEN TO ME!" she screamed louder until she was nearly hoarse, but no one noticed.

Two doctors took turns giving Kitty CPR and then zapping her body with jolts of electricity.

"Hey, stop it!" Kitty yelled again. ZAP! Another jolt with the electronic paddles did nothing to resuscitate her lifeless body. Kitty grabbed her chest in reaction from where she perched monitoring the unfolding crisis. "Ouch!" she said, sucking air through her clenched jaw. "That looks like it should hurt. I'll bet that's gonna leave a mark." Even though Kitty could feel nothing from where she watched the ensuing drama, her face distorted in pain with each increase of voltage.

The doctors traded comments until one turned and spoke to Luke in the corner. "You're her husband, right?"

Luke nodded and moved his lips like a fish left too long on shore without water. No sound was forthcoming.

"Sir," the doctor continued. "Does your wife have a history of heart problems?"

Luke shook his head no.

"Is she taking any drugs," the other doctor fired at him.

Unable to find his voice, Luke shook his head no, again.

"We've got to figure out why her heart stopped. We must have missed something," the doctor in charge said to his colleague. He turned once more to Luke, hoping to find answers for the unexplained heart failure in his patient. "How did you say this happened? How did she end up with a sucker lodged in the back of her throat?"

At six-foot-four inches tall, Luke O'Connell epitomized the phrase: tall, dark and handsome. A former college basketball star, now turned Landscape Architect, he usually commanded attention because of his striking good looks. The doctors probing him for details regarding his wife's accident were blind to his physical attributes and yelled at him, "Speak up, man! We're trying to save your wife!"

Luke tried again until finally he found his voice. "Treadmill," was all he croaked out.

The doctors and nurses all looked at one another with puzzled expressions, until someone finally coaxed more information out of him. "What, sir? Did you say, *treadmill?*"

Luke shook his head numbly. From where Kitty was suspended, she held her breath willing Luke to spill the details so she too could be enlightened as to what was happening. The doctors continued their tireless efforts to revive Kitty.

Luke shook his head and attempted to speak again. "She ... she was running on the treadmill — like she does everyday." He was wringing the over-sized U.C.L.A. tee shirt that had been haphazardly cut from his wife's body and tossed aside. He stopped to collect himself as emotion choked him, causing him to clear his throat several times before continuing. "She was on the phone and apparently had the sucker in her mouth. She must have tripped and fallen backwards and hit her head on the barbells." Luke let his tears spill over, too dazed to bother wiping them away. He raised the tee shirt to his face to inhale his wife's scent. He buried his face in the shirt and cried unabashedly.

One of the doctors, the one waiting to use the charged paddles on Kitty's exposed chest, shook his head and commented to the nurse off to his side. "Jeez. What the ... ? Aren't those things equipped with safety clips or something, for God's sake? It would have saved her life. What a waste," he offered the last more as a judgment, rather than sound advice.

Not sure if the young doctor had directed his comments directly at him or not, Luke wiped his face with the shirt and spoke as if in a trance. "She was always so proud of the fact that she was perfectly coordinated and extremely limber. She said the safety clip was for whimps. She never bothered to wear it." Luke sobbed openly. A nurse came in to offer him assistance.

"Hah!" Kitty exploded with emotion from where she watched the action and raised both arms like a marathon runner crossing the finish line after an exhausting race. "That's right, Baby. The safety clip is for little old ladies and heart patients with pacemakers! You tell them, Luke! Your wife is not a whimp!" Kitty looked all around her searching for someone to high five, then realized the stupidity of her reaction. Toning down her misplaced excitement, she mumbled, "Just you wait. You'll be sorry, Dr. Smarty-pants. I'm going to be just fine! Now hurry it along and fix me up! I want to go home now." Kitty watched as the nurse quickly ushered Luke out of the room. Suddenly without warning, the commotion ceased and the room went strangely quiet.

Kitty stared from her lofty perch. "Oh, this can't be good. Why did you all stop? Luke? Where are they taking you? Please ... you've got to help her ... I mean me. You've got to help ME!"

A short Asian doctor with a fierce scowl and presumably the physician in charge stepped back from the gurney and removed his rubber gloves with a snap. "How long has she been down?" he asked the young resident standing closest to the bed.

Kitty watched helplessly as they were about to pronounce her d-e-a-d.

"This can't be happening. I must be dreaming. That's it. This is all a bad dream and I want to wake up now. Wake up, Gladys!" And then louder, "C'MON, KITTY WAKE UP!"

She wanted to weep but no tears came. Feeling a rising panic, Kitty sensed a presence near her. She turned her head and suspended beside her was the most beautiful woman she'd ever seen. The woman's hair, an amazing shade of auburn rust shimmered like liquid fire. And her eyes. Kitty's own green eyes, so like her father's, paled in comparison to this stranger's eyes. They were a vivid shade of emerald green like the lush fields of Ireland in the springtime. The woman's skin had a ripe healthy glow. Whoever coined the phrase "a complexion like peaches and cream" must have used this breathtaking beauty as their model. Words to describe such beauty ricocheted in Kitty's mind. *She is truly amazing.*

The woman's beautifully crafted gown reached to the floor hiding her feet. Her dress, a lovely shade of ivory, was unlike anything Kitty had ever seen. Tiny flawless diamonds winked through the woven lace patterns making Kitty think of nighttime star constellations.

The flame-haired beauty laughed a light tinkling sound that wafted about her. "Why thank you, Katherine. You don't mind if I call you Katherine, do you? It sounds so much more *heavenly* than Kitty. Don't you think?" Even the sound of her voice was amazing, almost musical. Her words floated around Kitty cocooning her like a security blanket.

Kitty felt as though she had walked in on the middle of a conversation and somehow missed what had been said prior to her arrival. "Excuse me?" Kitty thought to herself. She looked around to be sure there was no one else this woman could be speaking to. Suspended high in the corner of the room, there was only Kitty and this woman. "Are you t-t-talking to m-m-m-e-e-e-?" Kitty finally stuttered out loud.

The beautiful woman brushed her long auburn hair back with a graceful sweep of her perfectly manicured hand. "Why of course, Katherine. Do you see anybody else up here besides us?" The woman gestured with open arms.

Kitty shook her head and thought, "*I must be losing my mind.*"

Again, though Kitty had spoken no words out loud, the woman responded. "No, Katherine, you haven't lost your mind. I can hear everything you're thinking."

Kitty sat wide-eyed for once at a loss for words. She stammered and found her voice, "But how? Who ...? What ... ? How do you know who I am?"

"One thing at a time, all right? First of all, my name is Grace. And earlier when you first saw me you thought I was amazing." She laughed. "Thank you. I *am* amazing.

"Okay, Grace," Kitty spoke with care. "It's nice to meet you. I think. Would you mind explaining to me why I'm hanging around up here on the ceiling? And what about them?" Kitty pointed down. "Can't they see us up here?"

The woman's smile warmed her eyes changing them to a deep hunter green. "Them? Oh, don't mind them. They can't see us or hear us. It's just you and me."

"Okay." Kitty drew the word out and chewed on the corner of her bottom lip. "All right. What about *that*?" Kitty pointed to the lifeless body on the gurney below her. "Is that really *me*?"

Grace's smile was replaced with a look of sadness and she nodded. "I'm afraid so."

Kitty's brow furrowed in a look of concern. "Am I ... I mean ... you know? Am I *dead*?" She spoke quietly, not wanting to force the hands of fate that would cement her future.

Grace spoke in a near silent whisper. "Yes."

With that one word, the room began to shift and spin. Kitty felt like she'd had one too many rides on a tilt-a-whirl. Kitty stared at Grace and noticed her eyes changed color again. The kaleidoscope of colors swirled from green to blue. Kitty saw her ashen face reflected in Grace's transforming eyes and in a mere instant she saw compassion, love and understanding shimmering there as well.

Kitty laughed. It started as a little chuckle until it snowballed into a giggle. Her laughter increased to giant guffaws, followed by deep belly laughter. Eventually the laughter gave way to hysteria and then sobbing. Grace moved close to her and put her arm around her. She began to hum a haunting melody in Kitty's ear. Eventually Kitty's weeping tapered off. Her tears subsided leaving Kitty with little hiccupping gasps of breath. The immense finality of her death was replaced with an unexplained calmness, which enveloped Kitty until there was nothing left to feel, except peace.

Grace produced a handkerchief with intricately laced edges and handed it to Kitty. Kitty blew her nose with gusto and heaved a sigh of acceptance.

When at last Kitty was able to speak, she pulled away. "Well, Grace. I'm hoping that this is all a very intense dream and that you're just something I've conjured up from the dark recesses of my fertile imagination. Man, when I wake up am I ever going to have a doozie to tell my therapist. Oh wait – I don't have a therapist. But when I wake up, I'm going to find a therapist and you can bet that the first thing I'm going to do is put her on speed dial." Kitty sniffed loudly, wiped her runny nose with the lace hankie and stuffed it in her pocket. "Grace. Please tell me this is all just a bad dream." She turned pleading eyes to Grace.

Grace's smile held reassurance and comfort giving Kitty a sense of peace in spite of her dire circumstances. "No, Katherine. You're not dreaming. This is real."

Grace looked lovingly at her as a lone tear escaped down Kitty's cheek. As she hugged her, Grace whispered in her ear. "But it's okay, Kitty. Everything is going to be just fine. Everything will become clear to you. But you must trust me."

THREE

Reality hit Kitty like an out of control semi-truck on a runaway truck ramp. Clearly she had little choice but to trust this mysterious stranger. Kitty knew from past experience reality could be a tough pill to swallow. She could feel a tiny bubble of fear churning deep in her stomach, but she did her best to squelch it. She pulled away from Grace's embrace. To combat her nervousness, Kitty began to jog in place. She didn't even question the fact she was no longer floating, but stood on solid ground now. She looked like one of those runners you see on the side of the road at an intersection waiting for the light to change, hopping back and forth from foot to foot. She quickly changed to jumping jacks, followed by a series of deep knee bends.

Kitty always believed in attacking every problem head on and with a good dose of humor. She figured death should be no different. She reasoned that if Grace was distracted with her calisthenics and odd behavior, perhaps she could delay the inevitable – whatever the *inevitable* might be.

Kitty continued to squat, contort and bend. She finished doing a toe touch and sprang upright like a giant jack-in-the-box. "Well, Grace, can you tell me what happens next? Clearly you must be some sort of angel or what I imagine an angel might look like. You're too perfect not to be an angel. If I was headed straight for Hell they wouldn't have sent someone so nice - I hope," she added nervously.

Grace smiled a confirmation.

"So does that mean I'm on the next outbound transport to Heaven, or what?"

Just as Kitty placed her hands on her hips and was preparing to execute near perfect lunges, Grace held up both hands to stop her.

Grace took Kitty's arm and gently guided her. "Not quite yet. We have a little business to conduct first."

They could no longer view the emergency room but walked along a wide corridor. The need to make sense of what was happening around her evaporated. For once in her life, she was content not to know all the details. Not knowing all the details was probably a good thing, she reasoned. She half expected clouds or misty vapors to rise from a hidden fog machine giving credence to a Hollywood version of what the afterlife should be. But there were no Hollywood theatrics here. Only the stark white-walled corridor existed. Kitty lost all sense of time and space.

As they walked, the corridor slowly transformed. Kitty stopped and stared transfixed as little beams of light burst through the floor. At first she saw only a few. Within moments spread before her like a runway carpet, hundreds of brilliant light beams burst forth from below.

Kitty grinned like a schoolgirl on her first outdoor field trip. "Wow! This is incredible! What is this?"

Still holding Kitty's hand, Grace stopped and closed her eyes. "Wait for it," she whispered.

"Wait for what?" Kitty asked.

"Those are the prayers, Katherine. Close your eyes and listen. Even though there are so many, each can be individually discerned."

Kitty looked puzzled. "Prayers. Prayers for what?"

Grace opened her eyes and looked directly at Kitty. "Why for you, Katherine. Can't you hear them?"

She shook her head, but then stopped as her daughter's voice rose up to meet her. Kitty turned her ear and closed her eyes.

The sound of voices rose to meet Kitty in the prisms of light. From the sound of their urgency, her family and friends were unaware of what was happening to Kitty in the trauma room. Although she couldn't see their faces, she somehow instinctively knew they were all huddled together. Heads bowed. Hands clasped.

"Dear Lord, please don't let my Mom die. I'm not ready for her to go yet. I need her! She was teaching me how to sew. We were going to make a special dress for me to wear to my first high school dance next month. I love her so much, Lord. I really do! I'm sorry I've been fighting with her so much lately. I don't know why I do it. I'm sorry! Please God, please! Let her be all right. I swear I'll never fight with her again if you'll just save her!"

Kitty recognized the pleading voice of her 14-year-old daughter, Sarah. She was the baby of the family. Her loud, boisterous nature charged the air with chaos wherever she landed. Although to hear her prayer, Sarah was acting totally out of character – even for her. Kitty wasn't used to Sarah's serious side. Her daughter tended to be a bit of a drama queen. Ordinarily her temper ignited quicker than a string of firecrackers. She may be temperamental, but she had a softer compassionate side as well. The flip side to Sarah's compassion was her painful honesty. Sadly she'd created a few enemies because of it. Poor Sarah had yet to learn the art of speaking half-truths in order to avoid hurting other people's feelings. Kitty couldn't help but wonder how she would ever learn such a valuable lesson without her mother.

Kitty's eyes welled with tears for Sarah. "My poor baby," she whispered. She barely had time to digest Sarah's plea, when another prayer followed.

The next one came from her husband, Luke. *"Heavenly Father ... please guide the doctors as they work on my precious love. Please be with Kitty and let her know you are with her. Please Father - we need her ... I need her so much. She's the only woman I've ever loved."* A choked sob escaped him before he could continue. *"I don't think I can bear being without her. Forgive me for the pain I've caused her lately. Please Lord ... it can't be her time yet! It just can't be!"*

"Whew, that one must have been tough for him." Kitty opened her eyes to explain to Grace. "You see, we've been having some problems lately. House stuff, kid stuff, money problems. The usual.

We're having a hard time agreeing on some major issues and neither one of us wants to give an inch." She trailed off.

Kitty closed her eyes again in order to hear the voices and prayers of her other two children. Anger filled her 19-year-old pregnant daughter, Rebecca's prayer. *"God, this can't be your will! How could you bring me through all the garbage I've gone through only to take her away now? Even though I've been so mad at her, she never gave up on me! She never stopped praying for me. I started believing in you again because of HER and her faith! I didn't abort this baby because of HER prayers for me."* Rebecca's anger gave way to sadness. *"Please Lord, I'll do anything you ask of me. I'll break up with Aaron if that's what it'll take. I know I can't have this baby without my Mom here. Please God, I beg you ..."*

Even though Kitty agonized over Rebecca's current crisis, she rejoiced inwardly. "Oh please God, let her break up with Aaron!" And then the situation hit her. "Oh Grace, I'm not going to be there help Rebecca through the tough months ahead, am I? I'll be the first to admit that Rebecca's headstrong and willful, but that doesn't mean she doesn't still need her mother. What kind of a life will she have without me? What if she's forced to stay with her boyfriend?" Kitty shuddered. "Rebecca is going to need her mother's wisdom more than ever." Kitty slowed her steps and stared off into space imagining Rebecca's dismal future.

"When she dropped out of college to *find herself,* obviously we were concerned. When she ended up with Aaron we thought she purposely was punishing us. She's behaved so childishly – but then, she's still a child herself in so many ways. But she's not a bad person. Just last week we had a terrible fight. I reminded her she was about to discover the "joys of motherhood" firsthand. I'm afraid I couldn't resist the temptation to mete out advice from generations of mothers long past. I unleashed the dreaded timeless curse of, 'I hope you have a daughter *just like you* someday!' Who feels childish now? My careless remark drove a wedge between us and we've not spoken since." Kitty slowed her pace through the corridor as she shared her worries for Rebecca. "Grace, I messed up with her. I need to fix this."

Grace took Katherine's arm pulling her along. "Well unfortunately, you're not being there will fix things now — although probably not in the way you would like. Come along, Katherine. Let's keep moving."

The more they walked, the more lights there were. So many light beams burst through the floor, it became non-existent. The corridor was a solid golden road of light. The effect was very "Oz-like." Kitty wondered if this was how the yellow brick road looked and then chided herself for thinking of something so stupid at such a serious moment. She concentrated on the light beams again and the accompanying voices and prayers. There must have been hundreds of beams all with petitions on her behalf. She could clearly hear separate prayers from her best friend Dani and Dani's husband and kids. Kitty recognized the voices of the women from her Thursday morning Bible study group. There were prayers from the youth group and the couples group she and her husband attended. Volleyball and soccer team moms all lent their voices. The prayers went on and on. Their heartfelt emotional pleas were overwhelming.

"Oh my goodness. So many prayers. I had no idea ..." Kitty inhaled deeply and let it out in a long sigh. "Are these all really for me?"

Grace smiled and nodded. "Yes, Katherine. You are very well loved."

"I had no idea. So many friends — so many people." Kitty shook her head in bewilderment. "Are all of those people down there at the hospital?"

Grace covered her laugh behind her hand. "Oh my heavens, no. These prayers come from everywhere. Prayers are not boxed in by logistics, Katherine. Once a prayer is spoken or thought they just immediately float upwards towards Heaven no matter where you are." Grace lifted both arms in the air to symbolize the flight of the requests.

The tortured prayer of her son, Matthew touched Kitty the most. Even though his laid-back personality caused him to march to the beat of his own drummer, of all her children, he was the most tenderhearted. Unlike his sisters, he tended to wear his emotions on his sleeve. Matthew considered his sensitivity more of a flaw and worried that it made him seem less masculine. Kitty knew it made him unique. She shared a special mother-son bond with him unlike anything she had with her two daughters. The raw emotion of Matthew's prayer was nearly tangible.

"Father God, I know you are with Mom right now. Send your Holy Spirit – surround her with your love. I feel your presence, Lord. Let her feel your presence as well. Let her know we all love her and need her. She is such an awesome mom. Please heal her, Father. Your Word says all we need is faith to believe for healing. I believe! I have faith for her healing, Father, and I know Mom does too! Your miracles still work today! She needs a miracle right now, Lord! She ..."

Kitty craned her ear to hear the rest of the prayer, but Grace pulled her along. "Wait, Grace. I want to hear the rest of Matty's prayer. It's filled with such ..." Kitty searched for the right word. "... such *power*. I always suspected he had a much deeper faith than he let on."

"You've had a profound influence on all your children. But enough of this. We really must move along. We have an agenda." Grace let go of Kitty's hand and moved on ahead, talking to herself as she went. She appeared to be going over a mental checklist.

"Can't we stay and look at the lights and listen to the prayers some more?"

"The prayers are lovely aren't they?" Grace answered.

"Oh yes. They're so beautiful. They fill me with ..." Kitty exhaled loudly. "I don't know. Something. They make me feel so *loved*."

"But you are loved, Katherine." Grace spoke with authority. "Surely you must know that."

Doubt washed over Kitty's face.

"If all those people knew what I was really like they wouldn't be praying so hard for me. I've made such a mess of things. I've not been a very good Christian, Grace. The harder I've tried to be what God wanted me to be, the farther I've fallen from that. I've really blown it. In fact, I'm pretty surprised I even get to go to Heaven."

"Well, you're not there yet," Grace said.

Kitty looked worried for a moment. "Then, does that mean that I'm not really going to Heaven?"

"I didn't say that. I just said you're not there yet. So many questions, child! Patience. You must have patience."

"Hah! That's never been one of my strong suits," Kitty sighed. She inclined her head one last time towards the direction of the lights, but all too quickly they passed through the corridor and stopped in front of a set of large double doors.

When Grace stopped so suddenly, Kitty nearly collided with her. Kitty excused herself and took a look down at herself. She suddenly became very aware that she was still wearing the workout clothes she had on at the time of her demise. She fidgeted nervously and bent down to tie her shoe.

"Hmm … I wonder when that came undone? Are we going to see *HIM* now? You know — *the man upstairs?*" She straightened and adjusted the strap of her workout bra. She lowered her voice to a whisper. "I'm not exactly dressed for a face-to-face with God."

A brief frown crossed Grace's face and disappeared just as quickly. "I hate it when people refer to him like that. So disrespectful." Grace shook her head as if to clear her thoughts and perused Kitty's outfit and smiled sweetly. "Not to worry, Katherine. There will be time for a change later. We have a little while before we meet Him," she said.

Kitty pulled the hair scrunchie from her long wavy hair and finger combed the thick mass. She shook her head unleashing the dark locks that tumbled freely just past her shoulders.

"But I thought to be absent from the body was to be present with the Lord. I always just assumed that the instant you died you would go to be directly with God. I know that's what it says in the Bible — somewhere. Or something like that." Kitty scratched her head. "Oh, I'm so bad with Scripture references. But I'm pretty sure it's a New Testament verse. I think." Kitty's smile lacked assurance.

Grace grasped both handles and opened wide the double doors. "Could you be thinking of 2 Corinthians 5:6? *Therefore we are always confident and know that as long as we are at home in the body we are away from the Lord. We live by faith, not by sight. We are confident, I say, and would prefer to be away from the body and at home with the Lord."* Grace recited the Scripture effortlessly.

"I think that might be it, but I'm not sure." Kitty looked down as if searching the toes of her cross-trainers might actually stimulate her memory and ability to recall Scripture.

Kitty stood apart from Grace. Grace turned and spread her arms wide to Kitty. "Come, come, Katherine. We need to go in and take a seat. Grace walked ahead of Katherine and entered the large room. The enormous space looked like a movie theater, of all things. The lights were dimmed but Kitty could distinguish several rows of high-backed theater seats with seven seats in each row. Each row was slightly elevated from the one in front of it. About 20 feet beyond the front row, an immense blank screen covered the entire wall from floor to ceiling.

Kitty entered slowly and took in her surroundings. Fighting her nervousness, she played with her hair tie and tried to appear indifferent. "Cool. Stadium seating. Wow, this is quite the movie room." Kitty tried humor to alleviate the butterflies in her stomach. "So, is this going to be like an in-flight movie or something?" she asked jokingly.

Grace walked over to the second row and gracefully sat in the center seat. "Please come join me, Katherine." She patted the empty seat beside her in invitation. "The rest of the Scripture I quoted, states in verses 9 and 10: *So we make it our goal to please him, whether we are at home in the body or away from it. For we must all appear before the judgment seat of Christ, that each one may receive what is due him for the things done while in the body, whether good or bad."* As she spoke the last verse, she turned to Kitty and gave her a fixed stare. Kitty was unsure whether the look Grace gave her was accusing or not. "Please come and sit beside me, Kitty." Using her familiar nickname for the second time. "We are indeed, going to watch a movie."

Kitty walked over and sat beside Grace. She wondered if her face revealed her mounting terror. She had an inkling of what was to come, but desperately hoped she was wrong. Kitty was terrified the deep dark secrets of her entire life were about to be projected on this huge screen. She trembled at the idea of her closeted skeletons being brought to light. Here in this place where there seemed to be no secrets, her carefully hidden sins were sure to be highlighted. Secrets Kitty had managed to keep hidden from her husband and even her best friend. Kitty knew with certainty that all would be on display — soon.

Grace reached for Kitty's hand and held it gently in her own. Were it not for the serene smile on Grace's face, Kitty would have fled in fear. "Here we go. It's time we had a look at what has brought you here."

The lights dimmed on cue from an unspoken command. Kitty sat at attention as the blackness enfolded her. She released Grace's hand and twisted her own icy cold hands in nervousness. The huge screen came awake as an unseen projector clicked to life, masterfully fitting the spools of film into designated slots.

Grace reached for Kitty's hand again and squeezed it reassuringly. "Okay, Katherine. For lack of a more fitting cliché ... *this is your life!*" Grace spoke the last, completely devoid of humor.

FOUR

It took a moment for the images projected on the screen to focus. Kitty's nervousness increased as her eyes adjusted to the darkness. She took a quick glance to make sure she and Grace were alone. If a heaping helping of humiliation were forthcoming, hopefully she'd have a little privacy. Though the chairs surrounding her remained empty, Kitty sensed another's presence. She massaged her arms to chase away the goose bumps that had risen on her bare flesh and turned her attention toward the giant screen.

A date appeared on the screen then slowly faded and was replaced with vivid color images of an old car groaning to a stop. As Kitty absorbed the action, a noticeable change occurred in the theater. Sniffing the air, the unmistakable smell of newly mown grass and car exhaust hung about her. Heat from the noonday sun warmed her face and arms chasing away her goose bumps. A slight breeze blew a wisp of hair into her eyes, causing the errant lock to dance out of control. The sound of cicadas chirping sprang up from beneath her feet. Kitty felt transported through time and space. She became a participant rather than a casual observer. She took a moment to pinch herself to determine if the sights, sounds and smells were real. She glanced at the seat in front of her half expecting a lap bar to roll down for her protection since she felt like she'd been forced aboard an amusement park ride. Clearly, this would be no ordinary movie-going experience. But of course there was no safety bar, so she hugged her arms and held her breath waiting and watching with a mixture of fear and excitement.

* * * * *

August 12, 1960

The 12-year-old Buick Sedan rumbled to the curb and stopped in front of the military base hospital sign. In smaller print under the hospital name, the words *Biloxi, Mississippi* were barely discernible thanks to the tenacious efforts of a small band of pigeons. A woman in an advanced stage of pregnancy got out and slammed the car door harder than necessary. She dropped the cigarette she'd been smoking and ground the remains with the toe of her black loafer. The heat of the midday sun bore down on her, creating a line of perspiration on her upper lip and underneath her heavy breasts.

The woman leaned in the open window and looked across the head of her three-year-old daughter, Maria, to ask rather nastily, "Are you going to wait for me, Henry?"

Henry barked back his response. "No, I can't. I'm going to take Maria over to Mrs. Lawson's house so she can watch her. I'll come back for you later. It's probably nothing. You're over reacting, Sophia. There's still almost two months until you're due." He pumped the accelerator revving the engine, anxious to be away.

Without a departing word for the toddler, Sophia straightened in anger. "Nothing! She screeched. "Damnation, Henry! You hit me square in my back with that stupid alarm clock. I've got this terrible pain in my spine now. Who knows what could happen?" She waved her hand in dismissal. "Well fine. Go on with you then. But you better hurry back. I don't want to wait out here all day for you. It feels like it's 115°!" She searched her imitation leather handbag for a hankie to wipe her perspiring face.

Sophia smoothed her smock over her protruding belly and lumbered off as best she could in her condition. She took one last look over her shoulder and spat out expletives in Italian as Henry sped away.

* * * * *

Kitty stared as the woman entered the hospital double doors.

"Wow! That was the weirdest thing I've ever seen before. I felt like I was really there. I could feel their feelings. I could sense their thoughts and emotions – even their anger. Those are my parents." She pointed at the screen, offering an explanation. "That was the day I was born, Grace."

"Yes, I know." She patted Kitty's hand.

"They looked so young. They were in their early twenties then, I think. I don't ever remember Daddy not having gray hair. He looked so different then. And Momma. She was so pretty back then. But she didn't look very happy, did she? I don't think those two ever got along. And oh my gosh! I can't believe Momma didn't quit smoking while she was pregnant! They certainly weren't very careful back in those days, were they? They weren't careful about a lot of things. Did you see my sister Maria? Didn't they have car seats — or laws back then? Good Lord! All in all, I'd say it wasn't a very magical day to welcome me, was it? I was always aware I'd been a prema-ture baby, but nobody ever bothered to tell me why exactly. Can I see what happens next, Grace?" Kitty turned expectant eyes toward her.

The scene on the screen had paused while Kitty talked with Grace. Grace inched her head in a slight nod and the action on the screen resumed. Kitty wondered if there was someone hidden in the shadows operating a remote control at Grace's request.

* * * * *

Several hours had passed and the old Buick slowly ambled its way into the crowded hospital parking lot. The engine continued to rumble and cough even after Henry had turned the ignition off. With one final hiccup of smoke and noise, the car quieted. Henry blew a perfect smoke ring before snuffing out the cigarette butt in the overflowing ashtray. He rubbed his irritated eyes that had been too many days without a good night sleep and looked towards the front entrance. Henry couldn't spot his wife amongst the crowd of emerging nurses. In irritation, he unwound himself from the driver's seat to saunter towards the building.

Henry shoved his hands in his pockets and forced one foot in front of the other. He exhaled loudly. This was one of those days he wished he would have heeded his mother's advice all those years ago. She had tried to warn him that mixing his hearty Irish genes with Sophia's strong Italian DNA would be a recipe for disaster. She had dared to compare him and Sophia to oil and water. It chapped his pride to think his mother may have been right. At the time, he figured his thrice married and divorced single mother was the last person who should be offering him marital advice.

Henry knew with certainty that way back then at the age of eighteen, he loved Sophia with all his heart and would have moved heaven and earth to be married to her. He defied her aged, immigrant parents and joined the Air Force two weeks after he and Sophia were wed just to prove to everyone that he was a man in control of his own destiny. Now, years later, he wasn't so sure.

Walking towards the hospital entrance, Henry slowed his pace and stopped to take in his surroundings. The hospital was abuzz with late day activity. He glanced at his watch. "C'mon, Soph. Where in the Sam Hill are you?" he spoke under his breath. He ran a hand through his hair and then patted his empty stomach absentmindedly. He walked over to a dilapidated park bench and planted himself. Hanging his head, he searched the ground between his feet staring at the dirt-filled cracks.

* * * * *

Kitty shifted nervously in her seat and gently poked Grace in the arm. "Psst, excuse me, Grace," Kitty whispered. The image of her forlorn father studying the sidewalk remained frozen on the screen.

Grace turned and a lone dim light, flickered overhead, illuminating the twosome. "Yes, Katherine."

"Okay, I know this is going to sound weird. But, I swear I can see everything that my dad is thinking inside his head up there." Kitty pointed at the screen. "How is that even possible?"

"I can't give you a scientific reason for anything that you are seeing or feeling right now. All I can offer is this. Just … *go with it*." Grace waved a hand towards the screen. "Don't think about it. Don't question it or try to figure it out. For the sake of argument, you have become part of Henry and Sophia Murphy for this short span of history. Their thoughts and emotions will be an open book for you. I don't know why. I just know you need to pay attention to not only what you see and hear, but to what you *don't* see and hear. Does that make sense?" Grace asked.

Kitty shrugged her shoulders. "No. Not really."

"Just watch, Katherine. Let's see where this goes. You are being given a unique opportunity to feel what your parents are feeling. To see what they are thinking. For right now, you get to be part of the circumstances of the day of your birth. It's a gift, dear. Don't waste it, okay?"

Kitty shook her head slightly not completely convinced about the "gift" she was about to receive. "Okay. If you say so."

"Good," Grace said. "Let's continue then. Shall we?" The light instantly disappeared and the projected images burst to life.

* * * * *

Deep in thought, Henry squished a wayward ant under the toe of his boot. He felt the pressure of his troubled marriage weighing upon his shoulders. He needed another cigarette. Smoking helped to clear his thoughts. Marrying at the age of 18 hadn't been the smartest thing he'd ever done. He was happy Sophia had been as desperate to get away from her family, as he was to get away from his. Her parents had offered her a life of forced servitude in their family owned Italian bakery. The promise of a life of adventure as an Air Force bride and possible foreign travel overseas had been a veritable brass ring to an 18-year-old Catholic schoolgirl. Sophia had jumped at the chance to become Mrs. Henry Murphy. Henry stole a glance at the hospital entrance sign housing a nest of pigeons above the double doors.

He had to laugh. Biloxi, Mississippi wasn't exactly the exciting foreign post that his recruiter had promised him when he joined up. Maybe Sophia had a right to be upset with him. So caught up in his desperation for a "normal" traditional family, he failed to notice the signs of Sophia's discontent. The last few weeks the signs were impossible to ignore. That little voice in his head taunted him that perhaps Sophia didn't really love him at all. While he, on the other hand, loved her so much, it sometimes scared him. He shook his head in sadness and tried to chase away those niggling feelings of doubt. Sophia was unhappy; that much was obvious. He was content to live in denial and ignore her constant angry outbursts and erratic mood shifts. He chalked it up to pregnancy hormones. He was so close to having his dreams fulfilled. He couldn't wait to surprise Sophia and show her the cute little house he'd found. It was definitely a real fixer-upper, but that made it all the more appealing. It even had a white picket fence. He was working on a deal to trade the sedan in for a used station wagon. Maybe they could even get a mangy little dog to greet him at the door when he came home at night. Yeah. A dog would be good. He fished in his pocket for his smokes. One quick one before he went in search of Sophia. He inhaled long and deep and let the nicotine work its magic. It was a nasty habit, but one he was reluctant to give up. Somehow the searing smoke helped to organize his thoughts.

Exhaling loudly he looked up at the sky, searching the heavens for answers. Who was he kidding? His dreams weren't lining up with his wife's. Sophia hated taking care of a toddler. She'd never agree to get a dog. She complained about being cooped up all day and the drudgery of housework. He sat there wondering how his tumultuous marriage managed to declare a cease-fire long enough in the last few years to conceive two children. Sophia had half-heartedly agreed to one child after they were married and refused to even consider having another. But Henry could be very charming and persuasive at times. One night of empty promises, a new Dean Martin record and free-flowing cheap Chianti had sealed the deal and the promise that Maria would not be growing up as an only child. For that he was grateful. He wouldn't have to worry about Maria should anything happen to him or Sophia. She wouldn't have a childhood like his, if he had anything to say about it.

God, he was excited about having another baby. He wished Sophia shared his enthusiasm. Henry smiled in memory of that night months ago when baby number two had been conceived. At the same it time it saddened him to think of the punishment Sophia had doled out for his duplicity and seduction. It was the last time Henry had been allowed to touch his wife in any manner. Seven months of celibacy was not his idea of the perfect marriage. Lingering memories danced in his thoughts; remembrances of intimacy and sweet caresses. Whoa, better not go there, he chided himself. Reining in his lustful thoughts, Henry straightened and forced the images from his mind.

Flicking the ashes from his cigarette, he turned at the sound of voices and laughter as two nurses emerged from the entrance, deep in conversation. He paid little heed to them until they passed directly in front of him and he caught a slight whiff of sweet smelling perfume. He looked up and gave them both the once over. Both uniform clad women turned and smiled as they crossed his field of vision. Always one with an eye for the ladies, Henry couldn't stop the boyish grin from lighting his face as they whispered and giggled in his direction. His slight smile coaxed the dimples in his cheeks and caused them to become more pronounced. The gesture was not lost on either of the nurses. Henry noticed the unmistakable blush of their cheeks and their increased twittering laughter.

He huffed out smoke and pent-up sexual frustration. He was a man with needs, after all. And seven months with unfulfilled needs and a man could think about doing all sorts of things that would lead to trouble. If his mind continued to wander where it shouldn't, he just might end up needing to go to church to light a few candles. Henry forced movement into his limbs and ordered his body to stand and move towards the entrance. He hoped Sophia's visit with the doctor this afternoon would put her in a better mood. Secretly he hoped there was a pill she could take that would make everything better. She had been worse than ever the last few weeks. He prayed he'd survive the last couple months of pregnancy. Henry extinguished his cigarette in the receptacle outside the door before he made his way to the information counter to inquire after his wife's whereabouts.

"S'cuse me. I'm looking for my wife. Her name is Mrs. Sophia Murphy," Henry barked at the elderly blue-haired volunteer behind the counter.

Looking bored, the woman in the blue and white striped smock gave Henry a slight smile as she pushed aside the gossip magazine she'd been reading. She did her best to appear well informed, although Henry suspected she wasn't. She removed a sharpened pencil from the chipped "Uncle Sam Wants You" coffee mug and used it to systematically check every name on her clipboard. Henry didn't even attempt to mask his impatience. He jingled the loose change in his trouser pocket and rocked back and forth on his heels. His obvious irritation was lost on this woman who licked her forefinger with each turn of the page. Henry removed the shiny silver cigarette lighter from his other pocket and began flipping it open and closed.

"Oh, yes ... yes, here she is, Mr. Murphy. Your wife has been admitted to the maternity ward. Second floor." She beamed at having located the patient in question.

Henry's agitated state heightened as confusion overtook him. "Whoa ... hold on there a minute, Grandma. Are you sure you've got the right Mrs. Murphy? My wife is pregnant, but she just came in for a check up. There should've been no reason to admit her. Would you check again, please?"

The smile vanished from the volunteer worker's face as she eyed him angrily. "Yes sir," she replied through gritted teeth. "You said Sophia Murphy, correct?"

Henry nodded. He slipped the lighter back into his pocket and drummed his fingers on the counter.

"Well then, perhaps you should talk to one of the doctors or nurses up on the second floor maternity ward. You'll find the elevators down the corridor there on your left." Puckering her face, she dismissed him with a wave of her hand in the direction of the bank of elevators. Henry turned on his heel and departed, muttering under his breath as he cursed whoever was responsible for this oversight.

As Henry stepped off the elevator, the smells and sounds of a busy hospital floor assaulted his senses. He fought the urge to cover his nose. The maternity ward was a beehive of activity. Nurses in prim white uniform dresses, starched caps and sensible cushioned sole shoes scurried past Henry. Two tired looking orderlies pushing carts laden with evening dinner trays, jockeyed for position in the narrow hallway. The pungent aroma of hospital food forced Henry to hold his breath until they pushed past him. Locating the nurse's station, Henry marched with purpose to the desk. He stopped in front of a nurse who was busy relaying orders on the telephone. He quickly scanned her nametag identifying her as "Nurse Whitfield." Henry leaned over the counter. "Excuse me. Can you ..."

The nurse looked up offering Henry a vague distracted look as she removed her tortoise shell glasses letting them hang suspended by a silver chain. Resting her glasses on her ample bosom, she held up her index finger stopping him mid-sentence. "Just a minute, sir. I'll be right with you," she said covering the mouthpiece of the phone with her hand.

Henry straightened and checked the time on his ancient Bulova wristwatch. He paced back and forth in front of the desk impatiently.

Ending her call, she became all business. "Thank you for waiting, Sir. May I help you?" she asked.

Henry forsook any attempt at polite niceties. "Yes you can. I was told my wife was admitted earlier and I need to find out why and I need to know where she is. Her name is Sophia Murphy. I'm here to take her home."

Nurse Whitfield reached for a nearby clipboard, replaced her glasses and checked for Sophia's name.

"Yes sir. Your wife was admitted. She is in room 236, bed 4."

"Why was she admitted? She just came in for a check up. She was having a little backache."

Nurse Whitfield appeared confused. "Sir, your wife won't be going home with you today. Didn't anyone phone you?"

"No. Why would they?"

The nurse removed her glasses once more. "Mr. Murphy, that little backache that your wife had turned out to be a baby girl. She was born a few hours ago. I'm sorry no one telephoned you."

Henry paled noticeably and grabbed the desk for support. The nurse responded quickly to his alarm and led Henry to the small waiting area adjacent to the nurses' station. She forced him to sit and offered to fetch him a cold beverage. "Perhaps you should put your head down between your knees, Sir," she suggested.

Too numb to respond, Henry let instinct dictate as he leaned over and took a deep breath. He needed both hands to support his head and hold his cart wheeling thoughts inside his skull. Intense guilt was the emotional forerunner. "It's all my fault," he whispered. "I shouldn't have fought with her this morning." He lifted unseeing eyes to the sympathetic nurse and babbled in guilt. "I knew I had crossed a line when I threw the clock at her. I was just so mad at her."

Nurse Whitfield soothed with little shoulder pats and compassionate words. "There, there. I'm sure everything will be just fine," she soothed.

Henry's gaze had become wild-eyed as he fretted with concern. "I've been walking on egg shells around Sophia for months. She's been harder than ever to live with these days. I blame myself for this. I should have controlled my temper. *Never hit a woman, no matter how mad she makes you!* That's what my dad always taught me."

The nurse offered Henry a scowl that was clearly meant as a reprimand for his confession.

"No ... geez ... it wasn't like that! I NEVER would really hit Soph. But blast it all! I *wanted* to. For the first time ever I was so tempted to just haul off and belt her. I'm not gonna lie about that. But I didn't hit her! I swear it! I threw the clock towards her and she pivoted in the wrong direction and it nailed her in the back. It was an accident! Aww, Lord, what have I done?"

As the news of his daughter's birth sank in, Henry stopped abruptly. "A baby girl? Oh my gosh. Is she — I mean, are they both all right?

"Yes sir. They're both doing just fine. If you would like, I could take you to your wife's room. She should be ready to wake up soon."

"Yes. I'd like that. I need to see Sophia." Henry stood and let the nurse guide him down the hall.

Grateful Henry wasn't about to faint on her, Nurse Whitfield smiled appearing to be relieved that she wasn't in the presence of some psychotic wife beater. Her attitude suddenly changed and she became an animated chatterbox as she led him down the corridor.

"Congratulations, Mr. Murphy! A new baby girl! That's so exciting! Your wife did just fine, in spite of her little alarm clock *accident.*" She turned a raised eyebrow his way and continued, unperturbed. "There were no complications that are common with premature deliveries. Your little girl was just anxious to get here, I guess. She is rather tiny, but that's to be expected when a baby is more than six weeks early. She weighs almost 5-½ pounds and is just as cute as a bug's ear. They'll want both your wife and baby to stay in the hospital for a few days, but that's nothing to be alarmed at. They ran some preliminary tests to be sure her heart and lungs are well developed and so far everything has checked out just fine. Here we are!"

The nurse steered Henry in the room that was occupied not only by Sophia, but three other women who were all busy eating their evening meal. Sophia was in the farthest bed from the door and had her back turned to the rest of the room; her dinner tray all but ignored.

Henry gave the nurse a cursory thank you and approached Sophia's bed with a light step, afraid of waking her. He pulled a chair over and sat staring at his wife's back now adorned in an unattractive hospital issue gown. Sophia, who was a light sleeper by nature, stirred and rolled over.

She opened her eyes and took a moment to get her bearings. Realization dawned as her hands immediately went to her stomach which now was a mere protrusion of what it had been only hours earlier.

"Oh God." She brought a hand to her face to massage her forehead. She groaned and looked over and found Henry staring at her with a guilt-ridden face. "Where the blazes have you been?"

Henry slouched lower in his chair as shame washed over him. "Ssshhh, Soph. Lower your voice."

Sophia struggled to sit up slightly, grimacing in pain as she shifted her weight. "Don't shush me," she spat. "You were supposed to come right back for me. Why weren't you here when this baby was born? I tried to tell you that my backache was something, but as usual, you wouldn't listen to me."

The room grew strangely quiet. Henry snuck a peek over his shoulder and noticed the other three patients stealing glances at

Sophia's loud accusations. "Sophia, please. Lower your voice, Baby. You want everybody to know our business?"

"Don't you 'baby' me. You were with *her* weren't you?" Sophia's expression became distorted in anger.

"Come on, Soph. There is no her. I already told you that. Why won't you believe me?"

"Because you're nothing but a good for nothing liar. Why should I believe anything you say? Admit it. That's why you threw that clock at me this morning. You were mad at me for figuring out your secret about your little hussy girlfriend."

"Sophia, stop this right now! I told you I don't have a girlfriend. I threw that clock at you because sometimes you make me so stinkin' mad I just lose all control." Henry stood up quickly, so agitated he nearly knocked the chair backwards. He paced back and forth in the small confined space. "Especially when you accuse me of something I didn't do. Now can we drop this once and for all?" Henry ran his hands through his dark wavy hair, stopped his pacing and stared down at the floor trying to regain his composure. Deciding a change of topics might be in order, Henry took a couple of deep breaths and sat down again. "So, how do you feel, Soph? How is the baby? Have you seen her? Has she got all her fingers and toes?"

Henry's barrage of questions did little to soothe Sophia's temper. "How do you think I feel? I just had a baby. There's a reason they call it labor, you know. God, I'm exhausted." She lay back and closed her eyes.

Henry made a weak attempt at charm and softened his voice and smiled.

"So, another girl, huh? I'll bet you were surprised. You thought this one was going to be a boy. Maria will be happy to have a little sister. She told me on the way to the sitter's she wanted a baby sister so she could dress her up in her dolly clothes. We'll have to keep an eye on that one. Have you thought of a name yet?"

Sophia turned pain filled eyes towards Henry. Tears glistened, threatening to spill over her dark lashes.

"No, I don't have a name yet, and quite frankly I couldn't care less. You pick something. In my mind this baby is just another mouth to feed and somebody else who's going to want something from me all the time. Why don't you just go home, Henry. I'm tired. I want to get some sleep." She closed her eyes as a lone tear escaped down her cheek. She swiped it away quickly. He wasn't used to seeing Sophia's weaknesses manifest as tears. More familiar with her unbridled anger, he found the tears very unsettling. He shoved his hands in his pockets and glanced around nervously, waiting for the moment to pass. Slow silent tears gently cascaded down her pale cheeks. Unable to bear her silent weeping any longer, Henry stood and drew near enough to wipe the tears from her face and reached for her hand.

"Sophia, please don't be this way," he soothed. "I'm sorry I wasn't here when the baby was born. I can't undo that. I don't know how to fix this. Please tell me how I can make you happy? We've got two girls now that need both of us. I need you to pull yourself out of this. I have to leave in a couple of weeks for a T.D.Y. assignment in Texas and I need to know you're going to take care of these babies."

Sophia snatched her hand away in anger.

"Temporary duty in Texas? For how long, Henry?" she snapped.

"I don't know. Six weeks, maybe longer. They haven't said yet. I'll see if I can get a one-week leave starting tomorrow so I can take care of Maria until you get out of here. Then I'll be home for a few days to help with the new baby."

The weight of his words settled upon Sophia and she visibly appeared to sink lower in the bed. Anger was replaced by despair. "You think that will make everything all right, Henry?" You'll give me one week and then be gone again? Big deal. Why bother? You're never home most of the time anyway. Why should having a new baby make any difference? Just go away, Henry. I don't want to talk to you anymore." She turned her back to him and let her tears flow.

Distraught and dejected, Henry turned to leave. Sophia rolled over and stopped him.

"Henry, wait. There's one more thing. You asked what you could do to make me happy."

Henry's heart beat double time as he turned his hope filled green eyes to her in anxiousness. He hurried to Sophia's bedside to avoid the prying eyes and ears of her roommates.

"Anything, Soph. You know I love you. I'll give you whatever you want, Baby."

"I told you after Maria was born that I didn't want any more children. But you insisted you didn't want an only child because of the way you were raised. You managed to trick me and get me drunk long enough to knock me up. Well guess what? Nothing's changed. I still don't want this baby. I don't want either of them. I just don't have what it takes to be a mother. I don't think I ever did. I want you to give me a divorce. I want a life of my own. That's what you can give me, Henry."

The knife of pain cut Henry to the core. The physical pain he felt at Sophia's remark made him take a quick step back from the bed as if he'd been burned by it.

"I'm sorry, Sophia. You know how the church feels about divorce. That's one of the reasons I married you. I never wanted to end up like my folks. No, Sophia." Henry's spine straightened with resolve. "The answer is no. No divorce."

Henry turned and made a hasty departure before Sophia could launch another missile of bitterness at him. He bit down hard on the inside of his mouth to keep the wellspring of emotional anger at bay. He stopped a passing orderly to ask for directions to the newborn nursery. Steeling himself, he prayed for strength to a God he wasn't even sure existed anymore.

Henry waited for a group of over zealous, cooing new grandparents to depart before he approached the window of the nursery. He knocked on the glass to get the nurse's attention. Any other time, Henry would have noticed the attractive auburn-haired beauty in the nurse's uniform, but not today. Too many monumental problems were heaped upon his shoulders for him to take notice of anything other than seeing his new daughter for the first time. He pointed to a tiny pink bundle in the second row off to the left. The card on the bassinet adorned with pink and blue balloons and a stork with a bundled baby in its beak, read:

IT'S A GIRL!
MURPHY, (Sophia)
8-12-60 2:14 p.m.
5 lbs. 6 oz. 18" long

The nurse, whose nametag identified her as *A. M. Grace, R.N.*, pushed the bassinet to the front row center where Henry could have a close up of her. The nurse beamed and used hand signals to inquire as to whether Henry wanted her to hold the sleeping baby up for his further inspection. He silently mouthed yes and nodded his head. Henry pressed both hands against the glass and for the first time in more than a decade, he was moved to tears. He shed tears of regret for having missed such a momentous occasion as his daughter's birth. And there were tears of shame for having disappointed his wife — again. And finally, tears of fear raced down his cheeks. Henry feared he was failing as miserably at fatherhood and marriage as his father before him had.

"Hello, you beautiful baby girl. What a precious angel you are. So, what are we going to call you?" As he continued his one-sided conversation, he swiped the offensive tears from his face and sniffed loudly. "Okay. I know this day didn't start out for you like it should have. But, I'm going to make it up to you. I don't know how, but I swear I will. How do you feel about the name Katherine? That was your great-grandmother Murphy's name, and that will be your name too. Don't you worry, little girl. Everything's going to be fine. Daddy's here."

Henry sobbed openly. He leaned forward, resting his head on the plate glass window separating him from his newborn daughter. He stood there for long minutes, uninterrupted, a solitary desperate shell of a man. He finally pushed himself back from the glass. He sniffed loudly and wiped his eyes and his nose with the back of his hand.

Henry straightened his shoulders and blew a kiss to the sleeping infant. He offered a casual finger wave good bye to his baby girl and to the nurse who'd stood rocking the infant from side to side the entire time Henry cried.

"Yes sir, Daddy's here, baby girl. You'll always have me," he whispered. Contrary to his words, Henry turned and made his way down the hall. His load of dejection so noticeable, his shoulders slumped under the weight of it.

Nurse Grace cuddled the tiny swaddled infant and pressed her close for a kiss on the top of her head. She watched the new father depart, his shoulders shaking with silent sobs. She continued to cuddle the infant and whispered prayers on the child's behalf.

"Father, this one is going to need lots of special care. Never leave her, nor forsake her. Help her to know that your Grace will always be with her."

FIVE

The large screen faded to black. Kitty sat transfixed. Tears silently streamed down her cheeks. She searched her pocket for the discarded lace hankie and turned towards Grace for explanation.

"Was that you holding me in the nursery, Grace?"

"Yes, indeed. Nurse A-Mazing Grace, at your service." Her warm smile provided small comfort to Kitty.

"You were with me the whole time?" Kitty's face mirrored her confusion. "But how? That was 43 years ago. You look exactly the same. How is that possible?"

"Isn't it wonderful? It's that whole time thing again." Grace waved her hand in the air to illustrate her point. "I've *always* been with you, Katherine. God's *grace* has always been available to you."

Kitty sniffed and wiped her nose again. "Is that supposed to be a play on words?"

Grace smiled and squeezed Kitty's arm. "Sort of. Surely you know that God's grace has always been with you, right? That *is* what His Word says."

"I know that in my head," Kitty answered. She stared off in the distance, eyes unmoving in a trance-like state. "It's what I've always been taught to believe. But I always believed that was more for *others* – not necessarily for me." She turned away and let her long hair shield her from Grace's questioning eyes.

"Why not for you, Katherine?" Grace probed.

"Because, I don't think I ever deserved God's grace." Kitty's confession was soft spoken.

"Why would you think that?"

Kitty shrugged her shoulders. "Because, I'm just … I have such …" Kitty struggled to put voice to her feelings. "I'm just not a very good person. I'm not worthy of God's grace. After watching how my life started, now I can see that I had problems from the get-go. It was pretty apparent that I was unwanted from the very beginning. That just set the groundwork for the rest of my life. Oh, Grace, I feel so ashamed." She wiped her eyes as twin streams raced down her slightly freckled cheeks.

"*Ashamed*. But why, Katherine?"

"Just look at the way my life started out." She gestured in anger at the screen. "It was so embarrassing. That was nothing like the way it was when my three children were born. My most wonderful memories are of the days my children were born. Luke and I *celebrated* the birth of all of our children. Why was the day I was born so awful? It made me feel so …" She struggled to find just the right word. "… so — oh, I don't know. It was just *wrong*."

Grace's confusion was obvious. "Wrong? Whatever do you mean?"

Kitty gave a half-hearted laugh that ended with a deep heaving sigh. "Well, where should we start? You want to talk about my dear, sweet mother who never loved or wanted me? Or should we focus on my father's Oscar-winning performance in the nursery with his bucket of tears?" Kitty's former shame was replaced with cynicism that seeped out like water through a sieve.

"You've lost me. Explain please."

Kitty shifted in agitation. "That whole thing in the nursery … where was all of that concern for me throughout my life, Grace? I've got to tell you, I'm pretty shocked my dad reacted that way, what with all the crying and stuff." Kitty pointed at the screen again to vent her hostility. "He wasn't even there for most of my life. He may have fooled you that day, but he didn't fool me. I'm not buying it. He wasn't around long enough to take care of *Daddy's little girl*. He didn't bother to show up when I had my tonsils out or I broke my arm. He wasn't there for my high school graduation, or for either one of my weddings. That little performance of his in the nursery that day clearly, fooled you," Kitty exhaled in disgust. "Now, shall we move on to *Mommy Dearest*? I think she requires little or no explanation, wouldn't you agree? Boy, I sure hit the familial lottery the day I was born, didn't I? How lucky for me to end up with those two." Kitty sneered.

"Oh Katherine, you have it all *wrong*." Grace shook her head and organized her response.

Kitty stopped ranting long enough to study her, then looked away, unsure what to expect. Kitty dared a glance in Grace's direction. She noticed that even though Grace's eyes were closed, her lips moved in what Kitty could only assume was a silent prayer. She worried her angry diatribe had somehow offended Grace.

Grace cleared her throat, turned towards Kitty and chose her words carefully.

"Katherine, surely you must know luck had *nothing* to do with the family you ended up with. You had no say in the circumstances into which you were born. Your life was pre-ordained by God."

"Pre-ordained by God? Well, I guess God doesn't like me very much then. But then I always suspected as much. Why did you have to show me that, Grace? I would be better off not knowing any of the events of my birth."

Unable to resist the urge to comfort her, Grace placed a gentle hand on Kitty's arm. "Because, dear — *every* beginning is important. Especially when the events that took place the day you were born were the foundation for everything that followed in your life. In the book of Psalms, David said, '*You made all the delicate inner parts of my body and knit me together in my mother's womb.*' God knit you together in Sophia's womb. He made all of your delicate inner parts. He had all of the hairs on your head numbered. He had a reason for making you exactly as you are and giving you to Henry and Sophia Murphy."

"But why? My mother didn't want me. My own mother didn't love me, Grace. I felt it my whole life. She and I struggled and fought and had a terrible relationship up until the day she died. What was so wrong with me that caused her to reject me? Am I really such a horrible person?" Kitty sobbed as her anger gave way to deep sorrow.

"There was nothing wrong with you. Look at me, Katherine." Grace placed a finger under Kitty's chin so she could turn her to look in her troubled eyes.

"Do you really believe Sophia didn't love you?"

"Wasn't that obvious? Weren't you watching just now? Didn't you see what I saw?"

"Yes and no. I saw a terrified young woman who felt alone and scared. I saw a woman without hope. I saw a lifetime of pain and a young woman who was fighting hard to keep that pain buried. Sophia was lashing out in anger at Henry, not you. I suspect there was love buried deep in Sophia, but she was afraid to show that vulnerable side of herself. Sophia's upbringing didn't start much better than yours. She had her own disappointments in life, as well. She didn't have any more choices in the details surrounding her birth than you did. Remember, it is God that chooses. And He chose Henry and Sophia for you, just as He chose each of their parents for them. Have you never read the book of Ephesians? It says, '*Long ago, even before he made the world, God loved us and chose us in Christ to be holy and without fault in his eyes.*' HE chose you on purpose, because HE LOVED YOU. Your birth was no accident. God did not make a mistake when He made you *exactly as you are* and gave you to Henry and Sophia." Grace's assuredness brooked no arguments.

Katherine wiped her eyes and runny nose and placed her hands in her lap.

"But what happened to her, Grace? What terrible things happened in her life that turned her into such an angry and bitter woman?"

"I'm sorry, Katherine, but I'm not at liberty to share any of the details of anyone else's life; only the details that occurred over the course of *your* lifetime as they interacted with you. Upon her death, your mother got to see the details of her life as she passed through here. I guess I know Sophia better than you. I know how she felt about her role as wife and mother. I know how she felt about you. She and I had a very similar question and answer period when she visited here. There are always so many questions."

"But that's not fair, Grace! Everything that happened in my parent's lives affected my life. Why can't I know what you know about my mother?" Kitty pleaded.

"I'm sorry, but those are the rules. I don't make them, I just enforce them. Is life always fair? Or *death*, for that matter. You are only 43-years-old. Ask your children if your falling off a treadmill and ending up here is fair? God is no respecter of persons. He treats everyone with the same love, grace and mercy. The choices people make ... the paths they choose ... oftentimes, lives are impacted by a casual or careless decision to go in one direction as opposed to another. God is fair in the fact that He gave *everyone* free will. If your mother never shared her secrets with you, it's because she had a reason not to. That was her choice. It wouldn't be *fair* of me to divulge those secrets without her consent. Don't you agree? And think on this for a moment, Katherine. Do you see any other observers here with us now?"

Kitty shook her head no.

"We are about to showcase the major events that shaped *your* life; the steps which directed your path to this point. How would you feel if we invited others to witness your life? Your successes. Your failures. Your secrets. Your *shame*?" Grace carefully enunciated each choice.

Fear crept into Katherine's red-rimmed eyes.

"No. Please. I couldn't bear it if anyone else were to know the horrible truths about me."

"Exactly. All of your secrets will remain here. As will Henry and Sophia's own private secrets. That's the rule."

Kitty sniffed loudly. "So it's kind of like that, *what happens in Vegas – stays in Vegas* thing?"

"Hmm ... well, we're not quite as commercial or decadent as Vegas. But seriously, you really must trust me, Katherine. This will all make sense to you before we're finished," Grace said with conviction.

"I'm so humiliated from watching the day I was born. Hearing my mom say those things out loud really hurt. And my dad's emotional reactions to that day caught me by surprise. Watching that brief passage of time has upset the balance of truths and lies I was brought up to believe about my dad and his character. Nearly 40 years of half-truths were just destroyed." Kitty paused to shake her head and clear the cobweb of thoughts. "This is all so heavy, Grace. I'm sorry if I'm not reacting the way I'm supposed to. But, I've never died before, so I don't know if there is supposed to be some sort of protocol. I hope you can forgive me for being so angry. I guess I wasn't prepared for this all to be so — informative. I hope you'll help me to make sense of all this, Grace." There was no joking in her plea, only a genuine need for understanding.

"It's all right, Katherine. Are you ready to see the next life-shaping clip?" Grace asked.

Kitty groaned. "Do we have to? I feel bad enough already. I *know* what my life was like. I lived it already. Thanks for pointing out all that stuff about God choosing me on purpose. I get it. God loved me. My life had lots of rocky moments. Parts of it just plain sucked. Is it really necessary to sit through more of this? It's just so *hhhaaarrrddddd.*" Kitty drew the word out in an annoying whine. Where moments ago she sought understanding, Kitty now crossed her arms and pouted like a petulant child who had been caught scribbling on the walls with a crayon. "Can't we just fast-forward to the end? It would be great if this all made sense, but I don't want to watch anything else unpleasant. No more bad stuff, okay?"

"No promises, Katherine. Unpleasantness is sometimes part of it. We have to complete the process. It's a cycle. You must come full circle in order to prepare yourself to meet God." Grace fluffed her flowing gown about her. Her silky mane resembled a molten halo and she casually brushed it off her shoulders settling it about her face making her look so relaxed, as if she hadn't a care in the world. Kitty wished she had the luxury of being able to abandon all care, but her inner turmoil was dancing to a beat all its own.

"Do you know how much more there is to watch, Grace?"

"Yes, I am aware of it all. I told you, God's *grace* has always been with you. We will see everything that happens together," Grace smiled.

"Do you know how long this will take?"

"Time doesn't exist for you now. There is no measure of minutes, hours or days. The passage of time is no more. This will take exactly as long as is necessary to bring you to understanding. It's up to you when that will be." Grace shifted her position and out of the corner of her eye Kitty caught a glimpse of delicate feet shod with strappy-jeweled sandals. Pale pink polished toes appliquéd with stars played hide-n-seek under Grace's flowing gown.

For a moment Kitty forgot her circumstances and smiled and thought, "How odd. An angel with a pedicure."

Kitty realized that nothing was as it should be. "Normal" could no longer be clearly defined. Death was nothing like she ever imagined. During bouts of depression throughout her life, Kitty occasionally entertained dark, macabre fantasies envisioning what death would be like. This wasn't it. She felt relieved there had been no physical pain thus far, just the gut-wrenching emotional pain. She wondered if she might have preferred a physical blow to her body rather than this emotional battering and humiliation.

Grace's assessment of the existence of time had been correct. It was impossible for Kitty to discern how long she'd been in the screening room. The events displaying her birth could have taken 30 minutes or three days. Time had no distinction. Kitty knew she remembered somewhere in Scripture there was a passage that explained, to God a day was like a thousand years and vice versa. She now wished she had been more diligent in memorizing Scripture. Kitty mentally added poor Scriptural recall to her ever-growing long list of things she had failed miserably in as a Christian. If this process took a long time, Kitty couldn't help but question if there would be an intermission later. Maybe one with snacks. Her obsessive mindset towards food kicked in and she worried if calories counted in Heaven. Or maybe she wasn't even in Heaven, but purgatory, sentenced to an eternity of watching home movies. Oh Lord, help me, she thought. She did a cursory internal inventory and seemed surprised that she didn't feel hungry or thirsty. Oddly enough, Kitty felt a sense of relief. After 30-some years of doing battle with everything that went into her mouth, she felt a wonderful sense of freedom.

Grace interrupted Kitty's thoughts as if she'd been reading her mind.

"We can take a break whenever you feel the need."

"No, Grace, I think I'm fine for now. Other than feeling like I'm emotionally bankrupt now, I feel okay — I guess. I don't know whether I should be hungry or tired. It seems as though I should feel some sort of urge but I don't. I can't believe I don't even have to go to the bathroom, which is odd for me. With all the water I drink, I usually have to pee a couple thousand times a day." She felt an instant blush heating her cheeks. "Oops. Can I see *pee* in here?"

"I think you just did say it. Twice, actually. It's okay," Grace laughed.

"Well all righty then. I guess we can go ahead with the next ... thingie," she said, pointing at the screen. Kitty lowered her voice to a conspiratorial whisper. "Grace, will it be as tough to watch as the one we just viewed?"

"I'm not sure, dear. Perception is in the eye of the beholder. Everyone who was present in the next event had a different interpretation than you. The circumstances changed the lives of everyone involved. How you perceive the episode is up to you. Only you can know your feelings. Shall we begin?" Grace asked.

Kitty shrugged her shoulders in response. "I guess so. But Grace, is this whole process just about the bad things that happened in my life? Will there be *anything* good or happy?" Kitty pressed.

Grace's face was unreadable. "We shall see, dear. We shall see."

Kitty resolved herself to the unknown and turned her attention once again to the screen as the unseen projector churned to life and a new date flashed suddenly and then disappeared just as quickly.

SIX

July 3, 1965

The pale yellow aluminum siding on the single-story houses had faded with the passage of time. Years of Texas dust storms had dulled the brick facades under the large plate glass windows from a bright brick house red to one of dingy rust. Throughout the neighborhood little boys ran barefoot and shirtless through struggling water sprinklers barely more than a trickle, while little girls in colorful rompers splashed in play pools and blew bubbles with reckless abandon. Lawns, which only weeks ago had been brilliantly green, were now a patchwork of lifeless hues and burnt brown splotches. The central Texas summer heat, searing and relentless, slowly robbed nutrients from all greenery so that by summer's end, only dry brown yards remained. Flags and banners dressed houses for the next day's 4th of July celebration. Many of the flags were tattered on the edges from too many years left to the defenses of the frequent Texas dust devils. Funding wasn't available for such expenditures. This was military housing at its finest.

An old station wagon came around a corner and the driver, mindful of children at play; slowly maneuvered his way to the last house on the street. Henry Murphy pulled into the shaded carport and cut the engine. He got out and high-stepped with caution around a smorgasbord of bikes, wagons, balls and doll strollers. His sweat soaked uniform was hopelessly wrinkled.

Before he turned the doorknob, Henry paused to listen to the sounds of his children playing inside. He could make out the faint sounds of the television mingling with the clatter of dishes in the sink. He steeled himself for what he was about to do to his family.

* * * * *

Kitty sat quietly, absorbed in the images of children playing and the sounds and smells of the dry Texas summer. She automatically began fanning her face with her hand to ward off the sudden change in temperature surrounding her.

"Poor Daddy. He looks like he's aged considerably, yet it's only been five years since the last scene. "He's going to walk through that door and tear our family apart, Grace."

"Do you remember this day, Katherine?"

"Vaguely." Kitty bit her bottom lip and continued the wild fanning with her hands. "I'm a little sketchy on some of the details. Lord, is it hot in here, or is it just me?"

"I'm afraid it's just you. You have become part of the action on the screen again. The sights, sounds, smells, emotions *and* temperatures."

Just then Kitty slapped her right calf. "Good Lord! Did you see the size of that horsefly? I think the little sucker just bit me," she screeched.

"Sorry, I couldn't resist," Grace grinned.

"What? You did that, Grace?"

"Guilty. I just want to make sure you're totally absorbed in what's happening. Just like you can feel the heat of the sun and the occasional breeze on your face, I think it's only fitting that you *feel* the insects as well. After all, they are all God's creatures, you know." Grace looked pleased with herself.

"Ha Ha! Not funny, Grace. I'm feeling quite enough, thank you. I could do without the bugs, if you don't mind. Yeesh! I hate bugs!" Kitty grimaced in disgust. She stood up and brushed off her seat and ran her hands over her arms and legs to be sure there were no errant insects hiding anywhere ready to crawl on her. Before she sat down she squatted and peeked below the seat to check the floor underneath.

"It's all right, Katherine. There's nothing else there. I promise. I'm sorry. I'll try to behave myself." Grace hid a smile behind her long shapely fingers.

"Fine." Kitty sat down, wary of Grace's motives. She pointed a warning finger at Grace. "But no more bugs. And no snakes, spiders, cockroaches or scorpions either."

"I promise, on my honor." Grace covered her heart with her hand. "Let's continue."

Kitty tried to make herself comfortable but felt somewhat edgy. She wasn't entirely sure whether she was more freaked out by the horsefly and Grace's ability to produce such reality, or by witnessing the upcoming destruction of her family. Within minutes, Kitty forgot where she was and felt so completely absorbed in the moment, she couldn't be sure if she was actually sitting in her old house in Texas or still seated next to Grace in the screening room.

* * * * *

Henry pushed the door open and a blast of warm air struck him as two fans and the window air conditioner fought for control of the small living room. Henry walked over, turned off the television and called out a greeting to his three children. He expected the kids to race to his side and fight to be the first to throw their arms around his waist and his legs. Instead he saw three little bodies scurrying out of sight and the slam of the hall closet door as they raced for refuge.

He could hear Sophia in the kitchen humming softly along with the radio as she washed dishes. The smell of lemony dish soap was barely distinguishable over the ever-pervasive odor of stale cigarette smoke, which hung in the air and clung to the cheap second hand furniture.

Oblivious to the fact that Henry had come in, Sophia yelled at the kids. "Hey you kids, quit slamming doors! Why don't you go outside and play before your father gets home!"

No response. Sophia turned the flow of water off and lowered the volume on the radio.

"Hey what's going on in there? Where did you little monsters go?"

Sophia laid aside the dish she'd been washing and reached for the towel on her shoulder to dry her hands. She reached up to check the dampness of her hair, which had been artfully arranged into neat little pin curls and secured with a mass of bobbie pins. She came out of the kitchen drying her hands and was surprised to find Henry standing in the middle of the small living room. He stood there unmoving, twisting his uniform cap in his hands.

"What are you doing home? It's only 3:30. I wasn't expecting you for at least another hour and a half."

Henry's mind was a jumble of thoughts and emotions. As he took in Sophia's unkempt appearance and her flawless, unlined face free of make-up, he placed a hand on his stomach to quiet the little flutter in the pit of his gut. He was still affected by her striking good looks. Even with her hair in pin curls and bobbie pins, he still believed she was the prettiest woman he'd ever laid eyes on — and the most difficult person in the world to love and to live with. Some days he was hard pressed to remember what it was exactly that he loved about her. The news he was about to deliver would shake Sophia's world upside down. But Henry knew if he ever hoped to have any semblance of happiness in his life, he needed to make the break soon – before he became as hard and brittle as Sophia.

Sophia's harsh voice jarred Henry from his musings.

"Well? What are you doing home so early? You know dinner isn't going to be ready for a while. So I hope you don't expect me to feed you this early."

"No that's okay, Soph. I wasn't expecting dinner to be ready. Can't a guy come home a little early once in a while?" Henry tossed his cap aside, pulled his wrinkled shirt free from his trousers and began to unbutton it as he headed down the hall towards the bedroom. "Man it's a hot one today, huh. Where're the kids? Why aren't they outside playing with the neighbors?"

Sophia retrieved Henry's cap and followed him down the hall as he talked over his shoulder at her. "I don't want them playing with any of those hooligans," Sophia snapped. "They're picking up all sorts of filthy habits from those monsters. All of their mothers are busybodies and their daddies stay out all night drinking. No! I don't want my children playing with any of them."

"Give it a rest, Soph. There's nothing wrong with the neighbors or their kids. They're no different than us. Give the kids a break and let them make a few friends. At least then they'd be out of your hair and you could stop complaining about them being underfoot all day." Henry removed his shirt, tossed it on the bed and began rummaging in the bureau for a pair of shorts.

"You make me sound like a snobbish shrew," Sophia snipped. "And besides, what's the point in letting them make new friends anyway? You know we're only going to be here for another few weeks. Once your new orders are confirmed, we'll be leaving. Pick up your shirt, Henry, and put it in the hamper," she ordered. "Do you think I'm your maid?"

Henry straightened and did his best to quash his anger. "Give me a sec, will you. I wasn't going to leave it there." Henry rolled his eyes heavenward and mumbled under his breath. "I just want to get out of this sticky uniform. I'm burning up. And I never said I thought you were my maid. I don't expect you to pick up after me. I'll do it in a minute." He grumbled and disappeared into the small bathroom to change his clothes.

Sophia's complaints increased in volume so she could be heard over the flush of the toilet and the sound of running water. "No you never said so, but you sure as almighty treat me like a maid. You go off to work all day and leave me here to take care of these – these *kids!*" She spat the word out like the very taste of it had set her tongue ablaze. "You expect me to cook and clean and do your laundry and do the shopping on what little money you bring home, and sometimes I feel like that's all I am is a hired servant." She shoved Henry's shirt aside and laid down in disgust on the bed. She stretched out and threw her arm over her eyes to shield them from the sun peeking through the window shade.

Henry emerged from the bathroom and tossed his uniform in the hamper in the corner, which was already steepled high with a mound of dirty discarded clothes. He shook his head, expelled his pent-up frustration in a long exhausted sigh and did his best not to comment about the mountain of soiled laundry. Sophia was quick to give him a litany of the chores she did, yet the overflowing hamper bore evidence to the fact that the laundry hadn't been touched in days.

He glanced down at his wife on the bed and quietly counted to ten to diffuse his mounting irritation with her.

Sophia's breathing had slowed as she lay on the bed. "Henry, since you're home so early, why don't you go watch the kids while I take a little nap." She inhaled deeply and exhaled a long weary breath. "Lord, I can't even remember the last time I had a nap in the middle of the day." She rolled over gingerly, careful not to disturb her pin curls.

"Yeah ... fine. Whatever. You take yourself a little nap, Soph. But we need to talk tonight after the kids go to bed."

Sophia mumbled something incoherent as Henry left the room. He closed the door softly behind him.

He waited until he cleared the hallway before he beckoned for his children. "Hey where's Daddy's babies? C'mon, ya'll. Where are you guys hiding?"

Henry headed for the coat closet and pulled the door open quickly and made scary monster noises as he jerked the door open.

"Boo!" he roared.

All three children screamed and then laughed at the same time. They gathered around their father waiting for even a moment of his attention. Henry gave eight-year-old Maria a hearty squeeze and a peck on the head.

"Hey, Darlin'. How's my princess today?"

"I'm fine, Daddy. Dopie Toby next door got his hand stuck in an old can in the back of his momma's tomato garden today. And when she came out and saw him screamin' like a stuck pig, she gave him a swat on the be-hind and started yellin' at him. When she helped him pull his hand out of the can, he had a big fat green worm in his fist. His momma was yellin' at him to put it down." Maria's eyes grew enormous and she gestured wildly to illustrate her story. "And he did too but not before he squeezed the guts out of it! It was juicy and green. It looked just like he had a hand full of slimy boogers! It was neat!" she laughed.

"Neat, huh?" Henry replied with feigned interest. Maria skipped out of the room, having spilled her exciting story.

He wondered when Maria had played with the next-door neighbor if Sophia had forbidden them to interact with the neighborhood children. It was obvious his wife wasn't watching the kids as closely as she implied. Maria's language was certainly colorful enough, which suggested she had been keeping company with someone other than her little brother and sister these days.

Henry reached down and picked up three-year-old Wesley and gently smacked his hand. "Get your thumb out of your mouth, boy. You're not a baby any more," he admonished the toddler. Wesley extracted his fat pudgy thumb, leaving a trail of saliva in its wake. Henry blew raspberries on Wesley's bare midriff until the little boy squealed in delight. Henry wrinkled his nose as he got a whiff of Wesley's overripe diaper. "Hey pal. Go get me a fresh diaper so we can change you before that stink peels the paint off the walls," he said, setting Wesley on the floor. He ruffled Wesley's hair, who promptly stuck his thumb back in his mouth and toddled off.

Shy, reserved, nearly five-year-old Katherine stood patiently by waiting for her turn. Henry hoisted her high in the air and then settled her on his hip. "Hey, how's my baby girl? What did you do today, sweet pea?" he whispered in her ear.

Katherine hugged him tight around his neck and covered his stubbled jaw with kisses. She pulled back and patted his cheeks. "Daddy, your face is all prickly. Does it hurt?" Her eyes widened with concern as she patted his face.

Henry obliged her by rolling his neck all around giving her full access to the contours of his face. "That's daddy's five o'clock shadow, baby girl. And no, it doesn't hurt. In fact, it feels lots better when you give me kisses." Henry smiled his affection for her.

She laughed and kissed him noisily on both cheeks. "I missed you today, Daddy." Her green eyes so like his own, turned suddenly serious. "Daddy, can I tell you a secret in your ear?" She lowered her voice and looked over Henry's shoulder to be sure they were alone. Henry nodded yes. Cupping her tiny hands she leaned in close to his ear. "Mommy slapped Maria on the face today cause she found out she went next door to play with Toby. And then she spanked Wesley when he got up from his nap cause he wet the bed again. And then she screamed at him cause she had to put a diaper on him again instead of the big boy underpants. Poor Wesley. It's not his fault, Daddy. He's still just a baby. Doesn't Momma know that?"

Henry walked out to the kitchen with Katherine still on his hip and grabbed a box of wafer cookies off a nearby shelf. He sat down at the scarred Formica kitchen table and settled Katherine more comfortably in his lap so they could share the cookies.

"No, baby girl. Sometimes I think Mommy forgets that Wesley is still just a little guy. But Wesley's not exactly a baby anymore, either. Your momma's just anxious for him to be potty trained. Where were you when Momma spanked Wesley and slapped Maria?" Henry nibbled cookies and fingered Katherine's waist-length brown hair.

"I was hiding in my closet so she wouldn't find me and spank me too. She was real mad the whole day, so I just tried to be imbizzable." She licked the end of her finger and stabbed at crumbs that had fallen on her shirt.

"You mean invisible?" Henry laughed. "You didn't want Mommy to see you?" he asked.

"Yes sir. That's it. I didn't want her to see me. She was on the phone for a really long, long time. I could hear Mommy yelling at Aunt Gina on the phone all the way in my room. I know it was Aunt Gina too cause I heard Momma say, 'damn it, Gina' a whole bunch of times." Katherine held an imaginary telephone, imitating her mother's angry phone conversation, complete with wild hand gestures and facial expressions.

The sight of her role-playing caused Henry to laugh, in spite of the worry niggling at his brain. Sophia and Gina screaming at each other? That's never good, he thought. The telephone trilled loudly interrupting his thoughts. Henry put Katherine down so he could answer it.

"Just a minute, sweetie," he apologized to Katherine. "Let me see who this is." Henry reached for the phone mounted on the wall next to the cabinets. As soon as he heard the voice on the other end, he turned his back to Katherine. "Hold on a minute," Henry whispered to the caller. "Hey, baby girl, why don't you go play in the other room for a few minutes while I take this call."

"Yes sir." Katherine turned to skip out of the room. Henry stopped her before she left as if remembering something.

"Wait a minute, princess. How come you and Wesley and Maria went to hide in the closet when I got home?"

She stopped and turned soulful eyes that were wise beyond her years, to Henry. "Cause we don't like the screaming."

Henry looked confused. "What do you mean, sweetheart? What screaming?"

"You know – the *screaming*, Daddy." She rolled her eyes the same way Sophia did when she was irritated.

Henry shrugged.

"Every night when you come home from work that's when you and Mommy start screaming at each other," she talked patiently like she was the parent and her father was the child. "We go hide in the closet cause it scares us. Specially Wesley. Maria has to hug him real close cause we don't want him to cry and make the screaming worse. Sometimes she puts her hands over his mouth to keep him quiet. Like this." Katherine covered her mouth with both hands to show her father what it looked like.

Katherine turned and left the room. Henry grimaced as though he'd been punched. *Idiot*, he chided himself. He smacked the wall with an open palm before he made his way out to the service porch.

"Son of a ..." he muttered, letting his curse hang in the air. He couldn't believe the kids overheard the heated arguments he and Sophia engaged in regularly. He thought they'd been more careful about shielding the children, but apparently – according to Katherine – they weren't doing a very good job of it. Henry stretched the telephone cord as far as he could and shut the door so he could have some privacy. Although he was alone, he continued to keep one hand protectively around the mouthpiece and talk in muted tones. Henry kept a wary eye on the door at all times.

"Vera? What are you doing calling me at home? I told you never to call me here. What if Sophia had answered the phone?"

The voice on the other end of the line purred an apology. "Oh, honey, I'm sorry to call you at home. But when I called your office they told me you already left for the day. I just had to hear your voice, Henry. I miss you so much. Did you talk to your wife yet? I need to know what's going on so I can give my boss notice before I quit my job."

SEVEN

Kitty's sharp intake of air didn't go unnoticed by Grace. The action on the movie screen halted momentarily while Kitty seethed.

"Are you all right, Katherine?"

"That snake! My mother didn't lie to me. He really *did* cheat on her! What a son of a ...?"

"Katherine! I will not tolerate that kind of language here," Grace warned.

Kitty instantly became defensive. "I wasn't going to say what you think I was. I don't use *that* kind of language."

"Well, I should hope not. We do have our limits here, you know?"

"If you must know, I was going to say biscuit!" Kitty cut her off. "My dad was a son-of-a-biscuit!" How dare he!" Kitty stood up in anger and fumed. Grace tried to calm her.

"Well, we won't even get into how silly that whole statement is. I mean, *really*. What would one actually classify as a *son-of-a-biscuit*? Would that be like ... I don't know – a bread nugget? A dough blob? No, wait. A dough boy!" She grinned at her pun. Kitty turned away in disgust. Grace shirked her shoulders. "Oh well, no matter. But admit it – it was *kind of* funny." Grace grinned at her own wit.

Kitty rolled her eyes and crossed her arms angrily, ignoring Grace altogether.

"Come now, Katherine. Sit back down, please." Grace shook off her attempted good humor and turned serious again. "I really don't think you should be so judgmental of your father and this particular situation."

"What? You of all people should have an unshakeable moral position on adultery. I don't care how cold-hearted and unlovable my mother may have been. Adultery, even the mere thought of it, is never justified!" She sat down in a huff. Her anger escalated to a boiling point causing a large vein to bulge and pulsate at her temple. Her green eyes turned ominously dark, looking like they could spit flames at any moment.

"You really should calm down, dear, before your eyes pop out of your skull."

"Grace, how can you sit there so calmly? Did you forget about *thou shalt not commit adultery?*" Kitty balled her fists in her lap.

"No, I'm very aware of the commandment. But your anger will not change the situation. Clearly your father made some mistakes. I am not making light of his adulterous relationship or trying to justify it. I'm merely suggesting that before you pass judgment and crucify your father, make very certain you know all the facts. Now ... shall we proceed, or do you need a few more minutes to simmer in your self-righteous stew?" Grace crossed her arms mimicking Kitty and cocked one eyebrow making it look like it had been snagged by a fishhook. She waited.

Kitty's anger disintegrated to be replaced by sudden shame. "I'm sorry, Grace. You're right, of course. I've always been way too judgmental. It's a nasty habit of mine. Might as well add that to my ever-growing list. I'll try and do better."

Relaxing a bit, Grace placed her hands in her lap. "Very well then. That's better. Let's see what develops."

Henry Murphy's larger than life figure moved to action.

* * * * *

Henry's smile was a mixture of guilt and abject pleasure. He took a deep breath to steady his racing pulse. He closed his eyes for a moment before he spoke.

"Oh, baby, it's good to hear your voice too. I really can't talk long, though. Sophia is taking a nap and she could wake up any minute. I think I've got all the details worked out." Henry absently picked at a piece of peeling plaster with his thumbnail. When the stubborn plaster chipped the end of Henry's nail, he stuck the ragged digit in his mouth. He nervously chewed his nail trying to even out the rough edge. "I'm going to tell her tonight after the kids are in bed. I heard from that Judge's office in Reno and I should be able to get a quickie divorce in a few weeks. If Sophia agrees, I can take her back to Jersey to live with her folks and then you, me and the kids can head to California."

The silence on the other end of the phone line gave Henry cause for concern. "Vera ... baby. Are you still there?"

"Yes. I'm still here." She offered nothing further.

Henry's nervousness grew. "Honey? We talked about all this. Remember? You said you couldn't wait to set up house and have a ready-made family. Why are you so quiet? You're not having doubts now are you?" Henry rushed on not waiting for her to respond. "C'mon, baby. I need you to support me one hundred percent on this or it's not going to work. I told you weeks ago that maybe we shouldn't be making all these plans. But you said you loved me and you wanted us to be together. *All of us.* It's not too late to change your mind if you're not sure about all this. I haven't told Sophia or the kids anything yet. So you better speak up now." Henry ran a nervous hand through his wavy hair then shoved his shaky palm in his pocket. "Vera?"

Vera's tone changed slightly. "It's just that ... well, Henry – I'm only 22 years old. How am I going to be a mother to three kids? I don't know nothing about being a momma. All I've ever done is cashiering at the P.X. That's the only reason we met in the first place. I never pretended to be something I'm not. How am I going to know what to do with them? I thought you were going to wait awhile before you sent for the kids. I've never even met them. How do I know if they're even going to like me?" Her voice sounded petulant.

"Why are you bringing this up now? Why didn't you say something earlier?" Henry began to pace as best he could in the small confined porch space. He stopped suddenly. "I told you on that first day I was married and had kids. I never lied to you. When we went out for coffee that first time and I told you what a cold unfeeling wife I had, you were full of sympathy for me *and* my kids. You said you had the same kind of life growing up. A house filled with fighting and anger. Do you remember what you did?" He rushed on before she could answer. "You put your hand on my arm and rubbed it back and forth and told me how sad it was for my kids to grow up that way. I told you all about my sham of a marriage. I swear to God, when you looked at me with those big baby blues full of tears, I thought – *finally* – somebody understands!" He threw up his hand in frustration even though she couldn't see him. "I tried so hard to stay away from you, Vera, I swear I did. But you kept telling me I deserved to be happy. You said my kids deserved to be happy. You pushed me into this affair because you acted like you cared about me and my kids!" His voice rose in agitation. "Was I wrong about everything, Vera?"

"No! You aren't wrong! Oh, baby! I do care," she cooed. "I'm so sorry, Henry," she sighed breathlessly.

Henry leaned up against the closed door and stared at the water stained ceiling tiles. "Lord, I've even been going to confession every week cause I've felt so guilty about us. Do you know how many extra *Hail Mary's* and *Our Father's* I've said over the last few months? Or how many candles I had to light at church?"

The voice on the other end of the line sniffed. Henry couldn't be sure if she was crying or not. "Oh, Henry. Please don't be angry with me. I love you so much. You know I'll do anything for you. For *us.* Only please don't be mad at me, okay? You're the sweetest, most caring man I've ever known. All most men want is sex, but you're not like that. You're different. I've never met a man who cared so much for his kids before. This is all kind of new to me. You know I adore you, baby," she said coyly.

For a man who'd been on compassion rationing for so long, he couldn't keep himself from grinning like a lovesick schoolboy. Her words were like sweet nectar. "You adore me, huh?" he gloated. "I've never been adored by anybody before."

"Oh, Henry," she twittered.

"Well, what's it going to be then?" His tone changed to one of seriousness. "Have you changed your mind? You've got to tell me now, baby. Before it's too late." Henry twisted the phone cord around his finger in nervousness.

"Oh, Henry. You know I love you. I do. I do. And I want to be with you – really. But three kids, honey. I'm just so … so *scared*," she sniffed loudly.

"It'll be okay, Vera. I promise. You know I love you too. We can make this work. I know we can." Henry wasn't sure if he was trying harder to convince himself or Vera.

"Okay, Henry. Whatever you say. If you say we can make this work, then I trust you, baby."

Henry closed his eyes and dropped his chin to his chest exhaling in relief. After getting the go-ahead from Vera, he did his best to cut his phone call short for fear that Sophia would discover him.

"Vera, I really can't talk anymore. I haven't told Sophia anything yet. Somehow I think she already suspects something's up. She's been accusing me of cheating on her since the first month we got married."

"Oh you poor thing," she said sympathetically, before her voice changed to one of concern. "Did you ever cheat on your wife, Henry? I mean before me?"

"How can you even ask that, Vera? I told you I've never done anything like this before, as God is my witness." He placed his right hand over his heart almost as a pledge. "You're special, baby."

"Oh, Henry, I love you so much."

"Listen, Vera. I gotta go. I promise I'll call you when I leave here tonight and everything's all said and done." Henry spoke in hushed tones for a few more minutes. Vera offered her support and encouragement on her end of the line. Hearing one of his children in the kitchen, Henry ended the call and went back inside to replace the receiver.

Maria was in the process of boosting Katherine up on the counter when Henry came in. He felt the sting of guilt-induced sweat in his eyes and took a second to wipe his damp brow with the back of his hand.

"Whoa, hold on there a minute. What do you two think you're doing? You know you don't belong on the counter," Henry scolded.

Katherine hopped down and fixed Henry with an innocent, *"who me?"* kind of look.

"We're sorry, Daddy, but we wanted to get a glass so we could have a drink."

Henry surveyed the kitchen area. The remains of lunch littered the kitchen table, which Henry had failed to notice earlier. Dishes were piled on both sides of the sink —some drying, some still soaking. It appeared as though every available space was cluttered with either dishes or food staples. Henry poked his head into the living room and noticed similar clutter there. Newspapers, toys and books were scattered everywhere. The threadbare rug looked as though it hadn't seen the carpet sweeper in weeks. A thick layer of dust covered the furniture and fingerprints dotted the small screen of the black and white television. With hands on hips, he shook his head and muttered under his breath, "What the heck does she do all day long?"

Henry herded the children into the kitchen for a family pow wow. "C'mon kiddos. We're all going to pitch in and get this place cleaned up for Mommy. She's taking a little nap and we're going to surprise her. When we're done cleaning everything up, we're going to work on getting dinner on the table. How does that sound?"

"Is Momma sick?" Maria asked innocently.

"No, your mother is not sick. She's just a little tired and needed some extra rest today, that's all." Henry ran hot water over the dishes in the sink and dug in.

"Toby's momma sleeps a lot too, cause his daddy says she's got a bun in the oven. Does Momma have buns in her oven too? I don't smell nothing cooking – but I sure would like some cinanimma buns. Could we have those, please Daddy?"

All three children cheered Maria's suggestion. Henry waited patiently for them to quiet down. He knew there was absolutely no chance Sophia could be pregnant again since it had been months since she'd let him near her. Something he never thought he would be grateful for – but in lieu of the circumstances with Vera, he was thankful Sophia had rebuffed his advances these past many months.

He really wasn't the kind of man who could sleep with two women at the same time. Even he drew the line there.

"No, no. Now hush. Nobody's having buns of any kind around here – especially not the kind Toby's mother is having. Is that clear?" All three heads bobbed in unison. "Now, lets forget about buns and let's get to work cleaning up the house. Who's with me?" Henry asked excitedly.

His suggestion was met with little or no enthusiasm from the children. But not to pitch in and help would be risking a spanking, so both girls got busy heeding Henry's commands. Even little Wesley helped by picking up his toys.

A couple of hours later, Maria and Katherine were finishing the job of setting the table when Sophia came in. She looked well rested with her face freshly scrubbed and her hair fashionably styled.

Sophia looked skeptical as she surveyed the tidy kitchen. She placed her hands on her hips as she eyed the Corningware casserole dish Henry was placing on the table.

"What's going on, Henry? What's all this?" she asked.

"No big deal, Soph. We all just thought we'd pitch in and give you a night off. C'mon over and have a seat." He patted an empty kitchen chair in invitation for her. "Maria, bring Wesley's booster chair over here by the table, sweetie."

"Maria, take your brother and sister and go to your room while I talk with your daddy," Sophia ordered.

Confused and unsure of which parent to obey, Maria turned pleading eyes towards Henry.

"Don't look at him!" Sophia yelled. "Go to your rooms, NOW!" Sophia pointed in the direction of the bedroom.

All three children leapt at Sophia's command and disappeared down the hallway.

"Sophia!" Henry's voice rose in defense of the children.

Sophia pulled out the nearest chair and sat crossing her arms over her chest, her suspicions on high alert. "All right. Let's have it. What's going on? You don't come home in the middle of the afternoon for no reason. You don't clean the house and cook dinner just to be nice. Something is up and I want to know what it is, Henry."

Henry hoped to have more time before talking with Sophia. He'd worked hard on the tuna casserole thinking that a nice dinner might put her in a better mood. He'd put the remainder of the afternoon to good use by rehearsing his *Hey honey, I'm sorry, but I'm leaving you and taking our children with me,* speech. Sophia wasn't going to allow him the luxury of buttering her up. Rather than sitting down, Henry opted to stand, keeping a chair safely between him and his wife. He forged ahead to get it over with as quickly as possible. He reassured himself it would only hurt for a minute if he spilled his news quickly – kind of like pulling a bandage off a scabbed over wound.

"Well, Henry? Did they confirm your orders today? Is that why you're home early?"

"Yeah, Sophia. That's part of it." Henry gripped the back of the chair for support until his knuckles turned white. "My orders came through for March Air Force Base near Riverside, California. I've got 10 days before I have to report."

Henry could see Sophia mentally calculating the timetable he'd given her.

"Ten days! Oh sweet Jesus, Henry. That's not enough time to get everything done!"

"Don't worry about it, Soph. I'll take care of everything." Henry searched his shirt pocket for his cigarettes and lighter.

Sophia got up and paced the small kitchen. "Riverside. Oh Lord, I hope it's not as hot there as it is here. I've had all I can stand of this God-forsaken Texas heat. If I never hear another tornado siren again, it'll be too soon."

Henry removed two cigarettes from the pack and lit one for each of them. Sophia searched a cupboard for an ashtray. She accepted the proffered cigarette and paced the kitchen, puffing away while she verbalized her priority list.

"Sophia, there's something you should know before you make too many plans. I'm ..." he trailed off, searching for just the right way to break the news to his wife. Henry stood at the intersection of painful truth or more lies. Now that the moment was here, he felt frozen with fear. *Just like a bandage* he reminded himself. *Just let*

82

it rip. He rested his cigarette in the ashtray and smacked his palms together stalling for time.

Sensing Henry's discomfort, Sophia stopped her pacing, turned and stared at her husband. "Well, Henry? What else is there?" She rested her cigarette in the ashtray alongside Henry's and placed her hands on her hips, assuming a combative posture.

Henry opened his mouth and let the words pour out like an upended bottle of milk spilling its contents everywhere. "Sophia – I'm going to California without you." He blurted the news out with a rush of air.

Henry could see the flush rising from Sophia's neck up.

"*Wh-h-h-a-a-a-t-t-t* ..." Sophia drew out the word in one long stutter.

"Soph, I'm leaving you and I'm taking the kids with me. I want to give you that divorce you've wanted for so long."

EIGHT

The screen faded to black once again. A single overhead light burst on scorching Kitty's eyes. Talking almost to herself in a near comatose state, Kitty filled in details for Grace.

"You know, Grace, even though I wasn't quite five, that is one of my earliest childhood memories. None of us knew all of the details of that night, but everything changed after that. We could hear Momma and Daddy screaming so loud. I think the whole neighborhood heard them yelling. We were so scared. Daddy came in and we could tell he'd been crying. I'd never actually seen him cry before that. Momma raced in after him. She was hitting him on the back trying to slap him. That's how I got this scar here." Kitty turned and pointed to the small jagged scar on her upper lip.

"I got in Momma's way as she was trying to hit Daddy and one of her long fingernails caught me just right. We were all crying and I was bleeding, but nobody noticed. I grabbed the pillow off my bed and buried my face in it to stop the bleeding." Kitty had a faraway look like she was reliving the ordeal. She reached up and self-consciously rubbed her finger over the jagged scar.

"I tried blocking out the yelling. None of us knew what they were fighting about. All I remember is their anger. Wesley was too little to remember any of it, and Maria and I only mentioned it a couple of times after that. I think they call that denial nowadays." She turned and smiled sarcastically. "We just wanted the fighting to stop. Daddy left that night with a suitcase. I only saw him a couple of times after that. I thought it was all our fault. Momma said he left because he got tired of us. Until just now, I always believed it was true. I grew up thinking my dad didn't love me after that night."

Kitty's emotional memories spilled out. She talked for what felt like hours. She filled in as many of the gaps in her dysfunctional childhood as she could recall. Nowhere in her recall was there a memory of the promise of a move to California with her father and the mystery woman, Vera. Kitty had no idea her father ever tried to fight for custody of his children. Those details had been conveniently omitted from Sophia's angry tirades. The common thread in every memory was Sophia's bitterness and hatred of Kitty's father.

Sensing Kitty needed to purge herself of all feelings, Grace merely listened, nodding at periodic intervals. She offered an occasional, "Oh sweetie," from time to time, but otherwise remained silent and let Kitty reminisce.

"Whew," Kitty exhaled. She stopped talking to give her feelings a chance to catch up with the rest of her. She put her head down and shook it, hoping to clear her mind. She looked up and continued. "I really loved him back then. He and I were close. I think it was easier to block out all of those good memories about my father after he left. It made it so much easier to believe he was a bad guy who didn't love me anymore rather than dwelling on what I had lost. I honestly had forgotten that Daddy and I used to love each other a lot."

"How was your relationship with your father as an adult?" Grace questioned.

"Relationship? That's a laugh. We had no relationship. He lived across the country from me. We never saw one another. We seldom spoke … rarely corresponded. It was *nothing*. After he left us, he was just gone. He never tried too hard to make things work. At least it didn't seem that way from my point of view." Kitty stood up and paced around the screening room. Unsure what to do with her hands she picked at the string tie on her workout pants until she'd frayed the end.

"I try not to remember too many details after Daddy left that night." Kitty's bad habit of talking with her hands chose that moment to assert itself. Needing more than just words to communicate, she flailed her hands and arms about to give movement to her words and voice inflections. "Momma moved us to New Jersey after my dad left. We lived in a small two-bedroom apartment above my grand-parent's bakery for a while. *Giovanni's Authentic Italian Pastries."* Kitty enunciated with a flawless accent. "I remember the smells of that apartment so clearly. It was this sickeningly sweet smell – like old frosting mixed with a yeasty odor of day old bread and grease." She scrunched up her face and wrinkled her nose in distaste.

"Momma worked in the bakery and left us with one of my many aunts while she worked. As if she weren't already cranky enough, throw in long hours in a backbreaking job *with her parents* and she was down right scary – and horribly miserable. We were all miser-able and unhappy in those days. She told us over and over again Daddy had a new wife and didn't want us anymore. None of us ever questioned her. Nobody argued with Momma. Eventually she got a job in Virginia and we left Jersey. I've tried to block out as much of my childhood as possible. There weren't too many happy things worth remembering. It's funny though, every once in a while I'll drive past a *Dunkin Donuts* and get a whiff of fresh-baked dough-nuts and poof ... just like that," she snapped her fingers, "... memo-ries of that apartment over the bakery pop right back in my head." Kitty sighed, her reverie slowly abating.

Kitty stopped her pacing. She looked at Grace and in the blink of an eye cartwheeled her thought process in an entirely new direction.

"Grace, I'm hungry. Is there any place we can eat around here? Do you have an employee cafeteria or something? Maybe a break room with a couple of vending machines?"

"We can get you something to eat, if that's what you really want, Katherine. Are you sure you're really hungry?" Grace asked.

"Well, of course I'm really hungry. Starving actually. It feels like I haven't eaten in days. How long have I been at this, anyway?" Kitty lobbed rapid-fire questions at Grace. "Do calories count up here, Grace? Is it still necessary to be careful about what I eat now?"

Grace motioned for Kitty to return to her seat. "Katherine, come sit down. And no – you don't have to worry about caloric values while you're here. But are you sure you're really hungry?"

Kitty returned to her seat and sat down in a huff. You could almost see the wheels turning in her head as she took an internal inventory of all her senses. She paused and looked momentarily confused. "I don't know, Grace. I really don't know if I *feel* hungry or not. But then, I'm pretty sure that never stopped me from eating before. I honestly can't even say whether I've *ever* felt hunger as an adult. Probably not. I eat on a schedule – like most people, or just because everybody else is eating. It was different as a kid. I think I was always hungry as a child. But then, that was probably Grandma Giovanni's fault. She was an amazing cook and always had something on the stove or in the oven. I couldn't wait for the next meal. The more Grandma cooked, the more I ate. I was pretty much a bottomless pit – which would explain why I was such a chubby kid. Momma never had to cook while we lived over the bakery, so at least she was happy about that. Grandma and the aunts provided all our meals back then. To this day, I think I can still inhale a half a dozen doughnuts in record time. Lord, I hated it when we moved from there to Virginia."

Grace took Kitty's hand and gave it a small squeeze. "Katherine, why do you suppose you got hungry all of a sudden after watching that last film clip and talking about your father?"

"Gee, Grace, I don't know. Good gosh, what's with all the third degree? Why don't you tell me what it is that you want to know?" Kitty answered sarcastically. "I mean, come on, Grace. I've just watched five years worth of my troubled beginnings on the big screen in living color. Five really painful years, I might add. I think that warrants a little snack, don't you?"

Kitty's anxiousness manifested with nervous twitching and a sudden inability to sit still. The change in her demeanor became even more physical as the minutes ticked by. The quickening of her pulse was evidenced on her neck and her pupils suddenly dilated. Beads of sweat appeared on her upper lip and her brow. Kitty sprang from her seat to pace again.

"Grace, come on – you're killing me here!" Kitty laughed nervously, covering her mouth with both hands in embarrassment. "Oops! I guess we can't do that *again* cause I'm already dead, right? Been there, done that! But for crying out loud ... aagghhh! Grace, I'm starving! Please just a little something. Get me a bucket of popcorn or something to nibble on and tide me over. I promise I'll be a good girl and sit down and watch as many segments of *the life and times of me* as you want." She folded her hands under her chin and smiled sweetly.

Kitty was a ball of nervous energy. She felt like a 10-year-old ADHD kid who'd been too many hours without medication, or an alcoholic in need of a shot of whiskey. Whatever it was, Kitty knew with a certainty that it had complete control of her.

"So how about it, Grace? Can you help me out? Is there a lounge or maybe an early-bird buffet? A hot dog stand? Tic Tacs? Something? Anything?" Kitty wrung her hands in desperation.

The lights in the room were perfectly timed to Grace's movements. As she pushed herself up from her chair, the single overhead light was joined by dozens of other lights throughout the room sparking to life like a well-choreographed dance. The lights illuminated large tables set up in a U-shape at the back of the room. Kitty blinked in confusion, certain the tables weren't there when they came in earlier. But now spread before her was the most magnificent display of food she'd ever seen.

The tables were laden with succulent meats of every variety. All were either roasted, charbroiled, barbecued, baked or fried. Juicy cuts of prime rib and expensive cuts of beef all nestled in warming ovens. Kitty inhaled deeply savoring the delicious aromas. The salad bar, a gorgeous display of brightly colored exotic fruits and veggies from all over the world, tantalized all of Kitty's five senses. Carbohydrates were well represented in the form of breads and rolls, as well as, potato variations and rice and pasta concoctions. And the dessert table! Holy cow! What a spread! You name it and it was there. All the tables were so artfully arranged, even Martha Stewart would have been impressed. And to Kitty's absolute delight, it looked as though all of her personal favorites were there, ready and waiting for her.

Kitty stared, awestruck. "Oh my goodness! This is magnificent, Grace. Absolutely beautiful — a veritable cornucopia of junk food. Now I'm sure I'm in Heaven," she breathed deeply, practically swooning with desire. Kitty licked her lips and rubbed her hands in anticipation. Like a contagious virus, Kitty's excitement seized Grace, who laughed openly at Kitty's appreciation of the buffet.

Grace clapped her hands and shooed Kitty in the direction of the plates. "Well you know, they say presentation is everything," Grace offered. She reached for an oversized tray and placed two plates and a bowl on it, offering it to Kitty. "Well, go ahead, Katherine. Dig in."

Kitty stood cemented to the floor, inner turmoil clearly etched on her face. Pondering all of the high-calorie choices, she chewed her lower lip in anxiousness. Tempted to indulge yet afraid of the adverse consequences – she waited.

"Well, Katherine, what are you waiting for? I thought you were *dying* to eat. Go ahead, help yourself." Grace tried to gently push the tray off to Kitty.

Kitty stood fast. She furrowed her brow in deep thought, hesitating. "I know that's what I said, but now I'm not so sure. I've had a system for mealtime for so many years. Everything has always had to be perfectly calculated before I allowed myself to indulge. All the fat grams, calories, fiber and carbs measured to an exact science. Even when I found myself on a binge, I still managed to set limits, you know?"

Grace didn't know and she said so.

"It's just that I don't think I've ever eaten a meal just for the sole enjoyment of eating. If I happened to overeat at one meal, I'd scrimp and starve at the next one. Or I would try to balance things out by spending extra time working out. Look at all of this food! I haven't had time to calculate the caloric value or fat grams of anything! How do you expect me to just sit down and eat, for crying out loud? I'm a career dieter, not some rookie." Kitty shoved her hands through her hair in agitation. She surveyed the tables and rolled her eyes heavenward praying for strength. She glanced down when something on one of the tables caught her eye. She inched closer for a more thorough investigation.

"Oh my gosh! Is that a ... Oh no ... it is! That's a Whopper with all the trimmings, isn't it? Do you have any idea how long it's been since I've had a real hamburger with the works?" Kitty nearly tripped over her own feet to lean in as close as possible so she could inhale the aroma of grilled meat.

Kitty floated back to an upright position, her eyes closed as if savoring the experience of letting her nose have a play date with competing smells. She lingered a moment longer in reverent silence before she turned towards Grace and launched in to what sounded like a well-rehearsed spiel. Grace stood back letting Kitty rant. Who in turn spouted off the differences between beef burgers versus soy burgers and the pros and cons of turkey burgers.

"I mean ... seriously, the healthy stuff doesn't even compare with the beef, you know? Sometimes the flesh just wants what the flesh wants. And the flesh wants the beef!" Kitty said. She growled deep in her throat in support of her conclusion.

Grace patiently balanced the tray pretending to be absorbed in Kitty's nutritional knowledge, until finally she interrupted. "So why don't you put the burger on your plate, dear?" Grace reached for the burger and placed it on a plate, spooning extra pickles and tomatoes next to it. "That's what they're here for."

Kitty turned her back on the table and closed her eyes. "Awww, Grace. This really hurts! You don't understand what it's like to be controlled by your fleshly desires, do you? I stand before you a weak-willed woosy! My will power is crumbling before my very eyes! How can you tempt me with all of this food? Have you no conscience?"

"The food isn't here to tempt or test you, Katherine. It's only here because you said you were hungry. Period. No games, no tricks. Grab a plate and enjoy the food. Don't you think it's high time you started enjoying one of the baser needs of the human body? It's really quite sad when you think about how you've allowed yourself to be in bondage to food for so long. Obviously it's important to find a balance and not step over into gluttony, but don't you think you've been out of balance long enough?"

Kitty turned around to face Grace. Her hands itched to reach for the dinner tray. She flexed her fingers a couple of times before she carefully reached for the tray. "Part of me wants to dive in face first and say to heck with the consequences. But at the same time, the logical part of me is trying to analyze everything that's here and make the smartest nutritional choices."

Grace shoved the tray at Kitty, releasing it to her care. She walked around so she stood directly behind Kitty. She put her hands on Kitty's arms and leaned in, whispering in her ear. "Suppose I told you, you can eat anything you want and you won't have to worry about it affecting your weight or appearance."

Kitty turned, eyeing Grace over her shoulder with eyes that had grown to twice their normal size. "Are you *kidding* me?" she screeched.

Grace shook her head. "Nope. Honest to goodness. You can have anything and everything your heart desires and I promise it will not add an ounce of weight to you." Grace held up her hand as if swearing an oath.

That turned out to be all the invitation Kitty needed. "Here, would you mind holding this for a second?" She shoved her tray back at Grace and rolled her neck from side-to-side. She inhaled and exhaled deeply and then reached down loosening the tie on her workout pants. She did a couple of toe touches and followed those by shaking her limbs like she was warming up in preparation for a workout. She reclaimed her dinner tray and turned her eyes towards heaven thanking whoever might be responsible for her good fortune.

"Whoever coined the phrase *died and gone to Heaven* must have been standing exactly where I'm standing right now. Well, here goes nothing! Stand back, Grace. Save yourself. You my friend are about to see something you don't see everyday. I feel it's only fair to warn you ahead of time not to get in my way or you're liable to pull back a bloody stump."

Heeding Kitty's words, Grace took one giant step backwards away from the buffet table.

Kitty started with cake – at least four different kinds. She then filled her tray with every type of caloric temptation within her reach. She loaded up on pizza and pasta, cannolis and calzones. It proved challenging, but somehow she managed to strategically arrange a little bit of everything on both plates and the large salad bowl. When her tray could hold no more, she turned and found a round table set for two, complete with candles, silverware and long stemmed crystal goblets. She transferred her heavy plates to the table, which was covered with a beautiful ivory linen tablecloth and matching cloth napkins.

"Wow, Grace, you've thought of everything. Will you be joining me, or don't angels eat real food?" Kitty asked.

"No, I won't be eating with you. I'll sit and keep you company though, if you don't mind. I do believe I'll have a glass of water while you indulge yourself. But please – go right ahead and get started. Don't let me stop you."

"Is that going to be a glass of *holy water*, Grace?" Kitty asked in all seriousness.

Grace smiled at the silliness of the question.

Kitty sat and picked up her napkin to remove the napkin ring. The ring looked to be made of platinum gold and was crafted in the shape of a small crown. Tiny rubies, emeralds and diamonds encircled the ring. Kitty was much too excited to satisfy the cravings of her palate to give the ring much attention. As she slid the napkin free, a beam from an overhead light caught the glimmer of a deep red ruby, creating a winking prism of beautiful color, distracting her.

"Oh, Grace, this is lovely," she breathed. "Heaven or wherever we are is certainly full of wonderful surprises. You ought to think about selling these napkin rings. You could make a fortune, you know. They're exquisite."

Grace smiled indulgently, shaking her head like a mother who finds it necessary to keep reprimanding their child on repeated common sense issues. "Oh, Katherine," she sighed.

"Oops, sorry. I forgot myself – again. Is it okay if I get started?"

"Yes, dear. But don't you want to say *grace* first?" Grace winked at her.

Kitty grinned until they both began to giggle.

"By all means, Grace. Would you care to do the honors, or shall I?"

"Would you mind if I did it? I do so love a good blessing."

Kitty shook her head and was surprised when instead of simply bowing her head and clasping her hands in prayer, Grace reached over with one hand and took Kitty's left hand in hers. She then placed her other hand on Kitty's head before she bowed in reverent prayer.

"Dear Father, thank you for all that you have provided. Bless this food to Katherine's body, Lord. Bless this food to Katherine's mind and bless this food to the very core of Katherine's soul, Lord. In your most holy precious name, I ask these things. Amen and Amen."

Warmth circulated through Kitty's limbs. It reminded her of the rare occasions when she drank wine. Alcohol made Kitty feel warm all over, but it especially caused an unusual penetrating heat in her shoulder sockets. Grace's prayer had the same effect on her. Kitty also thought it odd that food should be blessed to her mind and to the core of her soul. Weird. But everything to this point was lining up to be rather odd. Apparently dinnertime prayers were going to be more of the same.

Kitty attacked the food with gusto. She likened the experience to a marathon runner who trains their entire life for the single purpose of running in the Olympics. This meal was Kitty's Olympic bingeing marathon. All of her secret raids on the fridge had been preparing her for this once-in-a-lifetime food-fest extravaganza. Grace sipped water from her crystal stemware, content to sit silently while Kitty ate ... *and ate ... and ate!*

After a considerable amount of time, Kitty finally began to slow down. She'd had no idea her body was equipped to consume such mass quantities of food. None of her previous binges would ever come close to rivaling this experience. The fried chicken drumstick slid through her greasy fingers with a resounding thud. Kitty carefully inched her plate away. She was thankful she'd loosened the tie on her pants earlier. Sitting back from the table, she studied the front of herself. Crumbs dotted her workout shirt and littered her lap. Something resembling marinara sauce traced a path from her right breast to the tops of her thighs. Her fingers were covered with both frosting and some sort of condiment sauce. She didn't have a mirror, but felt certain her face probably bore evidence to her gluttonous debauchery as well as her clothes.

Kitty let out a noisy groan and followed it up with a slight hiccup.

"S'cuse me, she offered coyly and lightly dabbed at the corners of her food-stained mouth. Suddenly without warning, she further embarrassed herself by belching long and loud, the sound resembling a diesel truck backfiring. To cover her shame she promptly fell face forward into the remaining pile of food on her plate.

NINE

Grace studied her for a moment before speaking.

"Excuse you," she offered. "Well – was that everything you hoped it would be, Katherine?"

Kitty sat up slowly. Mashed potatoes clung to her chin. The complimenting gravy dripped from the end of her nose. Both hung dangerously by invisible suspension for a scant moment before plopping and squishing in a gelatinous mess on the table.

"Oh my gosh," she grimaced and shoved the plate to the opposite side of the table. "Why didn't you stop me, Grace? I am such a pig! How could you let me eat all of that?" Kitty grabbed her napkin and began trying to wipe the mess from her face.

"Well you never told me I was supposed to stop you at any point! I assumed you knew what you were doing."

"I think I'm going to be sick, Grace. Has anybody ever thrown up here?" she moaned.

"I'm not sure, dear. Although if there was ever a reason to purge oneself, I would say that you could certainly take the cake."

Kitty gasped. "Cake? Oh my gosh, no! No more cake, thank you." As her discomfort mounted, she laid her napkin down and forced her body to remain absolutely still. She leaned forward, cradling her head on her arms.

"Grace, are you sure that all of these calories won't show up on my thighs and my butt at some point?"

"Absolutely positive," Grace reassured.

"You know I don't usually eat that much food, right? I mean you do know that this was an extenuating circumstance, don't you?" Kitty dared a look at Grace.

"What are you talking about, Katherine?"

"Well – before, in my old life. I never would have eaten that much food at one time. In fact, I went to great lengths to keep that kind of food out of my house. Out of sight, out of mind, I always say."

"And your point is?" Grace prodded.

Kitty stood up carefully and waited to see if she was going to lose everything she just consumed. She brushed the crumbs from her clothes and spit on her forefinger to rub away the unidentified sauce staining her shirt. Grabbing her discarded napkin, she dipped the end of it into a nearby water goblet so she could wipe her mouth before she walked away. She moved slowly being careful not to jar her full stomach. She turned away from Grace as she spoke.

"Well, I'm not one of *those* kind of people, you know?"

"And who exactly are *those kind of people*, Katherine?"

"You know who I mean. Bulimics and Anorexics. I'm not one of those." Kitty turned around.

"Why do you say that?" Grace took a sip of water, fixing Kitty with a probing green-eyed stare over the top of her glass.

"Well, even though I have been known to sneak a little food here and there and perhaps binge *occasionally*, I would never make myself throw up afterwards. I never did that. I don't have an eating disorder. I just like to eat, that's all. In fact it rather pains me to say – but I was really, really good at it. Eating, I mean."

Unable to bear Grace's scrutiny, Kitty studied the floor. When she glanced up again she was dumbfounded to see that all of the food tables had disappeared. There wasn't so much as a stray crumb hiding anywhere.

"Whoa." Kitty turned questioning eyes towards Grace. "What happened, Grace? Where did everything go?"

"Away." Grace waved her hand in simulation. "Now what were you saying, Katherine? Something about the fact that even though you used to sneak food and eat until you *felt* like throwing up, you never actually did. So that means you never actually had an eating disorder. Is that correct?"

"Did I say I felt like throwing up?" Her brow creased with deep worry lines.

Grace shrugged her shoulders.

"Hmm, okay so *maybe* I might have said I felt like throwing up. Who knows? I'll tell you what I do know. All this food has addled my brain." She fidgeted in nervous agitation. "All those carbs are right now, even as we speak, wrapping themselves around my brain cells and vital organs and having a big giant free-for-all. They're sucking the life right out of me and suffocating me. They're making me so crazy I don't know what I'm saying!"

"You didn't have to say anything. I can see it on your face, Katherine. Well, that and – what *is* that mush on your cheek? Chocolate frosting?" Grace got up and walked over to Kitty pointing to a mysterious spot on her cheek. It was a big brown splotch that Kitty had somehow missed with her cursory cleanup. Kitty quickly swiped the offensive goo from her face with her finger. Not knowing what else to do with it, she stuck her finger in her mouth and sucked it clean.

"So tell me," Grace continued. "How frequently did you have your little eating binges in your previous life that were *not really an eating disorder*?"

Kitty attempted a nonchalant look. "I don't know. I don't think there was a definite pattern. I really only binged when I was upset about something." She bit down on the corner of her lip.

"When you were upset?" Grace proceeded to cross-exam. "There weren't any other times?"

"Well – maybe if I was worried about something. Or if I was having a fight with Luke or one of the kids. You know – usual stuff. And of course, when I had P.M.S. But we can't count that. *Everybody* binges when they have P.M.S. A woman wouldn't be normal if she didn't overeat during that time of the month."

Grace looked thoughtful. "You don't see any kind of pattern there?"

"No, I don't," Kitty became defensive. "I only overate or binged during times of stress. There is nothing abnormal about that, Grace.

Lots of women do that. No – strike that. It's not just women that do that. Men do that too!"

"Yes, I'm sure you're right. Feelings and emotions do tend to trigger some powerful urges." Grace paused in thoughtful repose. "What did you do *after* your little bouts of bingeing?"

"You mean besides feeling incredibly guilty and like the world's biggest failure?"

"Yes, Katherine. What else?" Grace's face revealed no condemnation, only compassion, but yet she wouldn't let it go.

"Well, sometimes I would take laxatives and hope that I could … *eliminate* a lot of what I had eaten." Kitty offered the information delicately, as if to talk about her bodily functions would be sacrilegious, given where she was. "But mostly, I exercised. I either got on my treadmill or the exercise bike. And then, I just exercised until I felt better." Kitty looked away in embarrassment.

"And how long did that take, dear? Until you felt better, I mean."

"Sometimes hours. There were times I walked on the treadmill for two hours at a time. And I could ride 30 miles on the Life Cycle if I needed to." Kitty started to feel the walls closing in on her with her confession.

Grace moved close enough to Kitty to take her hands in her own. "And did you feel better when you were done with all that exercising?" Grace asked tenderly.

Kitty couldn't look Grace in the eye as shame washed over her.

"No, Grace. I never did. I usually felt even guiltier, because not only had I spent hours trying to redeem my sin of gluttony, I'd ignored my family and my household responsibilities in the process. There were so many times when I wouldn't be able to spend time with the kids or help them with homework because I was too obsessed about exorcising away my inner demons."

"And how did that make you feel?" Grace pressed.

Kitty dared a look at Grace. Tears pooled in Kitty's emerald eyes. "Like the world's biggest loser," she croaked. "I felt like the worst mother on the planet and the worst wife in the world. I used to go to bed nearly every night and beg God to fix me. I mean really *beg*, Grace. I pleaded with God to make me stop the destructive bingeing and insane exercising. But He wouldn't take it away. I felt like He didn't care about me and didn't want me be normal. And then I would feel even guiltier for feeling that way about God. It was a vicious cycle that I lived with day after day, year after year, for as long as I can remember. I can't even recall the last time I went to bed at night and didn't hate myself for my lack of self-control. Then everyday I'd wake up and swear I would be better ... try harder. I'd vow to balance healthy food with normal exercise. I even promised I would pray *before* I ate anything and ask God to control me. But usually when I wanted to eat, I couldn't bother to pray because the voice of the enemy was so loud in my ear I couldn't hear God's voice. All I could hear was *'go ahead – you deserve that treat. You can start your diet tomorrow. You might as well eat what you want today – you've already blown your diet for the day. One more day won't matter.'* It was a horrible destructive cycle that I was powerless to control. Oh Grace, I'm sick."

Kitty returned to her theater seat and let her head fall forward until it rested on her thighs. She hugged her legs and slowly rocked back and forth. She took several deep breaths. For the time being she was in no imminent danger of bolting for the bathroom, thank goodness. So she merely moaned and rocked.

"What do you mean, Katherine? Are you in need of a facility?" Grace followed her and sat down beside her.

"No, not sick like that. I mean sick in the head. A nutcase. What makes me want to eat and exercise like that? Why can't I be free of this addiction? Thirty or more years of obsessive exercise, uncontrollable bingeing ... 30 years of feeling guilty about everything I ate." Kitty stopped rocking and stared at Grace, searching her serene face for answers. "Do you think that's when it all started, Grace? The day my dad left us?"

"What do you think, Katherine? How did you feel watching that episode unfold?"

"I felt abandoned. I felt like my dad didn't care about me and didn't love me anymore. I felt completely alone, Grace." Silent tears skipped down Kitty's flushed cheeks.

"As an adult, did your feelings for your dad ever change?"

"Some, but not much. I tried to keep as much distance between him and me as possible. But surely that can't be at the root of all my problems, can it? I'm not the only person whose father ever abandoned her. Plenty of other people deal with abandonment, so there's got to be more to it than that."

"I believe your father's leaving certainly impacted your life and had a profound effect on your behaviors. It certainly bears some further probing. You must keep in mind, that God created you to be an individual and every person deals with trials differently. People deal with life's disappointments in different fashions. You medicated your emotions with food and exercise addictions. Some people medicate their feelings with alcohol or drugs, or dangerous sexual practices or pornography addictions. Some people even use uncontrollable shopping and credit cards to deal with the stresses of life. I think there are as many different types of addictions as there are people. Your feelings are very valid and very real. It's a shame though that you spent so much of your life feeling guilty. I suppose even your guilt was an addiction of sort. Perhaps the rest of the footage will help to enlighten you further. I believe that with God all things are possible. I also believe he wants you to reconcile yourself with your past behaviors. Are you ready to move forward or are you in need of a restroom?" Grace asked.

Kitty stood up and did a couple of stretches to the right and the left. She raised her arms and stretched them overhead as far as she could. She bent over to touch her toes then stood up.

"No, Grace. Oddly enough, I'm feeling better. It's very weird. I think I'll be fine for now. I don't feel stuffed anymore? I ate enough food to feed a small third world country so how come I don't feel uncomfortable anymore? Did it all magically disappear in my stomach the way the food tables disappeared?"

Grace smiled, neither agreeing nor disagreeing with Kitty's assessment. "Perhaps," was her only offer of explanation.

Kitty resumed her seat once again, stretching her legs in front of her to get comfortable. "Or maybe ..." Kitty drawled. "Maybe I didn't even really eat anything at all. Maybe that was just my imagination. Grace?"

"Yes, Katherine."

"Was any of that real?"

"What is real, Katherine? Am I real? Is God real? For that matter, are you real or are you dead? Enough with the questions, missy. There will be a time and a place for everything to be made known to you. For now, please be still and let's watch the next installment."

Kitty smiled in spite of herself as she waited for her eyes to adjust to the sudden darkening of the room. She enjoyed the verbal sparring with Grace far more than viewing footage of her past. As soon as a new date appeared on the screen, Kitty felt the first flicker of panic deep in her gut. Everything she'd witnessed thus far would be nothing compared to what was about to come. The date that appeared signified the beginning of the worst period of her life.

Kitty instinctively drew her knees up to her chest and rested her feet on the seat. She hugged her legs in an automatic defensive reflex against what was coming. All thoughts of heaven vanished. With the appearance of the next date on the screen, Kitty knew to watch and relive the next segment would be a visit to Hell itself. She tried to steady her breathing. If she didn't know for a fact that she was dead already, she'd be worried about having a heart attack. Her quickening pulse and thundering heartbeat roared so loudly in her ears, she was certain Grace would comment on the noise. Stealing a glance in her direction, Grace was comfortably settled in her seat – waiting and watching.

Kitty silently prayed for strength. *Dear Lord, I can't live through this a second time. Please don't leave me. I don't think I can survive this day again.*

Grace reached for Kitty's hand and squeezed it reassuringly. "He's here, Katherine. Try not to worry. We're *both* here."

To Kitty – that was enough.

TEN

October 21, 1972

The house was unusually quiet for a Saturday afternoon. Twelve-year-old Kitty had been left home alone because of the nasty cold attacking her. But she didn't mind. Kitty liked the peace and quiet. Her mother and brother, Wesley, were off doing the weekly grocery shopping, while her sister, Maria, slaved away at the Burger Barn. Her stepfather of two years, Walter Devlin, had disappeared as usual, for which Kitty was profoundly grateful. Kitty much preferred Walter missing in action rather than having him at home. Her closest friend and constant companion, Mercy, lay contentedly on the twin bed by her side. Mercy, a beautiful five-year-old Golden Retriever, had come to live with her family three years ago.

Kitty stroked the big dog's soft fur and sang her favorite song. "Surely goodness and mercy shall fol-low me ..." The oversized fur ball howled her delight. "Oh Mercy, I'm so glad our house got broken into all those years ago so Momma let us get you to protect us, my big brave girl."

Kitty massaged both of Mercy's ears, who in turn panted her appreciation of Kitty's strokes by turning her head from side-to-side. Each time Kitty tried to stop her scratching, Mercy nosed her snout under Kitty's hand too keep her fingers moving. Kitty laughed at Mercy's persistence.

"You're so funny! But you really have to stop pestering me. I promised Miss Shirley, the church lady, I would send her a current picture of you and me so she can see what a beautiful big girl you've become. She must have been so sad to have to give you and your sister, Goodness, away. She was such a nice lady. I don't know why Momma didn't like her. I'll bet Shirley misses you and Goodness a lot." Kitty stopped stroking the retriever and bounded off the bed so she could rummage through her desk drawer for the picture she'd been saving to mail to Miss Shirley. "I'm going to write her a nice long letter and tell her how good I've been taking care of you."

Kitty sat down at the small desk and chewed the end of her pencil while she formulated her words in her head. Mercy hopped off the bed and obediently followed her, lying down on the floor next to her resting her head on Kitty's slippered foot. Kitty tried to use her best penmanship so Miss Shirley would be able to read it with her 70-something-year-old eyes.

"Let's see." Kitty thought out loud bouncing ideas off Mercy. "What should I tell Miss Shirley about, Mercy?" She thumped her pencil a couple of times and began slowly.

Dear Miss Shirley – I have been taking really good care of "our" dog, Mercy. As you can see by this picture of me and her, I keep her really clean and I brush her all the time. I am the only one she lets walk her, feed her and brush her. Most of the time I have to clean up her doggie business in the backyard, too, but I don't mind. I am so lucky that you picked us to be her family when you moved away to live with your son and his family. I sing her favorite song to her from the 23rd Psalm just like you taught me. Mercy "sings" with me!

Kitty wrote a couple more paragraphs filling in details for the elderly woman about school, teachers and her family. She paused and put her pencil down. Mercy sat at attention and placed her head in Kitty's lap when she sensed a change in Kitty's demeanor.

"Do you think I should tell her about Walter, Mercy?" The dog whined. "Probably not. I haven't said anything to anybody about how mean he's been lately. I sure hope he finds a new job soon. Maybe then he'll quit drinking so much beer and stop being so disagreeable."

Pushing her correspondence aside, Kitty stood and walked back over to her bed. She plopped down and Mercy was instantly beside her in the middle of the bed, lavishing her face with generous canine kisses. Kitty giggled uncontrollably turning every which way to avoid the dog's fat wet tongue.

"Stop it, you silly girl!" she squealed. Kitty sobered, sat up and kicked her slippers off and pulled her comforter close to ward off the sudden chill in the room. Kitty pulled Mercy close to steal her body heat. "Oh, it's cold in here," she said hugging Mercy tightly. Suddenly Mercy's head lifted and she sniffed the air, sensing something. She hopped off the bed, searching out the corners of the room. Whining and scratching the floor next to the dresser, Mercy lifted her head, pointed her snout up towards the ceiling and barked, turning in circles.

"What are you doing, baby? There's nothing there. Come back over here and lay down. You were keeping me warm." Kitty patted the bed next to her. Mercy gave a final whine and a yip and returned to her vacated spot. Once the big retriever settled, Kitty arranged the pillows on her bed to support her comfortably to lean against the headboard. She stroked Mercy's golden hair absently. "Oh Mercy. I can't tell Miss Shirley or anybody about Walter. I wish my mother wouldn't have married him. I don't like him. Last week when he punched Wesley, I got so scared. I didn't know what to do. Wesley begged me not to tell Momma, cause he said Walter would hurt him even worse if he told on him. I don't know if I can keep it a secret though. I know Momma is busy with her new job. I wish she wasn't gone all the time. Wesley just told me to try and stay out of Walter's way. That goes for you too, girl! I know he hates you and keeps telling Momma we need to get rid of you. But don't you worry. I won't let him take you away. I've been saving all my allowance and when I have enough, I think me and you should try and go find my real dad. He'll take care of us. Until then, it's just me and you, girl." Kitty snuggled the silky-haired dog and drew comfort from her presence.

* * * * *

"Grace." Kitty poked Grace in the arm. "Grace, I don't feel so well. Can we stop, please? I think I'm going to be sick." Kitty doubled over at the waist and moaned quietly.

"What's wrong? What's happened?" Grace tried to lean over to examine Kitty's face, but her long dark hair shielded her from Grace's prying eyes. Grace stood and leaned over Kitty's hunched body and lifted the armrests on either side of Kitty's seat. "Here dear. Maybe you should stretch out for a bit."

Kitty lay on her side, pulled her legs in tight and curled her body into a tight fetal position. She lay with eyes closed, lamenting softly. "No, no, no." Kitty spoke in short quick spurts of pain.

Grace squatted down to within inches of her face. "Katherine, I know this is going to be hard for you, but I really need you to sit up and watch the rest of this." She pushed the hair out of Kitty's face, searching for signs that she'd been heard.

Kitty swatted the comforting hand away. "Stop it!" she half moaned, half yelled.

"I really must take issue with you, Katherine. I'm only trying to help. You need to push past what you're feeling and sit up, please."

"Make it stop, Grace."

"Make what stop?"

"The movie. Can't watch anymore. No! No!"

Grace sat down near Kitty's head and tried again to comfort her. She gently massaged Kitty's shoulder and back. "Katherine, I want you to listen to me," she said sternly. "Open your eyes, Kitty. Look at me!"

Kitty slowly opened pain filled eyes and looked up at Grace. "What?" she croaked.

"We *must* watch this episode. I know how painful it is to relive this, but everything that happened triggered something in you that you must face. It affected the course of your life."

"I know, Grace. I was there already. Remember? I can't ww-aa-tt-ccccchhhh it," she stuttered through chattering teeth, as if suddenly chilled.

Grace half-leaned over and forced Kitty to a sitting position. "Katherine! If I show you something, will you sit with me and watch the scene unfold to the end?"

Kitty looked dazed and confused. "What? What are you talking about?"

"Katherine, look at the screen for a moment. Watch, please." Grace scooted over close to Katherine and hugged her in a comforting embrace. As Kitty watched, the scene came alive. So alive, in fact, that every direction Kitty turned, she became aware that she was now actually standing in the corner of her old bedroom. Her 12-year-old self was so close to her, she could actually reach out and touch her. She cautiously lifted a hand to do just that. Grace placed a warning hand on her arm and pushed it back to her side. "No. You can't. But I wanted you to see that you were never alone. I was here in 1972. My presence is what Mercy was barking at. Do you understand?"

Too confused to speak, Kitty shook her head no.

"Let's just continue. You'll see." Grace and Kitty became part of the small bedroom. They shrunk back and hovered in the corner next to Kitty's slightly cluttered dresser. The smells of young Kitty's room; a combination of inexpensive dusting powder, Bazooka bubble gum and warm dog, surrounded them. The air was chilly and both young Kitty and the older Kitty, hugged their arms around their midsections.

"I was there then. I'm here for you now. Okay?" Grace asked.

"Okay," Kitty whispered and shook her head woodenly.

* * * * *

"Mercy, do you think I should tell Momma that Walter hit Wesley last week? I don't want her to be mad at me for tattling. It's not that I hate Walter, exactly. I just never feel completely comfortable with him around. What my mother ever saw in Walter Devlin is a mystery to me. Walter is so short and round. He's barely taller than Momma. And that big jiggly belly of his. Ugh! Gross!" She puffed out her cheeks and laughed out loud. "Oooh, or the way he combs his hair over his bald head. It makes me and Wesley die laughing! I hate the way I can see all of his pink gums when he smiles at me. His fat fingers look like sausage links and have you noticed the way his neck disappears whenever he wears a shirt and tie?"

Mercy seemed to be nodding her canine head in agreement. "He sweats way too much and smells like cabbage, cigarette smoke and that nasty dandruff shampoo of his. Yuck! My mom is so pretty. She could have picked someone way better than Walter. I don't understand why she settled for him." Kitty continued stroking the dog and sharing her concerns.

* * * * *

Hovered in the corner, Kitty hugged herself and quirked a lopsided grin at hearing young Kitty's descriptions. "Oh, Grace. I had forgotten how Wesley and I used to poke fun of Walter. None of us kids ever cared for him. My grandmother and aunts all despised him. Grandma Giovanni always crossed herself whenever she was forced to be around Walter. Aunt Gina said it was because Walter wasn't a Catholic, but an atheist."

"What a terrible shame," Grace said.

"Apparently one of my aunts heard that Walter was married twice before he married my mother. Walter's second wife was supposedly Vietnamese. Walter had married her when he was in the Army and stationed in Vietnam. Supposedly he never brought her to the states because of all the military red tape, or something. There was even a rumor that he beat his second wife and nobody knows what became of the first wife, but foul play was suspected. My aunts loved to gossip, so there's no telling how much of any of that was true. Whatever the case, I spent my childhood wishing Walter the atheist wouldn't have left wife number two and stayed in Vietnam. Then he wouldn't have met and married my mother. My life would have been better for it."

"I sense that you're stalling, Katherine. Let's get this over with, please."

Kitty turned pleading eyes to her. "But why, Grace? Why do I have to relive this day?"

"I already told you. This day laid a very important foundation that I'm not sure you're even aware of. I've got to help you understand this, Katherine. It's vital."

"Vital, shmital. All I know is that I hated everything about my adolescent years. Every time I think ..." she rambled, a clear attempt to sidetrack Grace with an unrelated story. Grace was wise to her ploy and would have no part of it.

"Katherine! Enough! Now zip your lip." She made a show of sealing an imaginary zipper across her mouth, turning a lock and throwing away the key. "The sooner we watch this, the sooner we can put it all behind us. Now no more interruptions."

"Fine!" Kitty puckered her face and pouted.

ELEVEN

Kitty rolled over on her side and drew her knees up slightly. Mercy hopped over her next to the wall, circled around until she found the perfect spot and lay down, resting her head across Kitty's side.

"Maybe I should try praying about this whole Walter thing like Sister Mary Agnes at my Catechism class said. She said God loves the little children and He always hears our prayers. *All* of our prayers. I guess praying about it might be better than just trying to wish the problem away."

Kitty closed her eyes and silently prayed to God to help Walter find a new job so they wouldn't have to move again.

"And God, could you please make Walter be nicer and not hit Wesley anymore and help Wesley to listen better and do his chores so he won't upset Walter. And please, please God, don't let Walter send my Mercy away."

Kitty was in the middle of her prayers when Mercy hopped off the bed and trotted over by the closed door. The hair on her back stood upright. She growled low and deep in her throat. Kitty could see her lip curl back exposing sharp fangs. Kitty sat up and drew her knees to her chest, pulling the comforter close to her for protection – not from the cold, but from whatever it was that had Mercy's defenses on high alert.

The bedroom door flew open with a sudden loud bang, causing Kitty to jump in fright and Mercy to bark an alarm. Walter staggered in and made a move to kick the growling animal, but Mercy easily dodged his unstable jab. He lunged at the dog, grabbed her roughly by the collar and dragged her to the bathroom where he shoved her inside and closed the door, trapping her inside.

"Stupid, ugly dog! Shut the hell up!" Walter yelled and slapped the closed door with his open palm. On the other side of the closed door, Mercy whined, barked and scratched to be set free.

"So help me, I've had enough of that stupid mutt!" Walter came through the door and swayed unsteadily, cursing violently at the now imprisoned dog. He stared down at Kitty with glazed, red-rimmed eyes.

The offensive odor of alcohol was unmistakable on Walter's breath. His glassy-eyed stare made Kitty shiver in fear. She trembled and scootched as far away from the edge of the bed as the small space allowed. She felt the wall behind her back and silently prayed it would open up and swallow her before Walter came any closer.

"So what's the matter with you today, *Kit Kat*?"

Kitty had told him more than once how much she hated to be called that stupid name. Every time he used the much-hated nickname, he said it with a sneer, just to irritate and spite her.

Walter straightened slightly and puffed out his chest. He reached up and slicked back his thinning hair. In his obvious inebriated state his words slurred together and he stumbled as he made his way over to her bed. "Does Daddy's little girl have a case of the sniffles today, *Kit Kat*?" He half sat, half fell on the end of Kitty's bed.

Kitty sat straighter and attempted to appear unruffled. "My name is Kitty, not Kit Kat, and you're not my daddy." She stuck her chin out in false bravado.

In the blink of an eye, Walter reached over and backhanded her hard across the mouth, causing Kitty to cry out in fear. Surprised by the sudden change in Walter's attitude, she grabbed her mouth and covered it in protection against further battery. She tested her bottom lip by moving her tongue across it and felt the sting of a small cut. She felt the dampness from a slight trickle of blood. Walter's initial slap was well placed, causing her braces to dig into the tender flesh of her lips. The taste of blood on her tongue brought with it a rising nausea.

"Don't you ever back talk me, girlie. I'll call you anything I damn well please. And I'm the only daddy you got, *Kit Kat.*" He enunciated carefully just for the pleasure of watching her face distort in aggravation. He moved closer to her and pushed her dark hair out of her eyes. He tried to caress her cheek, but Kitty ducked under his short squat arms.

"Aw, Kitty darlin', I'm sorry. Daddy didn't mean to hurt you. Come over here and sit on my lap and let me kiss that boo boo on your lip." Walter leered at her and patted his tree-trunk sized leg.

Kitty took advantage of his slow movements and leapt from the bed, her feet barely touching the floor. She bolted for freedom, hoping to make it to the bathroom to release Mercy her protector, before Walter could stop her.

Walter anticipated her actions and jumped from the bed and barred her way. At 12-years-old, Kitty was short and pudgy for her age. She barely reached Walter's chest so it was no contest for him, even in his drunken stupor. He wrapped his sausage-like fingers in her hair and jerked her towards him, halting her progress. He spun her around so they were face-to-face. Hearing the noise and Kitty's cries from across the hall, Mercy frantically howled and clawed at the door for release.

Walter shoved Kitty up against the wall and pressed his fleshy body against hers. Kitty squirmed and turned her head from side-to-side to avoid Walter's whiskery jaw, which inched closer to her tear-stained face. Walter possessed a great deal of strength for a man of such short stature. He pinned Kitty to the wall with a surprisingly well-muscled arm, while his free hand moved to caress her pre-pubescent young body. Kitty managed to slap his roaming hand away. Sensing Walter's intention to kiss her, she reacted on pure instinct and raw adrenaline. As Walter's face drew nearer, Kitty stood on tiptoes and reached up and bit down hard on Walter's fat bottom lip.

He screamed out in pain. Surprised by Kitty's sudden assault, Walter reared back and punched her hard in the face twice, before shaking her and slamming her head against the wall. He threw her violently to the floor where she curled into a fetal position and lay moaning. *Dear God, please help me,* she whispered through bruised and battered lips. The prayer became her mantra as she repeated it over and over.

Walter left her lying there and went to Wesley's bedroom. Kitty could hear him opening and closing doors and drawers, but couldn't make herself move from the floor. He breezed past her room and she heard a door open followed by a loud hollow sounding thwack. She sat bolt upright as she heard Mercy's fierce barking, then a yelp ... and then silence.

"Mercy!" Kitty cried and clutched her chest absorbing Mercy's pain as if it were her own.

Walter came into her room, his hair disheveled and Wesley's baseball bat hanging limply at his side. His face contorted in rage, giving him the look of a madman. His crazy eyes bugged from their sockets and seemed to spin wildly. Kitty feared for her own safety. Walter Devlin was a man who'd slipped over the edge. Inside she silently cheered her brave protector, Mercy. The vicious blood-red claw marks rising on Walter's face and arms bore evidence to the fact that her would-be hero hadn't succumbed to Walter's brutality without a fight.

A look of horror crossed Kitty's face as Walter raised the bat, seemingly intent on bludgeoning her as he had Mercy. As he reared back to strike out at her, he stopped suddenly and glanced around the room in sudden paranoia. He turned around in circles, looking much like Mercy did when she chased her tail. He swung the bat in the air a couple of times even though there was nothing there. An unexpected look of concern hooded his eyes. He looked suddenly distracted. Using the bat for support, he dropped to one knee to snarl directives at her.

"Now, *Kit Kat* ... you tell anybody about what happened just now and I swear to God, you'll end up just like your little doggie in there. You got that, *Kit Kat*?" Walter spat. "When your Momma gets home, we're going to tell her that I came home and found old Mercy in there trying to bite you. Stupid dog just went plumb crazy. That's how your face got all messed up. I had to hit her with the bat to get her off of you, but not before she scratched the hell out of me. You got our little story straight, Missy?" He kicked her unprotected pajama-clad legs, as she lay there unmoving.

"Yes," she croaked through swelling lips.

"Yes, what?" he bellowed at her.

She raised her head in mock submission, even though she knew the gesture was wasted on Walter. She stared at his face contorted in anger, silently hating him.

"Yes, *sir*," she whispered.

"Good girl." He reached over and patted her bottom and then pinched her battered cheek before kicking her one more time for good measure. As a final blow to her dignity, before exiting the room, with one fell swoop of the baseball bat, he cleared the top of her bureau, hurtling her personal memorabilia to the floor. The slam of the front door rang throughout the house as Walter finally departed. She heard the sound of spewing gravel as his car raced down the street and out of earshot.

Kitty lifted her tortured body, crawling as best she could to the bathroom across the hall. She had to shove the door hard against Mercy's inert body, which blocked her entrance. Once inside the bathroom, she closed and locked the door. Mercy lay motionless on the floor, a pool of dark red blood staining the cheap linoleum floor under her head. Not wanting to incur her mother's wrath for using "the good towels," Kitty removed her terrycloth robe and gently blanketed the dog with it. She lay across Mercy and cried for what seemed like hours. Great gut-wrenching sobs poured from the depths of her physically and emotionally bruised body.

She cried and babbled at the horrible injustice of her sad young life. "Daddy! I want my daddy," she wailed. "Where are you, Daddy? Why did you leave me? I need you! Please come and find me and take me away from this horrible place."

Kitty cradled Mercy's lifeless form, rocking and crying until she was hoarse. It was there on the cold bathroom floor holding the still-warm body of her dead dog, she made her first attempt to pray for her enemy; albeit not in the way the nuns in Catechism class had taught her.

"Dear God, I hate Walter Devlin! Please make something really bad happen to him that will make him go away forever! I hate him with all my heart and I wish he was dead – as dead as poor Mercy. Make Walter die and please make it soon, God!" Kitty sobbed.

TWELVE

The lights slowly came to life in the screening room. Her childhood bedroom disappeared. Kitty sat and moaned in pain much as she had just seen herself doing over 30 years ago.

"Mercy," she silently mouthed.

Grace leaned over and cradled Kitty much like a mother would do with a distraught child. The two rocked. Kitty cried. Grace gently soothed.

"Why did he have to kill Mercy? She only wanted to protect me. She was just a big lovable teddy bear," she sobbed.

Grace continued to comfort Kitty. She pushed Kitty's hair from her eyes and soothed her with tender hugs.

"I don't know, sweetie. That was a very unfortunate incident, to be sure. Mercy was a trusted friend to you. That must have been very difficult for you to watch. Do you want to talk about what happened?" Grace gently prodded.

Kitty pushed Grace aside and got up to pace around the perimeter of the screening room. She hugged herself for comfort. Every few seconds she would make angry swipes at the never-ending supply of tears running down her cheeks.

"No! I don't want to talk about anything! I don't want to think about anything! I'm tired, Grace. I don't want to do this anymore!" Kitty stopped pacing and wrung her hands in agitation.

"Do what, Katherine?" Grace questioned.

"This!" Kitty opened her arms and waved them towards the movie screen and the hidden projector in the back of the room. "All of this! None of it's helping me to *understand* why I'm here. None of this makes sense! It only makes me feel worse. I don't know what you expect to accomplish by showing me all of these horrible things in my life. I have spent a lifetime trying to forget all of this!" Kitty shoved her hands through her hair and then wiped her runny nose with the back of her hand.

Grace shot up from her seat like a fully ignited bottle rocket to confront Kitty. "You're so close, Katherine! Don't you see it? It's so obvious to me! Surely you must recognize what has happened to you?" Grace forcefully turned Kitty towards her.

"See what?" Kitty yelled. "You're talking in riddles, Grace. What exactly am I supposed to see?" She turned away to escape Grace's penetrating stare.

Grace would not be ignored. She scurried around Kitty until she was standing toe-to-toe with her again. She held up both hands in surrender to halt Kitty's movements. "I told you, Katherine. You need to discover what brought you to the point of your demise. It's necessary to review the major life events that shaped you. Your father's abandonment was only the beginning. But this ..." she paused, pointing at the screen. A still photo of Walter Devlin stared back at Kitty. Walter, poised with a raised baseball bat and crazed fury turning his eyes into piercing black pinpricks of evil, loomed larger than life. "This cemented something in you that you yourself have yet to realize. I see it! Why can't you?" Grace's impatience rose with the tone of her voice.

Kitty grabbed her head with both hands and shook like a rabid dog. "Stop it! I hate this! I don't know what you want from me! I don't like this place any more! I want to go home!" With eyes pinched tightly closed, she kept her hands over her ears and started singing at the top of her lungs to drown out Grace's persistent badgering. "Surely goodness and mercy, shall follow me ..."

Grace inched closer and forced Kitty's hands to her sides. She placed both her hands gently on either side of Kitty's face and held her head still. "Katherine!" she scolded, and then a little gentler. "Kitty, please. Stop singing. Listen to me. Open your eyes, Kitty." Kitty obeyed. She slowly lifted her hands placing them over Grace's, which still held her face immobile.

"What?" she choked on the word.

"Ssshhh," Grace whispered. "You're going to get there. But apparently not just yet." Grace steered Kitty back to her theater seat, forcing her to sit. Kitty immediately drew her knees to her chest, hugging them with her arms and rested her head on them.

"Perhaps we need to try a little diversion therapy until you can see things more precisely," Grace mumbled, almost under her breath.

Kitty lifted her head like it was made of lead. "Diversion therapy? I don't like the sound of that."

Grace exited the row of seats and moved around to stand directly behind Kitty. She placed her hands on Kitty's shoulders and massaged ever so lightly. "Yes, I think we're going about this the wrong way. I think a different approach might be in order." Grace's face lit with excitement.

"I've got to tell you, Grace. I'm not feeling so good about this life-after-death thing. So far all of this has been worse than dying. Maybe this is really Hell. Is that it? When I died, I went to Hell and this is to be my eternal punishment – reliving all of the most painful moments of my life. Cause all I've seen so far has been really bad and really ugly. Am I right, Grace? Is this Hell?" Kitty's voice rose in panic. Grace stopped her shoulder massage. Kitty tilted her head back and locked eyes with Grace. Grace's emerald eyes were filled with compassion and hope.

"*Hell?*" Grace drew the word out making it sound like a question. "Oh my heavens, no. This most certainly is not Hell." Grace bustled about the room and headed for the exit doors. "Trust me on this, Katherine." Grace talked over her shoulder, then turned and stared at Kitty. "Hell is much, much worse than this." Grace brought a delicate hand to her chin to help her think out loud. "But perhaps you are right about one thing, Katherine. I believe you do need a little pick-me-up to help you get through the rest of this. Something good to go with the bad and the ugly." Grace turned and exited abruptly through the double doors.

Kitty sat rooted to her seat in confusion, unsure whether she should follow Grace or not. Suddenly feeling very alone, fear churned the acid in her stomach. *No more surprises*, she thought out loud.

"Grace?" Kitty squeaked, and then cleared her throat. "Grace, please don't leave me here alone. I'm sorry I yelled at you."

Before Kitty could move from her spot she heard a ruckus beyond the door. Loud noises, doors slamming and general commotion filtered through the open doorway.

Fear and confusion wrapped itself around Kitty. She buried her face in her upraised knees and covered her ears with her hands, much the same way she did on the few occasions when she watched a horror movie. She inwardly prayed for the fear to go away. The unidentified noises reverberated throughout the room, magnifying her fears. Everything about this "adventure" was uncontrollable. The unknown terrified her.

Perhaps seeing Walter again had triggered her panic and was now responsible for the clawing sense of alarm bubbling up inside her. Whatever the reason, Kitty let instinct take over and she started singing again, *surely goodness and mercy shall fol-low me*. The slow rhythmic tones of the Psalm always brought her comfort. It was her safe place. But something was wrong. The song wasn't helping. She didn't feel safe at all. She felt more afraid than ever. Singing her song over and over again, Kitty was so consumed with fear that Grace's return went unnoticed. Kitty nearly bolted from her chair when she felt Grace's soft tap on her shoulder.

Kitty's sudden movement and startled yelp caused Grace to gasp in surprise. Both women jumped simultaneously. Grace's hand flew to her chest to still her quickening heartbeat.

"Oh my, Katherine! You startled me!" Grace exclaimed.

"I startled you! Good gosh, Grace, you scared me to death!"

Grace rolled her eyes.

"Oops. Sorry, Grace. I keep forgetting," Kitty flinched at the death reference.

Grace smoothed her flowing gown and brushed her blazing mane back from her face. "I'm sorry, too. It took a little doing, but I think I have a nice surprise for you. You were right earlier. So far, I'm afraid that much of this whole ordeal has been a bit overwhelming for you. I think you are entitled to a little taste of heaven, if you will." Grace's smile enveloped her entire being. She was so excited about her *surprise,* she glowed. She turned towards the door and clapped her hands several times. "This should make you feel better," she beamed.

Bolting through the door, her oversized paws barely touching the floor, flew Mercy – looking exactly as she had before she died 30 years ago. Kitty had a scant moment to process her surprise when Mercy leapt into her lap. The dog lavished Kitty's stunned face with canine kisses. Kitty slid to the floor with the oversized fur ball and hugged her as tight as she could around the neck. She cried and laughed all at the same time, while Mercy barked and whined. The Retriever continued to bathe her with her long pink tongue.

Several minutes passed before their reunion was spent. Kitty couldn't stop hugging the big dog. She needed the continual affirmation of touch to cement her wondrous disbelief that Mercy was actually real. As Mercy settled, Kitty sat cross-legged on the floor and lovingly scratched her champion's golden ears. Kitty looked at Grace who sat in silence and watched the wild reunion in quiet delight.

"But how, Grace?" Speech was difficult with her throat constricted with emotion. "No ... no, never mind." She shook her head. "Don't tell me. I don't care *how*." Kitty's eyes sparkled with appreciation. "Thank you, Grace. Thank you." Kitty's tears fell on Mercy's head. She alternated between fierce hugs and generous ear scratching. Mercy was eager to wash away Kitty's unchecked tears of joy.

Grace smiled. "This is a special place, dear. *Nothing* is impossible for God."

No further explanation was required.

Kitty leaned over and placed loving kisses on Mercy's wide snout. The joy Kitty felt was unequaled to anything on earth. "Oh my brave Mercy. I love you so much. Can you ever forgive me for what Walter did to you? I'm sorry – so, so sorry, Mercy girl." Kitty hugged and kissed the silky-haired animal, letting her tears fall without shame. She half expected Mercy to answer with a human voice. This place had such limitless possibilities – anything was possible. Mercy sat contentedly by her side, silently communing the special language of love the two had shared long ago.

Grace stood and moved back to her original seat, inviting Kitty to rejoin her. "Come on, Katherine. Get off the floor and come sit here where it's more comfortable," Grace urged.

Kitty stood and Mercy was instantly by her side. "Just like the old days," Kitty said. She sat down and wasn't surprised when Mercy hopped up and sat beside her. She placed her big head in Kitty's lap. Kitty's hands were never far from the big dog and she continued stroking with loving hands that could not be stilled.

"Oh, Grace. This is the best surprise ever! How does Mercy even know who I am, though? The last time she saw me, I was only 12? That was over 30 years ago?"

"I told you – this is a special place and anything is possible," Grace's smile lit her face like a high wattage bulb.

Mercy nosed her snout under Kitty's hand when she suddenly stopped her stroking. Kitty felt tears well in her eyes once again.

"Oh you do know me, don't you girl? I always felt like Mercy's death was my fault. I should have done a better job of protecting her."

"That was an awfully big burden for a 12-year-old girl, don't you think?" Grace questioned.

Kitty shrugged. "I promised my mom I would be totally responsible for Mercy since Wesley and Maria didn't want much to do with her. I didn't do a very good job of taking care of her." Mercy's heavy body shifted so she nearly filled Kitty's lap. Kitty welcomed the heaviness of the dog's body. Mercy's senseless killing 30 years ago had left a heaviness of a different kind in Kitty. She never let the heaviness completely overwhelm or consume her. It became more of an annoying tightness that never strayed far from her heart. For survival's sake, Kitty had always stored the burden away, but now with Mercy's reincarnation, it felt as though a heavy yoke had been lifted from around her neck.

"That's not entirely what I mean, Katherine. I'm talking about the burden of responsibility of keeping those dark secrets of Walter's abusive behavior – the murder of your dog. That's a lot of secrets and responsibility for a child. Did you ever consider telling anyone about what was happening in your home? Your mother? A teacher?"

"I couldn't Grace. I was too afraid of Walter. You saw how crazy he was. I didn't know who else he might hurt. And as for my mother, I was sure she either wouldn't believe me, or worse yet – she'd somehow blame me. I was afraid she'd accuse me of encouraging Walter's advances. She seemed happy with Walter and I didn't want to be the one to mess that up for her. As disagreeable and difficult as my mom was, she still deserved some happiness. Even if it was with *Walter*." Kitty focused her energy on Mercy and spoke in hushed whispers.

"You poor dear. So many troubles for one so young."

"Grace, please don't make me watch anymore of what happened with Walter. Can't we simply skip ahead a bunch of years?"

"All right, Katherine. But don't you at least want to talk about this time period? It was after all, a pivotal time of your life. I noticed you are more upset about Walter killing Mercy than over what he did to you personally that day. Are you quite certain there's nothing you care to discuss?"

"What's there to discuss?" Kitty became defensive. "Walter was mean and perverted. Why should we dwell on anything else? After that day - I spent the next six years getting very good at staying out of his way. And I started packing on the pounds. I figured if I got really fat and gross, Walter the pervert would leave me alone. You know what's really sad, Grace? My mom was totally clueless about her disgusting husband. She started nagging *me* to watch what I ate. If I heard it once, I heard it a thousand times, '*boys don't like fat girls!*' I remember being so mad at her all the time. I just wanted to scream at her to 'wake up!' I don't know why she couldn't see that her husband was the real problem – not me. I had no control over the situation – but I could control the food. So the more she nagged me, the more I ate. I got really good at that too." She shook her head in disgust.

"So why didn't you stand up for yourself and tell your mother, for heaven's sake?"

"For all the reasons I told you. I think the bottom line though, was that it was a huge risk for me to trust my mother. I was worried she didn't love me as much as she loved her husband. I thought she'd side with Walter rather than me and that would have been worse than anything Walter could ever have done to me. I basically went into survival mode and thanked my lucky stars that Walter was fairly tame as far as perverts go. After he killed Mercy ..."

Mercy's ears perked up at the mention of her name. The dog turned adoring eyes to her master. Kitty smiled and treated Mercy to a vigorous belly rub. "Anyway," she continued, "after that day, Walter only tried to touch me a few more times. He slapped me around occasionally, but nothing as severe as that other day. Once I started gaining weight, he grew tired of me – or maybe he was afraid of the sheer size of my bulk. Who knows? I'm sure there are women who've suffered much worse than I ever did. It bothered me more that he enjoyed humiliating me."

"How so?" Grace asked.

"He was a bit of an exhibitionist," Kitty stammered, clearly embarrassed. "He got a kick out of *exposing himself* and touching himself in front of me." She shuddered. "Somehow that felt worse than the hitting. It always happened without warning. It was gross. I'd hear him laughing at me because I was so embarrassed by the sight of him." It was hard for her to continue. She cleared her throat and pushed on. "My first marriage right out of high school barely lasted a year, partly because I had a hard time letting my husband touch me. But, marriage at 18 was my only option if I was ever going to escape that house. I married the first guy that came along. Unfortunately, the guy ended up having as many problems as me."

"Hmm." Grace shook her head. "So – did you ever *forgive* your stepfather for what he did to you, Katherine?"

Kitty stretched, ignoring Grace. She yawned in a very unlady-like fashion. "Oh, excuse me. I'm so tired of talking about all of this – especially Walter. I've spent a lot of years trying to recover from the emotional damage he caused me to start opening up these old wounds now. Let's call it a day or move on to something else. What else have you got on that highlight reel of yours?"

Kitty got up and Mercy followed on her heels. The two romped around the open space chasing one another.

Grace halted them with a stern command.

"Katherine! We are not finished yet!" she scolded. "You will sit back down and finish this – now!"

THIRTEEN

Grace's words felt like a slap.

"It's important to know where you stand on this forgiveness issue with your stepfather."

Kitty stopped her roughhousing, giving Grace her full attention. A blush stained her cheeks. "I'm sorry, Grace. I didn't mean to brush you off. Please don't be upset with me. I couldn't stand it if you were mad at me."

"It's all right," Grace's tone softened. "I'm sorry to be so harsh with you, Katherine. The forgiveness issue cannot be compromised. Before we proceed further, it's imperative to know if you have any unforgiveness in your heart aimed at your stepfather."

Kitty and Mercy returned to their seats. A rush of air escaped Kitty after she sat. She exhaled in deep thought. "Well, I can say with all honesty, I *used* to hate Walter. You heard my prayers the day he killed Mercy. I wanted God to strike him dead in a very slow painful way. It was pretty childish, I know – but then I was only 12. I was a kid." She was lost in thought – a prisoner of her long-ago carefully stored memories.

"What happened to change your attitude?" Grace coaxed her from her reverie.

Kitty rubbed her temples hoping to free her thoughts. "Lots of things, really. For one thing, I got older. So I guess maturity had something to do with my attitude change. Then I met my best friend, Dani." Thinking about Dani brought a smile to her face. "She was a devout Christian. She took me to church camp with her one summer. I accepted Christ as my Savior and I knew it was wrong to harbor any bitterness. Thank goodness for Dani. I don't know what would have happened without church camp. And trust me – that took some doing. My mom was faithful to the Catholic Church even though she was practically ex-communicated for divorcing my dad. She thought it was a mortal sin for me to attend a non-Catholic church. She thought I'd come back from camp a *holy roller*, so she refused to let me go at first. Mom was always afraid of anything that was different. She finally relented because of my weight issues. She thought I'd get some much needed exercise at camp."

"Did you ever share your secrets about your stepfather with your best friend?"

"I was too ashamed. I think I was the original queen of denial before being in denial was popular. Dani is the best friend a girl could ever have, but back then I couldn't share my shame with anyone. Years later, I told her everything, but not until we were both nearly adults. It's so easy for people to judge you and tell you how they would do things, but until you actually live the nightmare – there's no way to predict a different outcome. My silence and denial was my way of dealing with the problem. I'm thankful for Dani. Until I met her, I didn't even realize I needed a deeper relationship with God through his son, Jesus. Pretty sad I know."

Kitty noticed Grace squirm and readjust her seat. Apparently angels get sore bums like everyone else, Kitty thought. Kitty had to hand it to her though, since she'd yet to hear Grace complain even the slightest. The woman was a veritable rock of stability. Kitty silently thanked her for her quiet strength.

Grace smiled, turning to Kitty, "You're welcome, dear."

Kitty laughed out loud. "Grace, you're the coolest. Mind reading is a great gift. I wish my husband had your gift. That would've come in handy a time or two."

"Oh my, yes," she laughed. "Definitely a blessing at times. But I'm certain God had a reason for creating his children the way He did and without that particular gift. Now – what were we talking about?"

"I was telling you about Dani and church camp."

Grace picked up the flow, "Oh yes."

Kitty quieted, offering nothing further.

"Katherine? Is there something else troubling you?"

"Well, there is something bugging me." Her brow furrowed in confusion. "Although, I realize I'm hardly in a position to judge anything."

Grace scooted closer to her, crossed her legs and rested her heart shaped face on her hands. "Go ahead ... shoot." You can ask me anything. I'm all ears."

Kitty stalled by picking at the cuticle on her right thumb. She avoided looking directly at Grace. "Well, it's just that ... I was wondering ..." she rambled.

"Oh good heavens, child. Just say whatever is on your mind!"

"Well, after watching what happened all those years ago and seeing that you were actually there on that day," she hesitated. "Well ... if you really were there when Walter killed Mercy, why didn't you stop him?" Her words rushed out like a giant balloon with a hole in it.

"I was wondering when you'd get around to asking about that?" Grace brushed imaginary lint from her gown and crossed her legs in the opposite direction.

"Well?" Kitty peeked at her out of the corner of her eye and spoke timidly. "It's just that – as an angel you can do all these amazing things, but ..." Kitty stopped short, uncertain how far she could go. She stammered and danced around the issue for a few more seconds. Grace focused on her, unperturbed by her stalling tactics. Kitty pushed on. "So, why didn't you stop Walter!" She didn't mean for it to sound like an accusation, but it clearly was.

"What makes you think I didn't stop him?"

"But he *killed* Mercy!"

"Yes, but he didn't kill *you*, Katherine."

Realization dawned. Kitty's lip trembled as she absorbed the details. Her face masked her conflicting emotions. Even though she struggled to hide her feelings of denial, anger and helplessness, tears welled in her eyes. She bit down hard on her bottom lip to stop from saying things she would regret later on.

"You're upset, Katherine." Grace waited.

"Yeah! You think?" Sarcasm gave way to barely controlled hostility.

"Lets, talk about it. What is the *real* reason you're angry?"

The struggle to stuff her feelings deep inside raged within. She squirmed, unable to find a release. Years of "stuffing" her emotions had honed her "stuffing skills" to near perfection. She silently counted to 10, balling her fists in repeated clenching motions.

"Katherine?" Grace was relentless in her prodding – digging to uncover the secret source of Kitty's true feelings. "Tell me. I know you want to. What is it?"

"Stop it. I can't. Not yet." She stood up so suddenly, Mercy yipped. Kitty made to leave, but not quickly enough. Grace grabbed the back of her shirt, pulling her back.

"Katherine, you can't keep running away. You've got to get this out. Tell me, please."

Trapped by Grace's staying hand, she sat down defeated. "I don't think I can yet."

Grace leaned her head back, searching the ceiling tiles before speaking. Closing he eyes, she breathed in a faint whisper. "Yes Lord." Turning to Kitty, her eyes blazed with patient understanding. "Okay, Katherine. We'll wait and talk about it when you're ready. I shouldn't have pushed you. I sense that you're close, but we won't go there until you say so."

"Grace, I haven't the slightest idea what you're talking about."

"I think you do. You simply aren't ready to commit to it."

"Commit to what?" She was genuinely confused.

"The source of your true inner turmoil," Grace said.

Kitty rolled her eyes. "Uh, sure, Grace. Whatever you say. If you know so much about me and my *inner turmoil,* why do we need to bother with all this?"

"What's obvious to me is clearly not getting through to you. Until it does, we'll continue dissecting your past. Eventually it will dawn on you. Everything happens for a reason. Apparently a few more steps are necessary for you."

Mercy barked as if to offer her opinion.

"Hey," Kitty scolded the big dog. "Whose side are you on?" she accused.

Grace laughed, lightening the tension in the room. "How about if we fast-forward to that summer right before church camp? We'll have a little look-see. It was no coincidence that circumstances lined up for you to be there, you know?"

Kitty exhaled and thought for a moment. "What are you saying, Grace?"

Grace turned, smiling at Kitty. She patted her arm affectionately. "Your steps were ordered by God from an early age. It was pre-ordained."

Kitty didn't bother to hide her irritation. "Yeah, yeah ... you talked about that earlier. But *if* God had 'pre-ordained' my life as you say and he knew exactly when I was going to get saved, why didn't he step in and intervene with Walter? Why did he let Walter ruin my life the way he did?" Staying calm was proving to be more difficult than she imagined.

Grace took a deep breath, exhaling slowly.

"Oh, Katherine," she sighed. "There are so many questions and I'm afraid I'm only going to be able to offer you a smattering of reassurance. God is ... well – he's *God*. He has reasons for allowing certain things to happen to his people – even the bad things. No one can explain it, not even me. Unfortunately, sometimes he *allows* bad things to happen to good people. No one is exempt from bad things happening, Katherine. The Scriptures speak of trials and tribulations that everyone must suffer. It's those bad things that cause people to turn inward and rely on God more. Sometimes the very thing you think will destroy you is the one thing God uses to draw you closer to him. God doesn't cause the bad things to happen, but he certainly can use them for his good when they do happen. Do you understand?"

Kitty nodded. "Yes, I think so. I don't necessarily like it, but I understand. Don't get me wrong, Grace. I knew all about God and everything from being raised in the Catholic Church, but I didn't have a real relationship with Jesus until I went to camp. What if I wouldn't have gone to church camp with Dani? Do you think I would have missed God? Was that my one and only chance to make Jesus my savior?"

Grace linked her hand with Kitty's. "No, dear. God doesn't want *anyone* to perish. He would have found you another way. Trust me on this – God is very persistent." Grace chuckled. "The day you accepted him as Lord, all of heaven rejoiced. But if it would have taken another year or two – or longer, all of the angels would still have rejoiced over your conversion."

Kitty's eyes grew round in disbelief. "You mean, your were there, Grace?"

"Well of course, Katherine. God's *grace* has been with you always."

Without warning, Grace waved her hand and the room was plunged into sudden darkness. Ready or not, Kitty steeled herself for the next film segment as the action exploded on the screen in full Technicolor and digital surround sound.

FOURTEEN

May 25, 1977

Sixteen-year-old Kitty checked the time on her inexpensive wrist-watch as she cleared away the clutter from the littered table. She'd gotten stuck covering the late shift for another waitress who called in sick. Watching the time inch towards midnight, she was now having second thoughts. Although she liked her part-time wait-ress job at the bowling alley, she didn't like riding her bike home late at night. Even though there would be very little traffic this time of night, she hated to admit she harbored deep-seeded fears of the dark. She very rarely worked past nine o'clock. She'd taken pity on the other waitress, Nicole, whose husband was home for 10 days on leave. Plus she could hardly say no to the overtime since she only had 15 months to go until she turned 18. She needed all the money she could get her hands on so she could move out on her own and be free from Walter the pervert.

Even though it was Saturday night, business was winding down. The crowd had thinned considerably in both the bowling alley and the snack bar area. This was small town North Carolina not some fast-paced big city nightspot. Most of the residents were safely tucked in for the night. Kitty glanced at the front desk at the sound of loud voices and raucous laughter.

"*Walter.* What's he doing here," Kitty said, spotting Walter at the front counter.

By the looks of him, Walter had started his Memorial Day celebrating several hours ago. He rarely needed a special occasion to drink. Holidays, weekdays, weekends – Walter imbibed in strong drink all the same.

The night manager, Max was busy in the back so Walter was yucking it up with some old guy who was every bit as snockered as Walter. He shuffled awkwardly with an unsteady gait towards Kitty. She could smell the liquor on his breath from three feet away. His blood shot eyes indicated he'd already exceeded an unhealthy level of intoxication. He twirled his keys with his fat sausage fingers and sat down - or rather fell down in a chair, resting his elbows on the table Kitty had just cleaned.

"Hey, girlie. You 'bout done here? I came to fetch you so you wouldn't have to ride home in the dark. It ain't safe, you know," he leered at her. He fished in his shirt pocket for his pack of cigarettes and lighter.

She avoided looking at him, busying herself instead by wiping off chairs. When she finished, she turned the chairs upside down to rest on the tables.

"I'll be fine," she said. "You don't need to wait for me. Besides, I promised Dani I'd spend the night with her so I'm going straight to her house when I'm done here. She's probably waiting for me, so you can go ahead home." It wasn't exactly a lie. She and her best friend Dani Waterman had discussed the possibility of a sleepover. Walter didn't need to know that it wasn't until tomorrow night though. The less he knew about her comings and goings, the safer she would feel.

Walter insisted on picking a fight with her about the safety of nighttime bike riding. Rather than create an embarrassing scene, she relented and agreed to leave with him.

"First, give me your keys," she said. She held out her hand, palm up waiting for him to hand the keys over.

"Whaddya want 'em for?" he slurred.

Rather than making him angry by accusing him of being drunk, she came up with a credible excuse to pacify him.

"I haven't had much nighttime driving experience since I got my permit, so if you let me drive home it'll be good practice for me." Inside Kitty shook with fear at the idea of driving on poorly lit country roads at night. But somehow it made more sense for her to drive rather than letting a drunken Walter get behind the wheel.

She finished the last of her cleaning duties and removed her apron. She retrieved her small purse from under the counter and trailed after a tottering Walter to the parking lot. Once she'd loaded her bicycle in the trunk of Walter's over-sized Chevrolet Impala, she slid behind the wheel of the monstrous car. Instinctively, she immediately pulled the armrest down separating herself from Walter in the passenger seat. The drive home only took about 10 minutes so Kitty felt fairly confident that not much could happen in such a short span of time.

The roadway between the bowling alley and home was extremely isolated and dark. Kitty hadn't been looking forward to riding her bike on that dark stretch of deserted road, so on some level she was grateful to have a ride. It would have taken her three times as long to get home on her bike compared to a car ride.

Kitty wasn't used to driving such a big car. She was learning to drive her mother's Pinto and felt more comfortable with a smaller vehicle. The sheer length of Walter's Impala made her skittish. She managed to safely maneuver her way out of the parking lot without hitting anything. Once safely on the road, she pressed the accelerator and picked up speed. Not used to so much horsepower, she gave the car too much gas causing it to lurch quickly. The unsecured trunk flew open with a loud bang. Walter yelled at her to take it easy. Kitty jumped at the sound of the banging trunk and the harshness of Walter's reprimand.

Walter pushed the armrest up and slid over to sit next to Kitty. She gripped the wheel with both hands until her knuckles turned white. She focused her attention on the road, ignoring Walter and keeping her eyes peeled for skunks or rodents that might dart out in front of the car.

"So, my little *Kit Kat*. Did you have a good night at work?" Walter's words ran together.

Kitty stole a quick look at him out of the corner of her eye pretending not to hear him. Walter played with the buckle on his trousers, which caused Kitty to drive faster. Perspiration dotted her upper lip. She wiped it away with the back of her hand willing herself to ignore him and keep driving.

"Guess I can't really call you my *little* Kit Kat now can I, Missy?" Walter pinched her fleshy upper arm.

She swatted his hand away, ignoring his remark.

Walter laughed at her and kept talking, slurring his words as he spoke.

"Yep. You sure have filled out real nice, Kit Kat. You've got lots of cushion now. A man likes something to hold on to, you know. You're not like your momma, girl. She's all skin and bones and sharp points. No, I like all the round places on you. It makes me itch to touch you."

Walter licked his lips in expectation and tried to reach over and push Kitty's skirt up so he could feel her generous thigh. From the way he reacted to the feel of her warm flesh, Kitty began to get panicky. Her breath came in short quick bursts. She fought to control her air intake worried she was going to hyperventilate. Walter's lust ignited and he wasn't satisfied with just touching her leg. In an instant, his hands wandered, grabbing Kitty everywhere. He pushed his hand under her uniform skirt and halted momentarily. He seemed to wrestle with indecision over which part of her anatomy to grab first; lower half, upper half? His arms flew about like a windmill.

Kitty had all she could do to control the big car and remain on the road. Trying to deter Walter's advances proved futile. It became increasingly more difficult for her to maneuver the unfamiliar car. The vehicle swerved from side to side as she repeatedly pushed Walter's roving hands away. She lifted her shoulder to swipe away her tears, still managing to keep at least one hand on the wheel. Her other hand continuously slapped Walter's groping paws. She silently prayed for a policeman to be hiding in the bushes some-where waiting to pull her over for her erratic driving. The smell of Walter's hot, stale alcoholic breath on the side of her face made her gag. Looking in her rear view mirror, she spotted a small drop of spittle working its way past the corner of Walter's mouth. He licked his lips, inching closer — his intention to kiss her quite clear. Seeing his fat disgusting tongue, Kitty new the moment to act was now. Glancing at the speedometer, it registered an excess of 55 m.p.h.

Thankful for the cover of darkness, she took her hand off the wheel long enough to quickly reach down making sure her seatbelt was securely fastened. Stealing a peek at Walter, she noticed he hadn't bothered with his seatbelt. Maybe his oversight would buy her some much-needed time. Before she could talk herself out of what she was planning, with split-second timing she slammed on the breaks with both feet. The car skidded, careening off the side of the road propelling them headlong into a nearby ditch where a huge tree took the brunt of the impact. Kitty managed to shield her face from injury by raising both arms at the last second to protect against the force of the crash. Her seatbelt held fast knocking the wind from her with a whoosh. She couldn't be sure if the stars dancing in her eyes were from the adrenaline rush or the one-ton vehicle losing its unexpected battle with the unyielding tree.

With the car's sudden stop, Walter was jettisoned forward slamming his face against the windshield. Blood appeared on his forehead instantly and gushed from his bulbous nose like a hot springs geyser. He slumped to the floorboard making no sound or further movement. Not bothering to check to see if Walter was still breathing, Kitty unfastened her seatbelt, grabbed her purse and ran around to the back of the car. The unlatched trunk had flown open and rested at an unnatural angle. With some difficulty, she wrestled her bike free from the trunk where Walter had carelessly placed it.

Kitty knew she was more than half way home but wasn't sure if home was the safest place for her to go. With only a scant moment for decision-making, she pedaled as fast as her shaky limbs allowed, heading in the general direction of familiar surroundings. The summer breeze blew her hair in her face. The coolness of it calmed her somewhat, helping to clear her head. Wanting to put as much distance between herself and Walter, she rode for nearly a mile before coming upon a shortcut that would lead her towards home. She stopped and pulled her bicycle into the bushes and waited for her breathing to steady. At 5'3" tall and 165 pounds, she silently prayed all this exertion would trigger a sudden heart attack. Death seemed preferable to facing her mother's wrath once she tried to explain what had become of Walter.

Kitty waited in the bushes watching for approaching headlights. The road remained deserted as far as Kitty could see. When she felt certain Walter was not giving chase, she squatted down and retched in the bushes until her stomach ached. When the vomiting subsided, she wiped her face and eyes. Right then and there she vowed she was done putting up with Walter and his perversions. Her natural inclination for self-preservation kicked into overdrive. She formulated a plan that would secure her freedom and release her from this hellish prison life with Walter. As she pedaled for home, she worked on a plausible lie to tell her mother regarding Walter's whereabouts.

"Where in the heck have you been?" Sophia yelled the second Kitty entered the house. The sounds of a late-night television program droned in the background. "And where's your father," Sophia asked through a thick haze of cigarette smoke.

Kitty cringed at her mother's referral of Walter as her father. "I don't know," she mumbled, making her way down the hall.

Sophia would not be dismissed so easily. She followed Kitty to her bedroom. "What do you mean, you don't know! He left here over an hour ago and said he was going to pick you up at work."

"Sorry, Mom. He never showed up. Maybe he stopped off somewhere for a drink. He does that sometimes, you know?"

Sophia reared back to slap her face, but Kitty had gotten too good at anticipating that move and ducked out of reach. Sophia backed down and settled instead for sticking a long, blood red fingernail within inches of Kitty's freckled nose. Kitty guessed the fact that she outweighed her mother by at least sixty pounds, might have had something to do with Sophia's acquiescence. Whatever the reason, Sophia more than made up for a physical slap by delivering a tongue lashing with nearly as much sting.

"Don't get smart with me, young lady! So Walter drinks. Big deal! It's none of your damn business and I won't have you taking that tone with me!" she yelled. "Do I make myself clear, Missy?"

Kitty knew the routine well by now. She quickly cowered, dropping her gaze to the floor in submission. "I'm sorry," she mumbled. "I'm tired, Mother. I'd like to go to bed, please."

"Fine. What happened to your face?" Sophia moved closer, examining Kitty's forehead.

Kitty backed away turning her head. She felt all around her forehead and winced as she touched a tender spot over her right eyebrow. Pulling her fingers away, a small spot of blood stained her fingers crimson. In the chaos of the crash, she must have hit her head on the steering wheel.

"It's nothing," she stammered. I had a little accident on my bike when I went over a curb. It's just a scratch." The lies flowed effortlessly from her lips.

"Well go put something on that before it gets infected. And don't get blood on my good towels."

"Yes ma'am." Kitty had nearly made it to the safety of her room when her mother's voice stopped her.

"You're sure you never saw Walter either at the bowling alley tonight or on your ride home?"

"No ma'am." She excused herself, locking herself in her room.

Since Maria had moved out three years ago, Kitty had the bedroom all to herself. She leaned heavily against the door and closed her eyes, grateful for the privacy.

Kitty knew she wasn't smart enough to figure this situation out by herself. Her best friend Dani would tell her she needed to pray for a solution. Dani and her family prayed about *everything*. Kitty felt strangely comforted by Dani's strong religious convictions and had started secretly attending church with them. There was a security at Dani's church Kitty had never known before. She still liked the Catholic services she attended at weekly mass, but somehow she had a hard time with the all the rituals and the traditions. It somehow seemed impersonal to her. Not to mention that the nuns always stared at her and made her feel guilty for no apparent reason. She felt safe every time she went to church with Dani and her family.

Maybe Dani was right. Maybe prayer could fix this problem with Walter. Kitty checked the door lock a second time wanting to insure absolute privacy. Prayer may be the way to get help from God, but it still felt weird to actually do it and she didn't want to risk anyone catching her in the act.

She knelt down beside her twin bed and closed her eyes. She took a couple of deep breaths, trying to relax. She hardly knew where to begin. She cleared her throat, hesitated, and then finally plunged ahead.

"Dear God, it's me – Katherine Murphy. My friends call me Kitty. You can too. God, if you're really there and if you really care about me and love me the way Dani told me you do … well then – I really need your help. I know I don't deserve your help cause I'm a big disappointment to a lot of people. Well – mostly my family. But God I still need your help. If you could help me out of this mess with Walter and stop him from touching me or slapping me … well – if you could do all that, then I promise I will …"

Kitty stopped for a moment to think of what sacrifice she could offer in exchange for God's help. She rubbed her temples and then twisted the ends of her hair as she pondered her options.

"I promise that if you help me, then when I graduate next year I'll become a nun. Men are pigs, so I don't think I'll be missing anything by not ever getting married. And if that isn't enough of a sacrifice, then I'll be a nun in Africa or the Amazon. Anywhere you say. I'm too ashamed of what's happening with Walter to tell anyone else about this problem. I know on some level it must be my fault. I don't want to be an embarrassment to my mom. So if you could help me without everybody finding out about this, that'd be great. Maybe while you're at it, you could help my mom to like me a little more. She's so angry with me all the time and I'm not even sure why. I wish things could be different. I really don't know how much more of this I can take. If you can't help me then give me the courage to end my life. I know it's a terrible sin and will probably keep me out of Heaven, but how could Hell be worse than living here in this house? I'm sorry to ask you for so much at one time. Please help me. Amen."

Kitty hurried to the bathroom after her prayer time and turned the shower on. She discarded her clothes and stepped in. She turned the water on as hot as she could stand it and let the scalding water run over her. She shampooed her hair three times and scrubbed her skin until it was raw, needing to wash away all evidence of Walter's roving hands. When she finished her shower, she toweled off and put on fresh pajamas. Kitty took all of the clothes she'd been wearing and stuffed them in the bottom of her laundry hamper. She wanted to throw them away, but she needed the uniform for her job. She didn't want any reminders of this terrible night. Tonight had been a close call and a sign that Walter was becoming more daring and more dangerous. With little more than year until she was 18, Kitty knew she was much closer to losing her legal safety net once she reached adulthood.

Before climbing into bed, she dragged the chair from her desk to the door and propped it under the knob to make certain no one could enter her room while she slept. After double-checking the window locks she finally dared to lay down. Even though the room remained fairly hot from the day's heat, Kitty pulled the comforter up to her chin and curled into a tight ball. Exhausted from physical exertion and emotional battery, she closed her eyes and fell asleep instantly.

She awoke the next morning to the sound of her mother's shrill voice. Checking the bedside clock, she was surprised no one had bothered to knock on her door to wake her for Sunday morning Mass. It was already well past eight o'clock and Kitty was certain they'd be late for the 10:00 a.m. service if they didn't hurry. She dressed quickly brushing her teeth and hair before unlocking her fortress to search out the cause of her mother's distress.

Walking into the living room, Kitty was shocked to find her mother yelling at two very large highway patrolmen. Sophia cradled the telephone under her chin and took turns screaming into the phone and then ranting at the officers. Wesley was in the kitchen making his breakfast and offering comments to no one in particular. He was all but ignored by everyone. Kitty shrunk back hoping to be ignored as well. The cops were doing their best to calm Sophia down, but they were having little or no success. Both men talked at once to be heard over Sophia's hysterics. Sophia finally spotted Kitty and turned her attentions on her immediately.

"Katherine! It's about time you got up! These officers are here about Walter. Did you see him last night? Did he show up at the bowling alley to pick you up?"

Sophia's normally perfectly coiffed hair looked like it had yet to see a hair brush this morning. In fact, Sophia was completely unkempt and still wearing her bathrobe. It was evident she'd been roused from her slumber by these two early morning visitors. Just last weekend Sophia was livid with Kitty for opening the door to a solicitor.

"You know my rule, Katherine. No one is ever allowed to see me without my hair and makeup being done!" Sophia had screamed.

If her mother was standing in the middle of the living room with mussed hair, no makeup and still in her bathrobe – it could only mean someone must have died.

Kitty inhaled sharply, fearing her prayers to God last night must have killed Walter the pervert!

All eyes focused on her as she did her best to compose herself and come up with a believable lie.

"No ... no, ma'am. I never saw Walter last night. You never called me to tell me to wait for him, so when my shift was over I rode my bike home as usual. I told you that last night. Why? What's happened to him?" Kitty's look of fright was genuine, but not out of concern for Walter's welfare. In a scant moment, visions of a courtroom trial and a lifetime of wearing a prison jumpsuit flashed before her eyes. *Oh dear Lord, if I've killed Walter, then going to prison would definitely be a creative way for me to leave home,* she thought. *That's not what I had in mind at all, God!* Her subconscience thoughts tortured her.

"He's in jail!" Sophia roared in anger.

"Jail?" Kitty nearly choked on that one word.

Sophia stormed back and forth in a small circle like a caged animal. "Lord, I need a cigarette. Wesley, find my cigarettes for me!" Sophia barked orders to Wesley in the kitchen. Remembering she hadn't disconnected her phone call, Sophia spoke harshly into the mouthpiece. "Howard, are you still there? Well see what you can do about posting his bail and then call me back! I'll get dressed and meet you at the courthouse shortly. NO! Don't tell anybody what's going on! Do you understand?" Sophia slammed the phone on the cradle ending the call.

Wesley hurried to do her bidding and brought Sophia her cigarettes. She lit one as soon as she had them in her hands. She inhaled deeply, unable to vent further frustrations until the smoke settled in her lungs. The nicotine gave her the boost needed to contemplate a course of action.

"Apparently, Walter had a car accident on his way to the bowling alley to pick you up last night, Katherine," Sophia said, exhaling a plume of smoke. "A cop came along and found him drunk, injured and unconscious. They took him to the hospital by ambulance and impounded his car. He suffered a mild concussion. They kept him at the hospital for observation and only just released him an hour ago. These officers arrested him as soon as he was discharged. They took him straight to jail. They're here to question us about Walter's whereabouts last night. They wanted to make sure the car wasn't stolen, since it's registered in my name because of ..." Sophia trailed off, becoming suddenly vague.

One of the officers sensed a change in her demeanor and probed for further information.

Kitty stood back, sizing the cop up and down. He probably weighed somewhere in the neighborhood of 275 pounds and stood well over six and a half feet tall. She couldn't help but think that must be some ridiculous neighborhood if it turned out a formidable giant the likes of him. Even Sophia curbed her hostility when she spoke directly to him.

"Excuse me, Ma'am. Is there something else you're not telling us," he asked curtly.

"No, no. Well, it's just that the car used to be in Walter's name, but when we relocated here from Virginia, it was necessary to change it to my name." Sophia purposely danced around his line of questioning.

"Ma'am, would you care to elaborate?" he asked.

Sophia avoided answering by puffing away on her cigarette. She excused herself to find an ashtray. "Hold on for just a minute!" She said in an unfriendly tone.

"Ma'am, if there is something relative to your husband's accident, it's imperative that you share it with us." Officer Jackson's southern drawl was as smooth as melted butter on a sidewalk in the middle of a warm day. "We're only here to try and piece together what happened." Officer Jackson was all business.

Under different circumstances, Kitty imagined her mother might have tried to charm these two officers. Since Sophia wasn't her usual self, Kitty almost felt sorry for her as she witnessed Sophia struggling to put the most positive spin on this very serious predicament.

"Well, it's nothing really. Just a little blip of a detail is all." Like Kitty and most of her Italian ancestors, Sophia could only verbalize herself by talking with her hands. "Before we moved here from Virginia, my husband Walter, was in a minor car accident and had his driver's license suspended." Sophia tried to brush the whole incident off as incidental with a wave of her hand.

Officer Jackson took out a small pad of paper and flipped it open to an empty page where he recorded Sophia's comments.

"Ma'am, was the cause of that accident alcohol related?" he drawled.

Sophia rolled her eyes and waved her hand.

"Pfftt ... there *may* have been something about that. Maybe. I really don't remember all the details," she said.

"Well, which is it, Mrs. Devlin? Was there alcohol involved in that accident? Yes or No?" He appeared to be losing patience with her.

"Well, yes – I suppose there was, if you must know. But it was nothing really. The judge over reacted and wanted to make an example of Walter by imposing an overly harsh sentence, if you ask me." She complained under her breath in defense of Walter.

"Ma'am, if this is a repeat offense for your husband, and he was driving under the influence without a valid license last evening, then I believe he's going to need legal counsel as soon as possible." Officer Jackson wrote a few more details in his pad before snapping it shut and returning it to his pocket.

Sophia was fuming by the time the officer dismissed her with a curt nod. He and his silent partner thanked her for her time and edged towards the door.

Sophia became wild eyed. She followed them, stopping them short of the front door. She casually touched Officer Jackson on the arm. "Wait ... is that all? Now what happens?" she asked frantically.

With one hand on the door, he tipped his head in Sophia's direction. He shot her an accusing stare as he looked down at her hand resting on his arm.

"Ma'am," he said politely, but clearly irked that she had dared to touch an officer of the law.

Sophia snatched her hand away like she'd been stung by an insect. She inhaled and took a step back. She brought her hands to her chest in what looked like a protective reflex.

"Like I said, I would suggest you contact a lawyer as soon as possible." And with that he nodded at her once again and ordered his partner outside.

Sophia's anger was palpable as her face contorted with rage. With one hand on the door and the other hand clenching in a fist by her side, Sophia looked like she was ready for a brawl. Kitty could tell her mother was fighting the urge to slam the door forcefully on the officers retreating backsides. Somehow she managed to keep a tight rein on her temper and merely closed the door sharply. She turned and leaned against it for support.

"Where did I put my cigarette down," she asked.

Sophia's anger bubbled so close to the surface Kitty would swear she could hear the snap of electricity coursing through her mother's veins. She and Wesley both rushed at once to find her ashtray. Sophia walked over to the sofa and perched on the edge. She took several deep calming puffs of her cigarette before saying anything.

"Well, hell … this is a fine mess Walter has put us in!"

Kitty did her best to mask her euphoria over the sudden turn of events. She hoped her face wouldn't give her away. She prayed she looked properly composed and solemn, even though on the inside she was dancing for joy over Walter's unexpected incarceration.

"Do you know if Walter said anything to the police yet?" Kitty asked with false seriousness.

"Like what? What do you mean?" Sophia barked.

"Oh, I don't know. Did he tell them how the accident happened or anything?" she asked.

"Well how should I know? He didn't come home last night, remember? I haven't seen or spoken to him since yesterday after-noon." Sophia ground her cigarette butt in the ashtray with a vengeance. "I'm going to take a shower and head to the courthouse. I'm waiting for a call from Howard Greene, our attorney. Come and get me right away if he calls. Understand?" Her words dripped venom and her scowl bore holes in both Katherine and Wesley.

"Yes Ma'am," they both answered in unison.

Sophia left the room in a huff, scattering a trail of Italian curse words in her wake. She left the house an hour later with specific instructions to both her children to stay off the phone. She made them promise they would tell no one what was happening within the walls of their family home.

Sometime later, Sophia phoned the house saying that things weren't looking so good for Walter.

"The judge has set a court date and implied Walter may have to serve anywhere from six months to a year in jail. Just what in the Sam Hill are we supposed to ..." She trailed off.

Kitty could hear her mother sucking furiously on a cigarette on the other end of the line. Kitty twined the phone cord around her finger waiting for her mother's next angry tirade.

"Exactly what are *we* supposed to do for that whole time? I can't believe he's put us in this position." She ranted non-stop, breaking periodically for tobacco inhalation and ear-piercing cursing.

Kitty tuned out while her mother rambled on the other end of the phone. Fear, anxiety and relief all danced an internal emotional jig. Kitty's racing heart kept time to the beat of a drum pounding out a rhythm all it's own. But in her head, all she could think was, *I'm free! I'm free! Thank you, Jesus! I'm free!*

FIFTEEN

When her mother hadn't returned by late afternoon, Kitty worried she was going to go stir crazy. A trip to her secret spot by the river and a long talk with her best friend sounded like the best solution. She didn't dare call Dani on the phone in case her mother should phone and get a busy signal. Kitty penned a note to her mother explaining she had a babysitting job and wouldn't be home until around 11:00. It wasn't a total lie; more like a half truth, Kitty reasoned. She did have to baby-sit, but not until seven o'clock. That left her with a couple of hours to sneak off by herself. Dani's house was in the opposite direction of their secret spot, so rather than ride out of her way, Kitty headed towards the river and sent silent telepathic communications to Dani. The two were so close, they usually sensed when the other one was in trouble and often-times responded to the unspoken silent commands. Kitty hoped she and Dani were in synch today.

Kitty sat on the bank of the slow moving river and listened to the late-afternoon calls of the summer wildlife. She loved this quiet tranquil spot. Moving her family to North Carolina four-and-a-half years ago was the only good thing Walter Devlin had ever done for her. She loved North Carolina more than any other place she'd ever lived. Mostly she was grateful for the lifelong friend she'd made in Dani Waterman.

She threw small rocks towards the water and was rewarded with an occasional fish breaking the surface. Kitty couldn't believe the sudden turn of events with Walter. What if he really was sent away to jail? Deep down she felt like laughing even though she knew the severity of his situation. She ignored the sting of guilt that negotiated with her conscience.

Fear clouded her eyes as the full weight of her responsibility settled within her. Was it possible Walter's arrest was the result of her prayers? After all, she was the one who'd caused the accident. Walter wasn't even driving, yet he might go to jail because of her. Kitty's head throbbed with blame. She never would've prayed for such a specific outcome to her dilemma had she known better. She had no idea prayer could be so powerful! Any future prayers would bear some thoughtful consideration from now on.

Needing absolution for her part in Walter's predicament pressed down on her like a heavy boulder. Even though it didn't come naturally to her, she knew with certainty she needed to pray again. Scanning the surrounding area first, she organized her thoughts before closing her eyes against the afternoon sun. She bowed her head.

"Oh God, what have I done? It's me, Kitty Murphy again. When I asked you for help last night, having Walter arrested wasn't exactly what I was expecting. I feel so guilty. I lied to the police and to my mom. Please forgive me for that. I really didn't think you'd answer my prayers quite so specifically and this quickly. What if Walter tells the police what really happened – that it was me that caused the accident. I'm so scared, Lord. I don't want to go to jail! Walter probably deserves what's going to happen to him, but I feel like such a horrible person. If you want to punish me for lying and for causing the accident, then I don't blame you. And I want to live up to my end of the original bargain. Next week when I go to Mass I'll ask Sister Carlotta how I go about doing that whole nun thing. I'm pretty new to this praying stuff, so you'll have to make it obvious to me what it is that you want from me. Thanks for listening to me, God. Amen."

Kitty opened her eyes and looked around. She felt ten pounds lighter. Purging the soul was very therapeutic. That must be one of the benefits of prayer, she thought. She breathed deeply inhaling a sense of calmness. Listening to the birds and drinking in the beauty of the river bathed her in peace. Kitty's musings were cut short at the sound of approaching footsteps.

Dani came around the corner humming a song Kitty recognized from a service she'd attended at Dani' s church a couple of weeks ago.

"Hey Gladys. Whatcha' doing?" Dani fished a packet of Bazooka Bubble Gum from her front shorts pocket before dropping down beside Kitty.

"Oh, Gertrude. I'm so glad to see you!" Kitty hugged Dani around the neck. Dani pushed her back so she could search Kitty's face.

"Have you been crying? What's wrong? Is everything okay?" Touched by Dani's insight and genuine concern, Kitty smiled.

"I'm fine – *now*. Everything's okay. I'm just glad to see you, that's all. It was kind of a rough day. I think everything's going to get better though."

Kitty filled Dani in on the details of Walter's accident and arrest, omitting her own involvement and what transpired prior to the accident. As expected, Dani was concerned and supportive. The two friends were content to sit watching the river, soaking up the quiet and sharing their worries until the sun started to slip low in the sky.

Kitty checked her watch and stood up brushing the dirt from the back of her shorts.

"I've got to get going, Gertrude. I'm sitting for Mr. and Mrs. Abbott tonight. It's their Sunday evening bridge night," Kitty said, righting her bicycle. "Hop on and I'll give you a lift home on my way. It's going to be getting dark soon."

Dani balanced awkwardly on the narrow seat as Kitty pushed off and rode standing up. The two giggled at the awkwardness of their jarring ride.

"Oh hey, I almost forgot the whole reason why I came out here looking for you, Gladys," Dani said. She had to hold on tight to Kitty's waist and lean in close to talk in her ear. "When I was at Sunday school today, I found out they accepted my application to be a camp counselor at church camp this summer. I'll be leaving next week and be gone for most of the summer."

Kitty deflated. She tried turning her head to talk to Dani, but found it nearly impossible. The pair nearly toppled when Kitty put her feet down suddenly twisting at the waist to talk to Dani. In her already fragile emotional state, Kitty's eyes began to sting.

"What do you mean *for most of the summer*? How long is that *exactly*?" Kitty asked.

"I leave a week from today and will be working straight through until the first week of August. The camp isn't just a camp for my church, but a whole bunch of different churches will be using the campgrounds. Once one group leaves, there's a day in between before another group comes. It's going to give me the opportunity to counsel a wide variety of groups and denominations. I'm so excited about it!" Mistaking Kitty's unexpected show of emotion, Dani tried to be uplifting. "But hey, don't worry. I'll be back in time for your birthday, Gladys. And I promise I'll be back in time for our weekend shopping trip to Raleigh for school clothes. I should earn lots of extra spending money for our shopping spree. We have to look especially cool for our senior year." Dani smiled, but it was lost on Kitty.

Kitty swallowed hard and then without warning covered her face with both hands and cried.

Dani climbed off the bike and hugged Kitty. "Hey what's all this, Gladys?"

Kitty continued to sob.

"Kitty ..." Dani rarely used her given name unless she was deadly serious about something. "Please tell me what's wrong." A worried frown creased Dani's brow.

Kitty hiccupped, wiping her runny nose with the back of her hand. She hugged Dani tight as if to let her go would mean losing her forever. She pulled back slightly to stare at Dani.

"I'm not crying about my birthday or the shopping trip, you dope. Its just ... do you have to go for the whole summer? I don't think I can stand it here by myself all summer. Especially with all the stuff going on at home with Walter and everything. You know how my mom is. Can you imagine how she'll be if Walter ends up going to jail? There'll be no living with her. Isn't there anyway you'd think about just going for part of the summer and then coming home to work? *Please*?" Kitty begged.

Dani's Cheshire cat grin started very subtly until it expanded beyond the boundaries of a normal smile. "Well ... I wasn't going to say anything to you until I knew for sure, but there may be a chance for you to go with me."

Kitty's face lit in surprise. "What do you mean?"

"One of the other counselors, Jessica something, may not be able to go after all because she got another job offer. She just graduated from high school and she's going to Duke in the fall. She was offered some sort of intern job or clerk thing. I really don't know the specifics." Dani's predisposition for rambling reared its ugly head, causing Kitty to groan inwardly.

Kitty grabbed Dani by both arms. "I don't care about the specifics, Gertrude. Just give me the facts, please," Kitty said.

"Oops, sorry." Dani waved her hand in dismissal, blew an enormous bubble unaware that Kitty was dying inside waiting for news that might change her whole summer. "Okay, anyway," Dani finally continued. "This girl should know by tomorrow if she's taking this other job. I told Pastor Skip I knew someone who could go in her place. I gave him your name. Even though you aren't quite seventeen, he said it would probably be all right since you're going to be a senior next year. So if he should happen to call you in the next few days, you have to say yes! I didn't know you'd be so upset about my leaving, or I would have told you my news right away. I'm sorry."

Kitty hugged her enthusiastically and squealed in delight. "Yes, yes! Tell me everything about the counselor job and the camp." Kitty fired questions at Dani in rapid succession. Dani filled in all the blanks for Kitty. She'd been attending the family owned camp since she was eight-years-old. Because she had such a long-standing history with the camp owners, they were eager to offer her a paid counseling job this year. The fact that Dani's boyfriend of two years, Peter Bauer, was going to be working there as well didn't hurt anything either.

Kitty turned serious. "What if my mom says I can't go? Or what if the other counselor ends up going after all so I can't? I think I'll just die if I have to stay home all summer."

"Well you know what I always say. If you want specific – you have to pray specific. Let's ask God to make it all work out, okay?" Dani was so convincing she could have sold snow cones to Eskimos. Kitty was a little jealous of Dani's self-assuredness.

Kitty looked around. "You want to pray right now? *Here*?"

Dani grinned. The wind picked up and blew her waist length brown hair in her face. She shoved it out of her way and playfully punched Kitty in the arm. "Sure you big dope. God doesn't care where you pray or how often. He's everywhere. It's easy. Don't worry about it. If you're nervous about praying, I'll do all the talking. I'm used to it."

Kitty breathed a sigh of relief. Kitty was thankful her friend was a "glass half-full" kind of girl. Dani did everything, including prayer with great gusto and enthusiasm. Dani wore her optimism and self-confidence like a pair of well-worn comfortable slippers. Kitty wondered if God ever told Dani "no" to any of her prayers. She could be pretty convincing.

The two held hands and bowed their heads close together. Dani started in with thanks and then proceeded to list every minute detail Kitty was stressing over. Dani's prayer was endless. She recalled everything the two had discussed and then some. No detail was too small or inconsequential. Ordinarily Kitty would become uncomfortable and start to fidget. Somehow she was strangely subdued and content to listen to Dani's long-winded plea. Dani's prayers were peaceful – reassuring.

With her eyes still closed, Kitty started to sense what it was that made Dani's prayers so different from her own desperate pleas. Dani didn't just talk *at* God. She talked *with* God. She believed God was real and he truly listened to her. Dani spoke from her heart, she didn't just give God a laundry list of things to do for her. More importantly, Dani had confidence that God loved her and cared about every detail of her life. Dani had a relationship with God.

Kitty felt a pulling on her heartstrings. A desire for unconditional love niggled at her insides, teasing her. She longed to know her Creator loved her. Heck, she'd be happy knowing *anyone* really loved her. As she stood with hands clasped with Dani, Kitty's logical reasoning and her heart of emotions began a slow methodical tug-of-war.

Dani quietly ended the prayer with a simple "Amen." She remained motionless, hands tightly joined to Kitty's. Neither girl moved, unaware of the silent battle raging within.

Lost in deep thought, Kitty squeezed Dani's hands periodically as her mind argued the logic of an unseen God loving her. *If* he was real, how could he possibly love her or care about her when her own parents didn't seem to care much about her? It didn't make any sense. It would be so nice to be loved by someone who didn't ignore her or forget her existence, like her father. To be loved by someone who didn't think she was too fat and needing to go on a low calorie diet, like her mother. Just to be loved without judgment for who she simply was. Her heart beat rapidly forcing her to take a couple of deep breaths. Somewhere in the back of her mind – deep in her heart, with the evening breeze bathing her face, she heard a quiet voice.

"Come to me, Katherine. The Lord is my shepherd, I shall not want. He maketh me to lie down in green pastures: he leadeth me beside still waters. He restoreth my soul."

Kitty was dumbfounded recognizing the words of the 23rd Psalm. The verses ricocheted around inside her head. It was the Psalm Shirley, the church lady, urged them to memorize before she'd agreed to let Kitty's family adopt Mercy all those years ago. Kitty couldn't believe she still remembered it so perfectly. A smile spread to Kitty's face as the words continued to pour out in her mind.

"Yea, though I walk through the valley of the shadow of death, I will fear no evil: for thou art with me; thy rod and thy staff, they comfort me. Thou preparest a table before me in the presence of mine enemies: Thou anointest my head with oil; my cup runneth over. Surely goodness and mercy shall follow me all the days of my life: and I will dwell in the house of the Lord forever."

Kitty knew instinctively that remembering that Psalm "all of a sudden" was no coincidence. God must have had something to do with that. It was at that particular moment that life, chance, coincidence and circumstances all aligned perfectly – pushing Kitty to the point of surrender. There was no clanging cymbals or great fanfare – only silent repentance … forgiveness … peace … and Kitty Murphy was quietly reborn.

Both girls opened their eyes and stared at each other. Dani seemed surprised to see tears in Kitty's eyes. Again Dani was the perfect friend for the simple fact she never pushed unless Kitty gave her permission. Dani gave her a reassuring smile and squeezed Kitty's hand one final time before giving her a hug. Kitty felt certain Dani sensed something was different about her. Kitty was reluctant to share anything just yet. She rested in the knowledge that not only would Dani patiently wait for her, but she'd be praying for her until the time was right to talk about today.

They climbed back on the bicycle laughing and giggling as they attempted their balancing act once more. As they headed for home, the girls were totally unaware that all of the angels in heaven celebrated and rejoiced over Kitty's silent conversion.

I tell you that in the same way there will be more rejoicing in heaven over one sinner who repents than over ninety-nine righteous persons who do not need to repent.

SIXTEEN

The screen images dissolved as the overhead lights slowly glowed to life. Grace's entire countenance changed watching the last few minutes of Kitty's spiritual transformation. She bounded to her feet like she'd been shot from a cannon. Kitty sat tongue-tied while Grace made quite a spectacle of herself.

"Bravo! Thank you, Lord. Simply magnificent. It really doesn't get any better than that!" Grace turned all around as if she was addressing unseen visitors watching from above. "No matter how many times I see a transformation, I still get all giddy and excited." Grace walked around the row of seats practically skipping around in circles. Grinning, she talked in hushed tones to herself. Kitty thought Grace was a nut.

Mercy picked her head up from Kitty's lap and followed Grace's movements with her eyes. After a few minutes the dog jumped from her comfortable resting place and wandered over to sit on the floor beside Grace. Whenever Grace moved to a new spot, Mercy followed. Kitty thought she was imagining things, but she swore Mercy's head was bobbing up and down in unison with Grace's. The whole thing was very surreal. Kitty sat drinking in the show Grace put on.

When Grace's euphoria was spent, she returned to her seat and sat down. Once again, she became the epitome of perfect angelic manners. Fanning herself with her hand, she cooled her flushed face. Grace clapped her hands three times in rapid succession and instantly a slight breeze wafted about them cooling Grace's warm flush. Kitty craned her neck in every direction but saw no thermostat or air conditioning vents. The air was blowing from somewhere, but Kitty was stymied trying to figure out from where.

Grace looked like she was covered in glitter. She was so sparkly, she shimmered. Kitty touched Grace's arm as if confirming her presence was real and not an apparition.

"Wow, Grace. Your skin is very warm. Are you okay?"

Grace turned to Kitty beaming with joy. Kitty raised her hand to shield her eyes from Grace's *glow.*

"Oh yes, Katherine. I'm fine. Quite wonderful, actually. Thank you for your concern."

"Can I ask what *that* was all about? Your behavior just now was a little ... *strange*, don't you think?"

Grace threw her head back and laughed. Her magical laughter tinkled melodiously making the sheer pleasure of listening a treat for the ears.

"Oh, Katherine, don't you remember the parable in the Gospel of Luke that refers to the lost sheep?" Kitty nodded her head yes, but remained silent. "That day back in May 1977 – you were that lost sheep. Your silent prayers for forgiveness and your inviting our dear Lord into your life was cause for celebration for all the angels in heaven – including me! And even though I'd already witnessed it all those years ago, it was so exciting to watch it play out all over again. Weren't you moved by watching your transformation just now?"

Kitty readjusted her seat and brushed Mercy's long golden hairs from the front of her workout pants.

"Well I have to admit, it was kind of a relief to see that I finally did something right. But after living it the first time and watching it happen all over again, I feel a little bit sad and somewhat guilty." Kitty tucked her hair behind her ears and watched and waited while Mercy came over to resume the vacated seat next to her. Kitty sat patiently as the dog searched for the perfect spot, before finally settling with her head nestled on Kitty's lap. Once Mercy found her spot, Kitty leaned over and kissed Mercy's wide snout.

Grace's radiant flush casually dissipated. Her color returned to normal. As Grace's glow faded, the cool breeze diminished, until it was barely more than a whisper.

"Guilty? Good grief! Whatever for *now*, Katherine?"

"At the time I asked God to come into my life, I knew I wasn't really doing it for the right reasons. I was scared because of the car accident I'd caused. I was responsible for Walter's concussion and his going to jail. I felt violated because Walter turned a simple ride home into another opportunity to feel me up. I hated Walter and couldn't understand why he was so twisted. I think I only turned to God as a cop-out." Kitty exhaled sharply. Out of nervousness she began absently chewing on her fingernails. A nasty habit her husband and children chided her for repeatedly, but one she was powerless to control.

Grace reached for Kitty's hand, pulling it from her mouth.

"We already talked about this. It's the trials and tribulations that propel most people towards God. You weren't unique in your conversion, Katherine. Most people need to come to that place of despair before they humble themselves and reach up and take God's hand. You shouldn't feel guilty about that. God has always known your heart. And whether you accepted Christ for the *right reason* or not – what matters is you said *yes* to God. He doesn't want anyone to perish. He doesn't care *how* you come to him – only that you come. The day you said yes to God, your name was recorded in the Lamb's Book of Life. There aren't any sidebars or postscripts noted in the Book of Life explaining extenuating conversion circumstances. Your name is recorded – period. Do you understand?"

"Yes, I think I really do understand, Grace. Thanks for clearing that up for me." Kitty visibly relaxed. "I feel ten pounds lighter all of a sudden – almost like a heavy burden has been lifted from my shoulders. Carrying around all that guilt for so many years, I'm surprised I managed to walk upright."

"Katherine, I wish I had the ability to turn back time for you to the day you accepted Christ. You were forgiven from all your sins that day. They were remembered no more. Just like that." Grace snapped her fingers in illustration. "It was your *choice* to carry the burden of guilt your whole life. You didn't need to wait to *feel* forgiven. You already were forgiven. It's a very simple concept – one that many Christians fail to recognize and accept. You lived your life based on feelings, stockpiling your guilt. You prayed for release, but never accepted it. So yes – just now when you said you felt ten pounds lighter – you probably really are. You've been liberated from your yoke of culpability. It's unfortunate it took you so many years to come to that realization. Think of how much you could have accomplished if you wouldn't have been carrying around such a heavy load all those years." Grace's words were tinged with sadness.

"I guess I never looked at it that way before. Being Sophia Murphy's daughter, I had a hard time letting go of all that stored up guilt. Guilt was ingrained in me from the day I drew my first breath I think. That's not something you can change overnight, Grace. I know I said I turned to God for all the wrong reasons, but eventually I had a genuine relationship with Christ. And I really did stop hating Walter a long time ago. My eventual confession to Dani about my home life helped with that. She helped me to understand the importance of forgiveness."

"So you told Dani your secrets while you were at camp that summer?"

"No way. I was having entirely too much fun to ruin my summer with serious stuff. I didn't confess everything to her until the following spring, right before our high school graduation. Walter was home and out of jail and as disgusting as ever. My mother was nagging me about losing weight and paying rent when I turned 18. I had so much pressure coming at me from every angle. I was going to church with Dani regularly and one night after an evening service I just completely lost it and told Dani the whole sordid mess – even about Walter's violence and killing Mercy."

"What was Dani's initial reaction?"

"She was outraged – begged me to tell my mother everything. Of course I couldn't do that and Dani never pushed. She has always been a great friend. She's shared my burdens, but never my secrets. Dani was always a better friend to me than I was to her."

"How so, Katherine?"

"She's always carried me spiritually – she knew more, prayed more, believed more. She's been my 'go to' girl whenever I've had a problem or needed a Scripture or an emotional pick-me-up. I'm sad to say I've shortchanged her as far as reciprocating our friendship. I've not always been available for her or been there to help her when she needed it. Sometimes I question why we've stayed so close. I can't believe she didn't dump me as a friend a long time ago."

"I think you're being too hard on yourself. You and Dani remained friends for 30 years. She must have found some redeeming qualities in you, don't you think?"

"Hmm. Maybe." Kitty bit her fingernail, snipping off a scraggly edge and spit it on the floor. As if suddenly remembering where she was and her social faux pas, she blushed all the way down to her expertly dyed roots. "Oops. Sorry, Grace." She dropped to her knees searching for the offensive scrap of fingernail.

"Get up, Katherine. You're being silly now." Grace offered her a hand up.

Once Kitty was seated, Grace reached over and forcibly stilled Kitty's hands, tucking them one in the other so Kitty wouldn't be tempted to chew on her nails again. Kitty's idle hands lasted about 10 seconds in her lap before she lifted one to her mouth to gnaw on another ragged end. Grace rolled her eyes at Kitty. Kitty shook her hands like she was trying to shake loose the annoying habit.

"Oooh! Stop it!" she said to herself. "Gosh, bad habits are so hard to break. Especially when they're used as a crutch for anxiety and nervous energy." She took temptation out of the way by shoving both hands one under each thigh to avoid doing any more damage to her already tortured fingers.

"Relax, Katherine. Why does talking about your perceived shortcomings make you so fidgety?"

"Being forced to re-examine all these areas of my life has been very eye-opening. When you start adding up all the places I fell short, I'm feeling a little overwhelmed. Now I can add mediocre friend to my ever-growing list of inadequacies. It's a little much to take in all at one time." Kitty pulled her legs up tucking them under her.

"Is that really how you've seen yourself all these years, just a mediocre friend?"

"Well I could probably count on one hand the number of real emergencies Dani's ever had where she needed me to drop everything and be there for her. The one time … the biggest crisis of her life and I dropped the ball. I let her down. I wasn't there for her in any way, shape or form."

"When was that, Katherine?"

"A few months after we'd graduated from high school. Dani and I both got married shortly after graduation. Her wedding was well planned and wonderfully romantic and happy. She married her high school sweetheart, Peter. My wedding shocked everyone and was totally impromptu. Anyway ... that's another story ... later." She waved her hand as if dismissing the topic.

"Dani and Peter wanted to travel the world and change lives. Peter was going to be a Youth Pastor and Dani was excited about their future. Peter's one weakness was fast motorcycles. He loved the speed and convinced Dani that they were completely safe. She confided to me that she loved the speed and excitement of riding behind Peter, hugging him close around the waist. Riding with Peter was the only rebellious thing Dani ever did to defy her parents. Dani was always so cautious and practical – still is." Kitty shifted her position finding it hard to sit for such long stretches without discomfort. Grace, on the other hand, seemed impervious to pain, rarely changing her position.

"One weekend Dani and Peter took a trip to the Outer Banks. On the way back they got into a terrible accident and poor Peter was killed instantly. Dani was in the hospital for weeks and needed several surgeries on her hip and leg. The doctors were sure she'd never walk again. More than a year of physical therapy and her parents' faith and support and thankfully, she recovered – physically. She still walks with a limp sometimes, but only when she's been on her feet too long." Kitty explained.

"Where were you when all of this happened to your friend?" Kitty wasn't sure if she heard an accusation in Grace's question or not. Kitty coughed to cover her discomfort.

"I was stuck thousands of miles away in Alaska. My husband, Jimmy had a job working on the Pipeline. I thought Alaska was a great idea since it was about as far away from my mom and Walter as I could possibly get. At the time, Alaska was a way to start over and be independent – *a great adventure*, Jimmy promised. Plus the job promised him thousands of dollars in income." Kitty checked

Grace's face for signs of judgment or boredom. Finding neither, she continued.

"Jimmy and I got married two days after my 18th birthday. Dani married about a month before I did. Dani and my family didn't know about my sudden marriage until it was over. I knew everyone would try to talk me out of it and I knew I'd buckle and not go through with it, so I kept it a secret until after the fact. Marrying Jimmy was my only option for leaving my mother's house. Because we left for Alaska within days of our marriage, I didn't see Dani for about six years. That was the worst part of my self-imposed exile.

"Jimmy had more emotional baggage than I did and the two of us together were a recipe for disaster. I hated him touching me and he hated that I had so many 'sexual hang-ups' as he called them. Most of all I hated being married. I simply traded one prison for another. I was looking for someone to take care of me for a change, and I ended up with a husband who was gone for months at a time. He also turned out to be a first class louse. He cheated on me pretty much from the get go and stole most of my savings."

"So what happened to keep you from helping Dani when she needed you most?" Grace asked.

"Their fatal accident happened about 10 months after they got married. Dani was about eight weeks pregnant at the time. She not only lost the love of her life and her soul mate, but their baby as well. I talked to her mom after the accident because Dani wasn't up for phone calls for quite sometime. Phone calls were the best I could do since I had no way of getting back to North Carolina to help her. I was literally stranded in Alaska. Jimmy kept all the money he earned in a separate account and sent a check to the landlord every month for my rent. I had to pay all my other expenses. I had a job making enough to get by on. We'd burned through all my savings just getting to Alaska, so I was flat broke. I was so miserable and alone; I had nothing to give to my best friend. By the time I actually did talk with her, I had little to offer. She went through a terrible depression and really needed me and I wasn't there for her. There are lots of things in my life I would do differently if I could, but abandoning Dani is probably my biggest regret of all."

"Obviously you mended your relationship with her."

"Of course. It was rocky at the start, but we recovered after a time. We went years without seeing one another because of our husbands and jobs and living at opposite ends of the country. But at least we talked on the phone regularly and thank goodness for the invention of email. Now ... I mean *before* my recent departure, we had regular weekly contact with each other. I love Dani more than I love my own sister. In fact, Dani and I were on the phone together when I ... well – when I *died*. Poor Dani! What a terrible thing to do to her!" Kitty shook her head. "Oh Grace, I must have hurt her terribly to die in the middle of our conversation! Is there some way for us to check on her and make sure she's okay?" Kitty asked hopefully.

Grace shook her head no, causing her silken auburn tresses to float about her shoulders.

"No, dear. I'm afraid that's simply not possible. And besides, Katherine, the purpose of this transition time is not to see how your passing affects your loved ones lives *after* you're gone. We're here for you to experience healing and restoration from what brought you here before your appointed time. Did I not make that clear to you?"

Kitty chewed her bottom lip in confusion.

"No, Grace, I don't think so! I don't know what I know anymore. I feel like we've been at this for days. There are so many memories flooding my brain and senses. So many things I'd worked hard to bury in my subconscious are floating to the surface. I'm totally confused by this entire process. I stupidly thought when you died your whole life would flash before your eyes in an instant. Once you draw your last breath you're supposed to either go and be with God right away or be cast into Hell. There is no mention of anything like what's been happening to me anywhere that I've read before. So what is all this, then?"

Grace inhaled slowly and held up her hand as if to interrupt her. Kitty, sensing the interruption, talked even faster preventing Grace from getting in a word.

Kitty waved her hand in dismissal. "I know what you're going to say! That whole time thing again. I got that much Grace. Time doesn't have the same meaning here. Blah, blah, blah! And speaking of time, what did you mean when you said that thing about me being here before my time? What's up with that? Why was it before my time?" Kitty turned in her seat gripping the armrest separating her and Grace with both hands.

"Well think about it, Katherine. You recently celebrated your 43rd birthday. You are a woman who exercises religiously. You're a healthy young woman with no apparent health problems with so much life ahead of you. Yet here you sit waiting for an audience with the Heavenly Creator. You don't really believe that your dying as a result of a treadmill accident was really the way God intended for you to go, do you? Did you even consider that the words of your own mouth are what brought you here so unexpectedly?" Grace pierced her with an unwavering stare.

Kitty hung her head momentarily trying to voice the growing anger building in her mind. "I'm here because I tripped on my shoe lace. I'm here because I was an idiot who had a sucker in her mouth while she was exercising. I'm here right now because I'm stupid, Grace! I probably deserved to die for being so irresponsible!" Kitty harrumphed in disgust.

"I have to agree with you that eating anything – especially a sucker, while on a fast moving treadmill was not the smartest thing you could have done. But don't you remember what you said right before you tripped and fell, Katherine?"

Kitty shrugged. "No, I don't remember, Grace. What did I say?"

"You said you were going to ..."

With a simple nod of Grace's head, Kitty heard her own confession booming loud and clear from somewhere overhead.

"I'm going to lose this last 10 pounds if it kills me!"

Stunned by her own words, Kitty was speechless. For good measure and with another casual nod, Grace let the message replay, not once, but three more times. Kitty closed her eyes. She covered her ears with both hands to block the incriminating words from seeping in and holding her accountable. The room grew suddenly quiet. Kitty sat absorbing her responsibility.

"So what happened," Kitty asked. "God finally got tired of my whining and complaining about losing weight? Is this whole experience supposed to be a sample of God's weird sense of humor or is God using me to set some sort of an example?"

Grace sat ramrod straight pursing her lips. "I'm sure you've heard the Scriptures about the tongue and the damage it can do? It's a flame of fire and can alter the course of your life. How many times have you heard the words, 'be careful what you wish for' or 'be careful what you say'?"

"I know; I used to say that all the time to my kids. Now look at me. I think on some level I was always worried I was walking a pretty fine line with my thoughts and my mouth."

"How so?"

"There's a verse in the book of Job that was always nestled deep in my brain. The one Job says about 'the thing he feared the most had come upon him.' I mean, there I was living what others considered to be the perfect life, yet I was always complaining to God about my weight and my looks – never satisfied. It was almost like I was waiting for the proverbial bolt of lightning from God taking everything away from me because I was so unhappy. I really won't be surprised if God doesn't let me in to Heaven. I'd give anything for a do-over right about now."

Grace's brow furrowed in puzzlement. "A do-over? What is that?"

Kitty laughed sarcastically. "You know — I messed up and would like to step into my time machine and do the whole thing over again. I could really use some serious do-overs in my life, Grace."

Grace tucked her hand under her chin in thoughtful repose. "Hmm ... a do-over, you say? I'm curious – besides changing how you handled things during Dani's accident, what else would you *do-over*," she asked with faint emphasis.

"Probably almost everything, Grace. I know I can't go back all the way to infancy, but in retrospect, I think I would have fought harder to stay with my dad versus my mother. And I definitely would never have married Jimmy ... maybe not even Luke, for that matter. And Luke ..." Kitty's thoughts trailed off.

Grace prodded, waiting for Kitty to finish her statement. "And Luke what? Are you saying you wouldn't have married Luke if you had it to do over again?"

"I don't know, Grace," Kitty shook her head. "Sometimes I wonder."

"But what about your children? If there were no Luke, there would be no children. What about the three of them?" Grace asked.

"Oh, Grace. I seriously don't know. I'm just thinking out loud. Don't get me wrong – I love them all. I have – or rather, I *had* a terrific family. Sometimes though, I felt so lost within them. I existed solely for them and apart from them I lost sight of who I really was. Sometimes I felt as though my only purpose in life was to be someone's mother or somebody's wife. Somewhere along the way, I lost track of *me*. Do you understand?" Kitty's eyes filled with uncertainty.

Grace's smile held only compassion. "Yes, I think I do. It does make me sad to hear you question your role as Luke's wife, though. That was one of my better arrangements, if I do say so myself."

"*What*?" Kitty blustered. "What do you mean, Grace?"

"Oh nothing much. *Chance* encounters ... timing, all of that. And then there was that whole disastrous first marriage thing of yours. Had to wait until that was caput, now didn't we? Whew, what a mess that was. Quite a struggle for you, to be sure."

"How could you know what I was struggling with, Grace? I was in Alaska when my first marriage fell apart and I met Luke. What did you have to do with any of that?"

"Perhaps we should take a look, hmm? Are you interested? It won't exactly be a do-over, but maybe a *look-see* will be enough for you to settle your misgivings. Then we can decide if you and Luke were really as unsuited as you seem to believe."

"I imagine that trip down Memory Lane can't be any worse than everything else you've forced me to watch so far. Maybe if I'm reminded of my beginnings with Luke, I'll have a greater appreciation for what I truly had."

"My thoughts exactly!"

Grace snapped her fingers plunging the room into a bottomless black hole.

SEVENTEEN

The noticeable change in the room was instantaneous. The temperature dropped by a good 20 degrees in their climate-controlled theater room. Goosebumps erupted on Kitty's arms causing her to rub them for much needed circulation. Inhaling sharply, she detected the smell of fish and thick mud wafting in with the bite of a salty sea breeze. Recognizing the date that appeared on the screen, Kitty closed her eyes breathing deeply the smell of the Cook Inlet mud flats at low tide.

The crisp August air and the scents of an approaching early autumn settled about her, transporting her back in time more than two decades. The cry of gulls assailed her ears, while the fleeting sun poked its head around heavy clouds, barely warming the sudden chill settling around her. Recollections flooded her senses. Long buried emotions began a slow resurrection. Every thought, every feeling and every minute memory of that historic date came hurtling back at her like a haphazard boomerang.

* * * * *

August 31, 1979

Nineteen-year-old Kitty Murphy, exited through the huge glass doors of the courthouse in downtown Anchorage, a newly signed Divorce Decree safely stowed in her shoulder bag. Once outside, the pungent air filled her lungs. She exhaled the tension of the past few hours slowly through her nose, grateful to be free from the stifling confines of the small courtroom. Pulling her jacket tight against the rising chill, she forced movement to her shaky legs. It was done, at last.

When she filed for her no-fault dissolution six months ago, she thought this day would never arrive. Patience was definitely not one of her virtues. In the last months she'd wasted more energy worrying about what people would think of her for giving up on her marriage after so short a time than the actual divorce itself. Somewhere along the way though, she stopped caring what anyone thought. She just wanted this whole fiasco behind her.

No one could possibly know what she'd endured being married to Jimmy Maxwell. Lord willing, no one ever would. Adopting her mother's philosophy on life, she decided denial was the best course to pursue. Pretend the last year never happened. At least with her name restored to Murphy, the charade would be easier. Masquerading as Mrs. Jimmy Maxwell the last year in her sham of a marriage lent an air of hypocrisy to her otherwise well-ordered life. Pasting on her "life is perfect" face everyday to face the people at work had only served to make her a master at subterfuge. She'd become an imposter in her own life. Well – no more. Today was the first day of her new life. No more subterfuge. It was time to come up with a new plan!

She walked without purpose, pausing to browse window displays secretly hoping a miraculous sign would appear pointing her in the direction of this new, yet non-existent plan. Stopping long enough to rifle through her handbag in search of her wallet, she searched all the hidden compartments for forgotten money. She counted her meager funds, the sum total of which amounted to all of $8.64. She sighed in exasperation. Well, it's not going to be much of a new plan with less than $10.00, she mused.

She debated whether a celebratory lunch, although much needed and desired, would be the most frugal course of action. Grateful now that she had enough foresight to park several blocks away when she arrived three hours earlier, at least now the remainder of her cash wouldn't have to cover parking fees. Along with her divorce decree, she now boasted sole ownership of the battered station wagon parked blocks away. Or as Jimmy had called it, "their honeymoon hotel love machine." The car was a piece of junk. It was a wonder the beat up old death trap had ever survived their trek from North Carolina to Alaska. It was even more of a mystery how the paper-thin tires would survive the first snowfall this season. The tires were so bald at this point, Kitty swore if she ran over a piece of gum, she'd be able to tell you what flavor it was. Clearly her "new plan" better present itself before winter arrived.

She shivered as a breeze blew her hair into her face. Good Lord, would her body ever acclimate to this constant cold? She'd best get used to it she thought. Alaska may very well be her home for a while. Chilled by the bite of the late August air, she relished the long stroll to the car. The fresh air stirred the melting pot of emotions in her brain, swirling them about adding additional chaos to her already cluttered mind. She gave her thoughts over to their own casual meandering. They seemed hard pressed to open all the doors lining memory lane.

Crossing the street, she found a vacant bench beckoning her to stop. Come and sit, it seemed to say. Open all the doors of your hidden closets – air your disappointments so they can be banished to the darkness once and for all. Granting permission to her damaged self-worth to sit and wallow in failure took little effort, since she'd be languishing in the deep end of the self-pity pool for some time now.

Marriage was nothing like she'd ever envisioned. Granted, there had been some initial excitement when she and Jimmy arrived in Anchorage last year. The best thing about Alaska was the geographical blessing of being thousands of miles away from her family. Moving so far from home made her feel like a real grown up, although at the time, she was barely more than 18. What a difference a year made. It felt as though she'd aged a decade since then rather than only a single year. Maybe the time attached to her life was accelerating like dog years, she thought sarcastically.

She and Jimmy had rented a tiny semi-furnished one bedroom apartment and "played house" for little more than a week after they'd arrived last year. The ink was barely dry on their rental agreement when Jimmy left to start his new job on the Alaskan pipeline in

Prudhoe Bay, far to the north. Even if joining Jimmy had been an option, Kitty would have declined due to the extreme temperatures and harsh conditions in the Arctic Circle. While the oil company provided every amenity imaginable to occupy employees in their down time, the lack of "normal" daylight and sub-zero cold was enough of a deterrent to keep Kitty in Anchorage by herself. Jimmy assured her his six-week work rotation would pass quickly. At the end of the rotation they'd have a whole week together before he had to head back north. The company paid him an exorbitant salary, furnished his transportation to and from Anchorage and provided great medical benefits. Not that two young adults ever worried about such things, but it was one more argument Jimmy provided her for why the job was so perfect.

"It's a win-win situation, Babe!" Jimmy promised her.

Kitty leaned her head back on the bench and let the wan sun kiss her wind-blown cheeks as she recalled those early days. Closing her eyes, she invited the unwelcome memories of the past year to come in and dance around – one more time. Just one more waltz, she told herself, and then I'll close the door and put them to rest – finally and forever.

* * * * *

"Come on, Babe. You're going to be fine. The next six weeks are gonna fly by. You'll see."

Athletic and boyishly handsome, Jimmy Maxwell, ran his callused hand through his thick shoulder-length, sandy blonde hair. He gave her a quick hug, a pat on the back and reached down grabbing his over-sized duffel bag. He shifted nervously from foot to foot, anxious to be on his way to begin his new adventure.

Kitty noticed him scanning the terminal before he gave her a cursory peck on the lips. Heaven forbid he should be caught giving into a public display of affection. She silently fumed. She knew it wasn't that he disliked showing affection so much as it was the fear of some "hot girl" catching him in a lip-lock with her, branding him as "unavailable." She wasn't stupid; she knew her husband had a wandering eye. Thank goodness, his new male-dominated job would put an end to that wandering.

Watching Jimmy disappear through the tunnel walkway, a feeling of abandonment made her gag with sudden fear. Treading just beneath the surface of the rising panic however, was a simmering relief. Two days later, relief boiled over to a full-blown liberation that drowned out the fear altogether. For the first time in her life, Kitty Murphy Maxwell was accountable to no one and finally free and independent. Everyone told her the first year of marriage would ultimately be the hardest. But since her husband would be gone for long stretches at a time – how hard could it be? Pushing past her initial fear of abandonment, Kitty spent her first full week of solitude exploring her new city.

Anchorage was different from any place she'd ever lived. It was almost as if the geographical separation from the lower 48 states gave Alaskans a detachment from the rest of the country and reality. Alaskans embraced the division. Kitty quickly learned when a local referred to a trip they'd taken "outside," it meant they left Alaska to travel somewhere in the lower 48 states. To most Alaskans, going "outside" was a necessary evil.

Anchorage was a beautiful city surrounded on three sides by majestic mountains, whose peaks were topped by late summer with a dusting of snow called termination dust. It signaled the end of the "warmer" summer months. The early snow was an indicator heralding the coming winter. If one had intentions of relocating "outside," they'd best be on their way, as winter wasn't far behind the termination dust.

Kitty loved the isolation Anchorage offered. Kitty's landlady, Mrs. O'Hara, a tiny Irish widow, was a host of information when it came to Alaskan history and trivia.

"Oh to be sure, you could drive for hours on end – sometimes days, and still be in the middle of nowhere," the elderly woman told Kitty the first week in her new apartment.

The woman probably had crested just over five feet tall in her younger years, but Osteoporosis had robbed her of several inches due to the hunchback piggybacking on her shoulders. Her springy orange curls seemed dull and lifeless compared to the sparkle in her bright blue eyes. "Of course, most of your driving has to be in the summer months, darling, because once the winter weather sets in driving anywhere is too bloody scary." She crossed herself and fingered her rosary beads that never seemed far from her twisted hands.

Mrs. O'Hara went on to explain about the non-existent freeways and two-lane highways ravaged from repeated years of frost heaves and over-sized potholes.

"But pretty near everybody has themselves some sort of small plane up here, to be sure," she explained. "Mr. O'Hara and I had one with floats on it – God rest his soul." She crossed herself again at the mention of her deceased husband. "And then you will most likely want to get yourself a good four-wheel drive truck or such, lass. I got an old Jeep out back, but the bloody thing don't run no more."

The old woman would talk forever if Kitty let her. She seemed particularly animated relating stories of cabin fever and the high rate of alcoholism due to the long winter days. Kitty suspected the old woman might have her own problem with demon whiskey, and opted to ignore the tales the old woman spun. Kitty was certain she couldn't spend the rest of her life in Alaska, but for the time being, it was home so she vowed to make the best of it and to heck with cabin fever.

After familiarizing herself with the city, Kitty managed to secure a job as a receptionist in a small accounting firm her second week in Anchorage. Her salary was twice what her waitress salary back home was, but still a mere fraction of Jimmy's earnings. She opened a savings account in her name and after paying her few bills, religiously deposited whatever was left over. True to his promise, Jimmy sent her nearly his entire first paycheck, which enabled her to pay her rent several months in advance. Her paycheck would have to cover everything else.

Life settled into a comfortable routine. She adopted a stray kitten for companionship, which she instantly dubbed as Jonah. Like his namesake from the Bible, her tiny tabby had been abandoned as well. Her Jonah, however, wasn't lost in the belly of a big fish, but in the bowels of an over-crowded animal rescue shelter. Jonah was only hours away from being destroyed when Kitty stumbled upon the shelter after making a wrong turn. Grateful for whatever coincidence had led her to the shelter, she and Jonah became fast friends. Jonah was the only other pet she'd ever owned besides her dog, Mercy. Jonah exercised his independence, for which Kitty was grateful. She and the kitten both required certain amounts of personal space, but both enjoyed the occasional snuggling under the down comforter on chilly nights.

The local library near her office became Kitty's home-away-from-home. Initially it was her love of mystery novels that claimed most of her free time. But with little or no social life and limited funds, she capitalized on the wealth of knowledge available to her. Since attending community college wasn't in her budget, she schooled herself in areas of interest including both Theology and Psychology. Her insatiable hunger to learn could not be fully satis-fied. The more she studied, the more she craved. Her large book bag went with her everywhere. The girls at work labeled her as both a bookworm and a Bible thumper and kept a conservative distance from her.

One month after she'd hired on at the accounting firm, a small fire forced the evacuation of her building, requiring Kitty to sprint down ten flights of stairs. After barely surviving the descent, she vowed to do something about her eating habits and excess weight. In a matter of weeks she discovered that by limiting her food portions and adding a few healthy options to her diet, she managed to lose 10 pounds.

Motivated by the weight loss and a desire for change, she joined a small gym next to the corner grocery store. She devoured all the books at the library on exercise physiology and nutrition. She not only pumped iron on a daily basis, but she pumped the employees at the gym for tips and information regarding exercise technique and form. Within three months, she shed 25 pounds from her frame. She had only a few more pounds to go to reach her goal weight of 125 pounds. She became a full-fledged exercise junkie and thought of little else except losing those last few pounds. She was in such good shape and knew as much as the instructors at the gym that she was offered a full-time job as an Aerobics Instructor. It was the perfect job for her. She embraced her role as a fitness guru and spent long hours at the gym.

The extended hours at work filled the void of her otherwise empty life. Jimmy's first six-week rotation soon turned into a 12-week rotation. Married four months and already the newlyweds had been apart for three of those months.

"Babe, I can't pass up the overtime," he told her over the phone, at the end of his first six weeks. "But I swear, I'll make it up to you as soon as I get back. I should be home for Christmas and we'll do something special."

"But what about Thanksgiving, Jimmy? Will you be home for that?" She could hear the whine in her voice and hated herself for it. It wasn't so much that she missed Jimmy, as it was that she was simply lonely for companionship.

"Listen, I gotta go, Babe. I'll call you next week and we'll talk about it then. Take care. Talk to you soon."

Standing in the living room of her small apartment, her feeling of abandonment resurfaced. The fact that neither one of them had said, "I love you," niggled at her conscience raising a red flag she chose to ignore.

Well, that's six extra weeks to continue my transformation, she thought. She knew she was looking her best ever. Compliments from co-workers and clients flowed freely, but Kitty had a hard time believing them. No matter how good she looked on the outside, she couldn't find the inner peace she craved. Exorcising her low self-esteem demons proved to be a far harder task than exercising her physical body. She was anxious for Jimmy to come home and put her fears to rest.

"Wow, you look great, Babe!" He told her meeting her at the terminal gate six weeks later. "But hey, I haven't seen many women in the last three months, so any girl would look pretty good to me," he joked.

Kitty felt her ego deflate.

He kissed her soundly and stepped back to give her a total once over.

She pirouetted self-consciously for his perusal. Jimmy let out a low wolf whistle and licked his lips suggestively.

"Um mmm, you sure look good." He pulled her close and pressed himself against her. "You still got a little meat left here on your backside though, but that's okay, a guy needs a little cushion." He chuckled, smacking her backside. He set her away from him and finger poked her saddlebag thighs, which were minimal in comparison to what they once had been. "You know Babe, with just a little extra hard work, I'll bet you could trim away some of this excess fat hanging below your butt here. What do you do all day at work, anyway? Can't they teach you how to get rid of this stuff?" He continued to poke her thighs like they were made of modeling clay until she stepped away from him.

Kitty bit down on her bottom lip to keep from crying. She refused to let him see how much his words hurt her. Jimmy was totally oblivious to how deeply his words cut her.

"But hey, don't get me wrong. You still look pretty darn good to me. I can't wait to get you home!"

Kitty couldn't wait for him to leave again.

Jimmy's week home flew by. He headed back up north for another six-week rotation. Rather than the abandonment she felt the first time he left, she only felt immense relief when he was gone. With his harsh criticism ringing in her head, she volunteered to lead extra aerobics classes and beefed up her personal workout schedule. Maybe by the time Jimmy came home again her excess fat wouldn't disgust him so much.

Returning home six weeks later, Jimmy barely acknowledged her physical appearance and was more subdued than the last time he'd been home. Long hours of strenuous, physically exhausting work had added 20 pounds of pure muscle to his lanky frame. He'd grown a beard and mustache to protect his face against the Arctic air, which lent an air of danger to his normally good looks. His physical changes weren't the only ones Kitty noticed about her husband. Much to her chagrin, she discovered her 22-year-old husband brought home a brand new drinking problem.

The drinking wasn't the only discovery Kitty uncovered. Her husband had apparently developed a severe gambling addiction as well. Poker was his game of choice and wagering most of his paychecks was the pound of flesh extracted for payment of his debts.

He arrived home with pockets full of I.O.U.'s and a vicious mean streak that gave Kitty cause for concern. To add insult to injury, the last straw came for Kitty one week after Jimmy returned to his job up north.

During his week home he casually mentioned the arrival of a dozen or so secretaries hired by the oil company. Kitty didn't give the comment much thought until she began experiencing some rather unpleasant symptoms in the lower nether regions of her body. Laying exposed and vulnerable, legs uncomfortably positioned in metal stirrups, she received a shocking diagnosis from a county health physician.

"It's the clap, Mrs. Maxwell. Gonorrhea, if you need a more technical term. It may be none of my business, but as a health care professional, I'm encouraged to remind you that the use of condoms is highly recommended, especially if you intend to be indiscriminate with your selection of sexual partners." The doctor removed her gloves with a snap and a judgmental look down the bridge of her nose. She excused herself, leaving Kitty alone in the examining room to absorb the shock and criticism.

A nurse returned with a loaded hypodermic needle filled with a powerful antibiotic, which she jabbed in Kitty's derriere. Her assessment of the situation was far less critical as she handed Kitty a box of condoms.

"A girl can't be too careful, you know?" the nurse offered in sympathy.

Stinging from the injection as well as embarrassment, Kitty headed straight to the courthouse to inquire about divorce papers. Shame coursed through her at her own naiveté and blind trust mistakenly placed in her unfaithful husband. Her marriage was quickly educating her in the School of Hard Knocks. This painful lesson would be filed away in her backpack of grievances she carried around unwittingly.

Kitty met Jimmy at the airport a few weeks later, confronting him with accusations and ultimatums.

"So, who's the little tramp you've been sleeping with lately, Jimmy?" She spat, before he'd barely had time to clear the tunnel walkway.

Dropping his gear, he took one look at her angry face, placed both hands on his hips and threw back his head in laughter.

"Good to see you too," he answered with a cocky smirk.

"Well?" Kitty shifted back and forth nervously, eyes ablaze with mounting fury.

"Relax," he ordered, although his own face was anything but. "Lower your voice," he commanded through clenched teeth as he leaned over to retrieve his bag. He grabbed Kitty roughly, dragging her away from the gate and inquisitive onlookers.

She shook free from his iron grip, planting her feet firmly. "Don't touch me!" she yelled. "I want to know who you've been sleeping around with."

Vehemently denying her accusations, he laughed walking away from her. Kitty followed at close range, hurtling threats as his retreating backside, oblivious to the snickers and stares from the throngs of airport patrons. Sensing his wife was close to hysterics, he stopped so abruptly Kitty nearly toppled backwards from running into him. He spun around quickly, his amber eyes glittering with disdain.

"You're crazy and neurotic!" he yelled. His jaw continued to clench. He moved as if to strike her and Kitty recoiled instinctively. Drawing glares from passersby, Jimmy lowered his voice and his hand. He backpedaled his anger in a mere fraction of an instant. He leaned towards her kissing her noisily. He chuckled an evil snicker, a disturbing sound devoid of mirth and grabbed her arm. "Come on, Babe. Let's get outta here."

Kitty jerked away from him and sprinted down the stairs past baggage claim and through the automatic double doors leading outside. She never looked back. Jimmy stood alone shaking his head, the sound of a muffled announcement barely distinguishable over the garbled loud speaker.

"Women! Who needs 'em," he snorted. Searching his pocket for a cigarette, he winked at a voluptuous blonde in tightly clad jeans and headed for the nearest taxi stand. He spent his week home at a local hotel alternating between begging Kitty to reconsider the divorce she'd filed for and berating her for her jealousy and mistrust of him.

Kitty was adamant in her refusal for reconciliation. Jimmy returned to his job on the pipeline. His final act as her lawful husband was to gain access to her bank account, completely emptying it of her hard-earned nest egg. Prior to boarding his plane for Prudhoe Bay, he took the courtesy of dropping her a good-bye note in the mail. It read:

Kitty,

Sorry how things ended, Babe. I never could have made it to Alaska without your money to get me here. Thanks for the little going away present you left me in your bank account. You've been a busy little bee while I've been gone! That should help pay off a few of my I.O.U.'s. If you weren't so dull between the sheets maybe I'd think about keeping you around a bit longer. But hey, life's too short to sleep with boring, ugly cows! Stupid women like you are a dime a dozen. There's always another sucker out there to be had. Take it easy, Babe!

Your loving husband,
Jimmy

EIGHTEEN

A loud barking dog interrupted Kitty's reverie. Jimmy's hurtful words and his rejection still stung months later. She needed to figure out a way to move past this divorce and get on with her life. It would be so easy to use this situation as an excuse to build the wall higher around her already damaged heart, but somehow she knew instinctively that it wouldn't solve anything. Besides, she'd already built that wall about as high is it could go. If it got any higher, she'd need a stepladder just to see daylight.

Kitty stood and forced movement to her legs as she glanced around getting her bearings. "Men!" The single word rushed out. "They're all pigs. Are there any good ones out there, God? How can I ever trust one again?"

The temptation to wallow in self-pity seemed to bubble just beneath the surface. Words of Scripture rattled around in her brain until it caught hold. *Cast all your cares on him ...*

Breathing deeply, she inhaled and exhaled a few deep belly breaths before she moved on. "Out with the old – in with the new," she breathed once more for good measure. "Here I go, Lord – I'm casting all my cares. In. Out." She drew air deep into her lungs several times until she felt a little light-headed.

The simmering anger she'd been feeding on the last six months slowly dislodged itself from her insides. The void filled with a leisurely unfamiliar peace. An easy smile lit her face.

"Hmm, okay. That's better. Maybe this is what maturity tastes like," she whispered to the wind.

Looking up at the Chugach Mountains to the east, her brow crinkled in concern. The overnight appearance of powdered snow on the peaks wasn't a good sign. After Jimmy had cleaned out her bank account, she'd switched banks and been barely scraping by the last few months. She'd only managed to save a few hundred dollars, far less than was necessary if she were to leave Alaska any time soon. The thought of staying another winter in Alaska turned her thoughts darker. Spotting her car, her legs dragged her towards it as if she were on autopilot. Leaning against the hood of her rundown wagon, she bit her lip pondering her dismal future.

She glanced around the neighborhood she'd parked in noting the cute compact houses and the neatly manicured lawns. The street was quiet with little or no traffic and only a few pedestrians. Dog walkers and moms with strollers all gravitated towards the park running the length of the street. Taking advantage of the calm setting and the fleeting sun on her face, Kitty closed her eyes and prayed quietly in her spirit.

Well, God, it would seem as though I've gotten myself into another fine mess. I know you hate divorce, but in light of the fact that my husband was cheating on me, I was kind of hoping you wouldn't hold mine against me. From this day forward, Lord, I'm not doing anything without your okay. I'm getting kind of tired of trying to do things my way. Obviously, my way doesn't seem to be the right way. I don't have very much money so I can't leave Alaska, although where I'd go, I couldn't say anyway. If you could send me a sign – a really clear sign, that'd be great. I can be pretty thickheaded sometimes, so if you could make it a sign that even I could understand ... well, I'd appreciate it. In your name I ask these things – Amen.

Opening her eyes, she was surprised to feel the tears on her cheek. Tears of failure? Perhaps. Most likely these were stress-induced tears regarding her bleak finances and uncertain future.

"But, I will not worry about things," she told herself walking around to the driver's side of her car. "It's not my job to worry about it anymore. It's God's job. I'm casting my cares, God," she reiterated.

Fumbling with her cumbersome shoulder bag, she fished her keys from the bottom of the bag amidst a hodgepodge of junk. Kitty juggled her large purse and transferred her over-size key ring with the attached mace cylinder to her other hand. She wrestled to pull the edges of her coat closed against a sudden gust of wind. Failing miserably at all tasks, she ended up dropping her keys in the street next to the car. As she bent over to retrieve them, she noticed a woman with glorious red hair and arms laden with packages step off the curb directly into the path of an oncoming pickup.

The driver of the pickup had no chance to react. With split second timing he swerved to avoid hitting the woman. He over corrected and started to lose control of the vehicle. Fear seized Kitty as she processed the situation in the span of a mere heartbeat. The driver had two choices; swerve right and plow into a woman with a baby carriage or swerve left and smash into Kitty's parked car. Almost too late, Kitty realized the driver opted for her direction as the out of control truck veered towards her. With strength she didn't know she possessed and a spring in her legs equaled to that of an Olympic hurdler, Kitty launched herself away from the oncoming vehicle. She landed with a hard jolt in the middle of the street. The screams of startled pedestrians could be heard over the sound of screeching brakes and crunching metal. The battered station wagon that she'd only legally owned for the last hour, absorbed the force of the collision.

Kitty lay immobilized in the middle of the street assessing her injuries. The first thing she noticed or rather felt, was a searing knife-like pain to the front of her skull. She half pushed herself up and rolled into a sitting position. Her arms and legs appeared to all work. Thank goodness, she thought. She tasted blood and ran her tongue around the inside of her mouth relieved that all her teeth remained intact. Reaching up, she tested the throbbing hot spot in the middle of her forehead and was surprised when she pulled her hand away to see blood staining her fingers. Never one who was comfortable with blood, especially her own, she rolled backwards resting on the pavement until she could calm her racing heart and the shaking of her limbs.

Within seconds a small band of onlookers hovered over her offering help and assistance.

Suggestions and comments were bandied about like shuttlecocks in a badminton game.

"Keep her still," someone said.

"Is she breathing," asked another.

"Don't move her neck," was spoken more like a harsh command from somewhere in the cluster.

Suddenly the crowd parted as a tall figure loomed overhead.

"Get back folks." The slightly accented voice was unmistakably male and instantly dominated control of the situation.

"Give her some air."

The commanding voice brooked no arguments as the onlookers all took one giant step backwards in unison like players in a *Mother May I* game. The stranger knelt down, barking orders as he did so.

"Someone find a phone and call for an ambulance. There's a blanket behind the seat of my pickup. Could someone go and get it please before she goes into shock."

Strangers scattered at his command. From her vantage point, Kitty couldn't quite make out his face. The sun was directly in her eyes forcing her to bring her hand up to shield them. She'd all but forgotten her bloodstained fingers, but when she caught sight of her crimson digits she turned as white as the newly fallen powder on the Chugach Foothills and passed out.

* * * * *

Bounding from her chair as if her seat were electrically charged, Kitty leapt to her full height.

"Whoa! Wait a minute, Grace! Stop the movie! Oh my gosh! Was that *you* stepping off the curb in front of the truck?"

Mercy jumped from her seat to stand next to Kitty. Kitty ran down to within inches of the silver screen and stared at the images frozen in place. Unable to clearly identify anything at such close range, given the enormity of the screen, she circled back behind Grace's seat. She studied the stilled figures. She moved to another side of the room to view the screen from a different angle.

At the top of the screen walking away from the scene of the accident, an auburn-haired woman turned for one parting glance over her shoulder. Her emerald green eyes appeared fixed on Kitty's prostrate form sprawled in the street. Kitty gestured wildly with both hands. She pointed first at the red-haired woman suspended on the screen then to Grace who was forced to crane her neck to see Kitty standing behind her.

"Aha! It is you, isn't it, Grace? That's what you meant when you said you arranged my meeting Luke?"

Grace pursed her lips, the picture of innocence. She examined her fingernails and fluffed her hair pretending to ignore Kitty, although Kitty suspected Grace was stalling.

"Well," Kitty pressed.

Grace meekly raised her right hand. "Ahem ... guilty," she said.

Kitty skipped around the seats and moved in close to sit beside Grace. A grin stretched Kitty's face from ear to ear.

"So ... you were like, what? Destiny? Fate?"

Grace waved a hand in dismissal. "Pish Posh. Call it what you will. You and Luke O'Connell were meant to be together. I merely gave destiny and fate a little push in the right direction."

"Wow, that's quite a revelation. If I tell you something can you promise to hold your judgment, Grace?"

"Certainly."

"I know this is going to make me sound really vain and horribly self-absorbed ... but watching that whole *accidental*," Kitty used air quotes to stress her emphasis, "meeting between Luke and I, all I could focus on was how I looked. I mean – hel-*lo!* I was really hot looking." She clarified her modern day vernacular for Grace.

"I was in the best shape of my life, but I was still so unhappy with myself just because of the stupid things my ex-husband had told me. What was wrong with me? I'd give anything to have that body back! Good Lord, it's a wonder God didn't strike me dead years ago because I was so self-involved. Why couldn't I just be happy with the status quo?"

"Pity that, isn't it dear?"

"So, Grace – back to this other thing."

Grace supplied her with a quizzical look. "What other thing, Katherine?"

Sinking back in the plush leather seat, Kitty relaxed and threw her head back in laughter.

"Try and keep up, Grace. I'm talking about me and Luke."

Kitty's change of topics was sudden, like a train suddenly rerouted on a switched track.

"You certainly went to a lot of trouble to arrange our meeting, Grace. What would have happened if Luke ran me over? What if I didn't have those lightning fast reflexes? It seems like there were a lot of chancy variables that could have created a different outcome altogether. Pretty risky, Grace, wouldn't you say?"

Grace smiled with confidence. "You forget who I work for, Katherine. Who do you think gave you those lightning fast reflexes? Factor in your prayer for a sign and the prayer Luke had prayed prior to the accident and you've got the perfect recipe for a *chance encounter*." Grace copied Kitty's earlier air quotes.

"That's right, I'd nearly forgotten Luke was praying at the same moment I was? He confessed that to me later after we'd known each other a while."

"Fate may have provided the opportunity, but you and Luke did the rest. After all was said and done you could simply have walked away that day. You didn't have to accept his lunch invitation."

Kitty flushed with embarrassment. "Yes, Grace. But I only accepted his invitation because Luke seemed more shook up than me. Plus I was starving and didn't have much money. Remember?"

"Is that the only reason you went out with him? For a woman only divorced for an hour, you certainly jumped at the invitation." Grace smiled that all-knowing grin of hers.

"Well maybe it was the bump on my head. I probably wasn't thinking clearly." Kitty threw her hands up in surrender.

"Hmm. Perhaps. Let's finish watching, shall we?" Grace winked and turned to face the screen as the action resumed.

* * * * *

Kitty thanked the paramedic as he finished bandaging her head. On his orders, she remained seated on the curb so she wouldn't run the risk of fainting again.

"You really should let us take you to the hospital, Miss. It's for your own safety. You don't appear to have a concussion, but an x-ray could rule out any serious injuries," the young man said, packing his supplies away robotically as if he'd performed the task hundreds of times. He stopped to check her pulse one last time.

Kitty didn't dare confess to him that she had no insurance to cover unexpected ambulance rides and emergency room visits. She shoved her long curly mane out of her eyes with her free hand. "I told you, I'm fine — really. I'm sure I was only reacting to the sight of so much blood." She shuddered at the memory. "I don't do well with blood. That and the fact that I haven't eaten anything since last night probably made me all woozy. It's nothing, I'm sure."

The paramedic released her wrist and looked directly in her eyes, commanding that she follow his finger one more time.

"Well, everything checks out fine," he said. "Scalp lacs tend to bleed like crazy. You really suffered more scrapes and bruises than anything. Since you don't require stitches and don't appear to have any blunt head trauma, then you're free to go."

Kitty stood slowly to leave. The paramedic helped her to her feet with a parting warning. "I believe it would be in your best interest, Miss, to follow up with your regular physician as soon as possible though — just to be on the safe side." He gave her a snappy nod of his head and gathered his supplies and departed in the waiting, now silent ambulance.

The driver of the pickup that had struck her car shook hands with the police officers he'd been talking with and walked over to join Kitty. With his hands shoved in the pockets of his worn jeans, he strolled casually over to Kitty and removed his sunglasses. Squinting against the afternoon sun, he extended his hand in introduction.

"Luke O'Connell, Miss Murphy. We were introduced earlier but I believe you were still a little shaken. I wasn't sure if you remembered my name or not."

Kitty couldn't help but notice that he towered over her petite frame by a good foot or more as he stood waiting for her to respond. She had to crane her neck to look up into his face. The distance her eyes traveled was more than worth the trip as she lingered on his handsome features. Her emerald eyes focused on his smoky gray ones, which were generously trimmed with the longest ebony lashes she'd ever seen. Not ordinarily the type of girl whose head could be so easily turned by a good looking guy, Kitty found herself quashing nervous stomach butterflies every time she dared a look at Luke's extraordinarily attractive face.

He had a rugged appearance with a strong square jaw covered in a days worth of stubble. The scruffy shadow only lent to his sensuality and was not at all unpleasant to look at, Kitty noted. His hair, the same jet-black color as his long lashes, without so much as a hint of curl or wave, brushed the collar of the white tee shirt hiding beneath his lightweight sweater.

Don't forget – *men are pigs,* logic and memory reminded her. *Tell that to my quickening pulse,* her weak willed flesh argued without much conviction.

"Mr. O'Connell." She smiled shyly and let his large hand swallow her much smaller one up in greeting.

"Please, Luke is just fine. Mr. O'Connell makes me want to turn around and look for my father." He returned her smile; his much less shy and with a warmth that reached all the way to his lovely gray eyes making them snap like they'd been sparked with flint.

When he smiled, he coaxed wonderful parenthetical creases, that weren't quite dimples in his cheeks, to show themselves. His smile revealed straight white teeth and a small scar under his bottom lip that pulled taut with the effort of his grin. The smile was the source of her undoing nearly causing Kitty to swoon into a faint for the second time that day. She reluctantly pulled her hand away from his and grabbed the strap on her shoulder bag with both hands like a security blanket.

"Okay, Luke," she offered timidly, testing his name on her tongue. A blush started at the bottom of her toes and worked its way all the way up to the part in her hopelessly wind-blown hair. She picked a spot in the middle of his broad chest and fixed her eyes on it to avoid looking directly at him. Looking at him was kind of like looking at a solar eclipse. Oh she wanted to look at him all right, but she was afraid if she studied him too closely, his gorgeous looks might burn her retinas.

Aside from wanting to get lost in his beautiful face, the thing that worried her most was while she was looking at him, this handsome stranger would search her face and find her lacking. Always uncomfortable with members of the opposite sex, Kitty fidgeted in nervousness and played with the zipper on her jacket.

Luke shoved one hand back in his pocket and swung his sunglasses around carelessly with his other hand. "And you are ... Katherine?" He asked politely.

She dared another peek at his face and blushed noticeably, managing only to answer with the shake of her head. After a few uncomfortable seconds passed, Kitty finally found her voice and shook her head no.

"No, not Katherine. I actually prefer Kitty. Only the teller at the bank calls me Katherine." Her splotchy red stained cheeks accentuated the freckles dotting her nose, causing them to pop out noticeably.

Luke smiled warmly at her. Kitty wanted to thank him for apparently sensing her shyness. He talked casually, drawing attention away from her discomfort.

"Yes, I think Kitty suits you. You don't strike me as a Kathy or a Katie. I like Kitty. How about if I buy you lunch, Kitty?" She started to interrupt him, so he pushed on before she could decline. "Now I realize that a simple lunch in no way will begin to make up for the trauma of nearly running you down, smashing your car and ruining your day. But hey – a man can hardly dismiss such a pretty girl without at least trying to make up for the wrongs he committed." He glanced casually at his watch. "It's almost two-thirty. We could make it a late lunch. I know this great Chinese Restaurant. They have the best egg rolls in town. *And* I heard you tell the paramedic that you hadn't eaten all day. I'd lose my membership to the Gentlemen's Chivalry Society if I didn't at least buy you lunch."

Her look suggested she was considering his idea.

"Please, Kitty. I feel so responsible and I'm totally to blame for all the trouble I've caused you. You've got to at least let me *try* to make it up to you." He grinned sheepishly and put his sunglasses back on before shoving his hands in the back pockets of his jeans.

Kitty wanted to accept his invitation so bad she could taste it. Knowing how socially inept her conversational skills were though; she stammered and bit her lip in indecision. She released little breaths one at a time stalling her decision. She glanced around the neighborhood where they stood before turning to look at Luke. Touching the over-sized bandage affixed to the middle of her forehead, she faltered.

"I couldn't possibly go anywhere looking like this. You'd be embarrassed to be seen with me," she said self-consciously.

"Hardly!" He smiled casually. "You won't embarrass me, I promise. And you've got to eat. If you're too shaken up or in any pain, I could just go and get you something and take you home, if you'd rather."

Kitty saw concern darken his smoky gray eyes. "No, I'm fine, really," she reassured him. "But unless you have a magic carpet hidden somewhere, I'd say we might have a little transportation problem. They just towed away my car and your truck – so, I think we're kind of stuck here."

He laughed out loud. He brought a hand up to support his strong chin pretending to be lost in deep thought. "Hmm, you're right. I forgot about that little detail." He snapped his fingers suddenly causing her to take a step back. "As luck would have it, I was actually on my way home when I ran into your car. I live two blocks over." He gestured in the general direction. "If you're up for it, we can walk to my house. I have another car parked in my garage."

Kitty thought about if for a split second and decided to trust her instincts. Luke O'Connell seemed like a perfect gentlemen. And it wasn't like she had to actually go inside his house. She could wait on the sidewalk for him. Her growling stomach cast its vote trumping all paranoia and Kitty accepted his invitation for lunch.

Luke's social skills were the antithesis to Kitty's. Perfectly at ease with small talk, he filled the distance with polite pleasantries.

"I really am very sorry about your car. I was driving my work truck. It's an old beater I bought when I got here last year. I moved here from Southern California and I'd rarely had an opportunity to see snow, let alone drive in it. I was completely terrified by the thought of getting behind the wheel my first winter here."

Kitty relaxed at his confession. So the perfectly handsome man had some normal fears. She was secretly glad. It made him appear more human and less like the larger than life persona she'd judged him to be.

"And I didn't stop with merely an old clunker. I over insured myself so I've got coverage coming out the wadzoo ... *just in case.*" He grinned at her like a mischievous little boy and shrugged his shoulders. "Sorry. My mother would have a fit if she heard me using such language in front of a lady. Anyway ... believe it or not, you're my first car accident. I don't think you'll need to worry about your car. With all of my insurance, I imagine you'll be able to get a loaner while yours is getting fixed – and anything else you might need. If you need to go to a doctor, don't worry about the bills. If my insurance company doesn't take care of everything, you have my guarantee that I'll personally handle everything."

Kitty smiled her gratitude. "Wow, thanks. That's really a load off my mind. I was already starting to worry about how I'm going to get around. You know what really stinks? As of a couple of hours ago, that beat up old station became legally mine." She chuckled at the irony. With a little encouragement, Kitty volunteered a few sketchy details of her morning visit to the county courthouse dissolving her marriage. She touched only on the highlights omitting personal details.

Whether he was a mind reader or not remained to be determined, but somehow he managed to take control of the conversation and masterfully steered them to a more neutral subject rather than her divorce.

"When I moved here last year I was tempted to hang a sign in my back window warning other drivers of the dangers of following too closely to my vehicle," he volunteered.

They laughed easily together.

"I bought the old truck because I didn't dare take a chance driving my sweet baby in the snow." Kitty gave him a puzzled frown. He answered the unasked question without prompting. "My sweet baby is a 1966 GTO and someday she's going to be a classic. I know it's silly, but I have a tendency to pamper her a bit because she's the first car I've ever owned. Bought and paid for her all by myself.

She stays covered up in the garage most of the time and I only use her for really perfect summer days and emergencies. I guess taking a beautiful woman to lunch would constitute a real emergency." He looked over at Kitty and gave her another devilishly charming grin. If he noticed the reddening of her face, he kept it to himself.

The struggle to keep from laughing out loud at his remark nearly proved too much for her. Never in her entire life had anyone ever referred to her as beautiful. His comment prompted a few second thoughts about having lunch with him. What if he was some sort of Prince Charming serial killer? She stole a peek at him. His easy gait, laughing gray eyes and the overall knight in shining armor demeanor made him appear as anything but dangerous. But – a girl couldn't be too careful, she reminded herself. Either he was the world's best liar or he was terribly near-sighted. Not wanting to seem vain and dwell on his "beautiful girl" myopic distortion, she searched her brain for something to say on any other topic rather than physical attributes. The thoughts in her brain whirred around like a hamster on a wheel trying to think of something that would make her seem worldly and sophisticated.

"So ... what was it that brought you to Alaska last year," she asked, changing the subject. As soon as the words escaped from her mouth she wanted to yank them back in like a yo-yo on a string. He's going to think you're a nosy simpleton! IDIOT! She inwardly screamed at herself.

Luke didn't seem bothered by her question at all. He merely smiled that wonderfully warm smile and continued his slow unhurried pace. "Well, when I graduated from U.C.L.A. last year with a degree in Horticulture and Landscape Architecture I'd never felt more lost in my entire life. I stupidly assumed that at the ripe old age of 24 and being the proud owner of a brand new college degree that I should have everything figured out. The stupidity of youth, I guess." He shrugged his shoulders. "My best friend from college convinced me to vacation with him in Alaska – you know, take some time off, *find myself* — that sort of thing. As it turned out, it ended up being a working vacation. His uncle was a commercial fisherman and the two of us went to work with him on his fishing boat."

"That doesn't sound like much of a vacation," she smirked.

"Oh no, it was amazing. Don't get me wrong, it was incredibly hard work, but for some reason, I loved it. My friend however, hated everything about it and he jumped ship as soon as he could. He went back to California but oddly enough, I ended up staying. After the fishing season, I got a job with a construction company that kept me busy all winter. When springtime rolled around, it was fishing season again, so I went back to work for my friend's uncle. I've actually only been back in Anchorage a couple of days. I guess I must still have my sea legs. At least that's the excuse I'm going to give as the reason for my terrible driving skills today." His laughter at himself flowed effortlessly. Kitty couldn't help but laugh with him.

"Well, in your defense, the accident really wasn't all your fault. The way that woman stepped out in front of you, there really wasn't anything else you could have done."

He shook his head in deep thought. "Yeah, I guess. The police weren't able to locate her to question her, but at least there were a couple of witnesses to the accident. The mystery lady seems to have vanished. Well, here we are. This is my house." He stopped and pointed at the small cottage style house. "I'll just be a minute if you want to wait here while I go get the keys and pull the car around. Promise you won't leave."

He treated her to a full blown perfect toothed, double cheek crease, award winning smile that Kitty felt all the way to the tips of her toes. She nodded her ascent and sighed with relief that he hadn't asked her to come in. This guy was starting to seem too good to be true.

Lunch ended up lasting nearly two full hours. Luke was so friendly and easy to talk to, Kitty felt as if they'd been friends forever. She did however, steer clear of any details she considered too personal. Not ready or willing to put her trust in someone she only just met, she promised herself she would keep this chance meeting with Luke in perspective. But he was making it very difficult to resist his charms.

Before they ate their meal, Kitty noticed Luke bowed his head momentarily. He could have simply been adjusting the napkin in his lap or he could have bowed in prayer. She couldn't be sure. She couldn't read anything into that, she told herself.

Lunch was a pleasant enough experience rich in witty banter and a comfortable conversational fencing and paring. Later when Luke took her home after lunch, he offered in parting to *keep her in his prayers*. His casually spoken comment shook Kitty's belief in men in general. She wasn't sure real men prayed. At least in her short life, she had yet to meet any that admitted to it.

The next morning as she was cleaning her apartment, she choked on her diet soda when a beautiful arrangement of flowers arrived for her from Luke. The card simply stated: *"I'm sorry I ruined your car, but I'm not sorry I met you. Are you the answer?"* He'd signed it simply, *Luke O'Connell*.

Her expertise in relationship protocol was sorely lacking and she worried over proper etiquette. Should she call him to thank him or wait and see if he called her? Should she let a relationship develop or blow him off right away and avoid the risk of possibly getting hurt at some point? Maybe this beautiful gift was merely a ploy to butter her up so she wouldn't sue him for the accident. Kitty reread the card and turned it over and over in her hands. Her cat Jonah sidled over rubbing against her making figure eights between her legs.

"Well, Jonah – what do you suppose I should make of this?" She asked the cat. "And what does he mean by, *Am I the answer?* The answer to what? Hmm … What to do … what to do?" Kitty tapped the card on the edge of the counter lost in deep thought.

Luke took all guesswork out of the situation when he phoned her later that day. He said he'd been thinking about her and wanted to make sure she wasn't suffering any after affects from the accident.

"Just a couple of bruises and a little stiffness," she reassured him. She purposely kept her answer short, unsure as to whether she should invite further conversation or not. Deep down she hoped he wouldn't simply dismiss her and hang up right away.

Kitty could hear Luke on the other end of the line as he hesitated. "Listen, I was wondering if you might be available to go to a concert with me tonight. I know it's short notice and all, but …" His words trailed off.

Kitty was too stunned to interrupt him. This handsome man was asking *her* out on a date.

Luke rushed on in response to the deafening silence at the other end of the line. "There's a free concert at the park downtown tonight with a bunch of groups playing. A friend of mine from church will be performing and I thought you might like to go with me." Luke paused and waited.

Kitty wound the phone cord around her finger absent-mindedly. "Well," she drew the one word out before launching into all the reasons she couldn't go. But truth be told, she was dying to go with him.

"I know it's in bad taste to ask a woman out at the last minute," he said. "Especially one as beautiful as you. You probably are booked up weeks in advance." He paused awkwardly.

Kitty found his sudden uncertainty endearing. She couldn't stop the blush from staining her cheeks. "Okay, now I know you're joking, right? Did you suffer some sort of head trauma during the accident yesterday?"

Always uncomfortable with compliments, today was no exception, so she did what she usually did and joked her way around the discomfort she felt. From her end, she sensed the instant the seriousness came into his voice.

"Why would I joke about something like that? I thought women liked it best when a man was honest and didn't play games. That's what my sister-in-law tells me all the time, anyway."

She couldn't tell if she'd offended him or not. She covered the mouthpiece with her hand and looked at Jonah for advice. "Help Jonah. What should I do?" she whispered.

"I'm sorry. I probably shouldn't have called. I'm being too forward. I apologize." His voice became somewhat tight and controlled like he was reeling his feelings in.

Panic engulfed her as she sensed he was about to hang up on her. "Luke ... wait! I'm glad you called. I don't have any other plans for tonight. It's just that ... well, I told you yesterday that my divorce was just finalized and I don't think I'm ready to jump right back into any kind of dating thing this soon. I ..." she felt herself waffling.

Luke took advantage of the opening and forged ahead. "Well, how about if we don't call it a date, then. Just two people going to a Saturday night concert together. No strings. I happen to know that you don't have a car right now — and well — I do, so how about if I swing by your apartment and give you a lift. No pressure. Just an innocent ride to a concert, okay? One friend helping out another friend."

"Well, I guess when you put it that way." She melted. It ended up being one of the best decisions of her life.

She and Luke O'Connell were married on New Year's Eve, two years later.

NINETEEN

Grace held her hand in front of her and examined her perfectly manicured nails. She brought her hand close for further inspection all the while downplaying her role in Kitty and Luke's *chance meeting.*

"So. You're not too upset about me causing that little *accident* are you, *Mrs.* O'Connell?" she asked nonchalantly. Her emphasis was obvious.

Kitty leaned over and hugged Grace tight around the neck. "Oh, Grace. How could I be? I ended up with a wonderful man. How could I be upset about that?" She pulled away to study Grace's face.

"You know, after hearing your desperate prayer about needing a sign and then vowing to never trust men again, I'll admit – I was a little concerned that the car accident might be a bit over the top. But it certainly seemed to do the trick, didn't it?" Grace beamed like a lighthouse beacon.

"Hmm – a bit over the top? Absolutely. But what is it that people are always saying? *Be careful what you wish for.* Or in my case, *pray for.* Luke was so opposite of any guy I'd ever known – it was easy to trust him. He'd confessed that at the precise moment of the accident he'd been praying and asking God to bring him a woman he could fall in love with and marry. Someone who needed to be taken care of. Can you imagine? Boy, did he get more than he bargained for. He told me later than he was getting impatient waiting on God, but that God had specifically told him to be patient and keep his focus on Him. God had the perfect answer for his prayers. Remember the oddly worded card attached to the flowers he sent me?"

Grace nodded her head.

"He wrote that because after the car accident he wondered if I could be the answer to his prayer. It always struck me as odd that at the same time I was praying for a sign, Luke was praying for a wife. God sure can be funny sometimes."

"Exactly! You both needed answers to prayer. And voila! Ask and ye shall receive." Grace laughed. "I must say though, Katherine – you and Luke certainly took your time figuring things out. If you don't mind my saying so, you were a tad stubborn. You had built so many walls around yourself you didn't make it easy to give yourself over to love."

Kitty grabbed a fat lock of hair and wound it around her finger. "I know, Grace. Once burned, you know? I'd had so much emotional damage done to me already. My self-esteem had pretty much been through the shredder. Meeting Luke on the very day my divorce was final was a little surprising."

"Yes, but you and your ex-husband had been separated for six months. You barely had a marriage the entire time you and he were married."

"I know. But after that experience, I had a hard time convincing myself I was worthy of love. My husband rejected me, as did my parents. I felt pretty certain there was something fundamentally unlovable about me. I didn't want to love Luke and I pushed him away for the longest time. Luke is, if anything – very tenacious. He stuck it out even though I kept him at arms length for the longest time. I didn't even let him kiss me for the first year we dated. He agreed to be just friends and seemed okay with that. He extended his stay in Alaska and turned down a great job opportunity in Seattle just to be near me, though. He obviously had hopes for something more. He told me later he fell in love with me at first sight. Good Lord, that's a scary notion, isn't it? I don't know if I necessarily believe in that sort of thing. We spent a long time cultivating a really deep friendship. It took some doing on his part, but eventually Luke wore me down and I let my guard down. Not exactly the stuff you read about in romance novels, but it worked for us." Kitty smiled in remembrance.

"So, are you sorry then, Katherine? Would you really do it over again with Luke and make a different choice?"

"Honestly? No. After watching our beginning story, I don't think I would, Grace. I don't think I'd change anything about our relationship together. I would have married him under any circumstances. I really do love him like crazy, you know?" Kitty felt emotion constricting her throat muscles and she had to force a swallow past the growing lump. "We had a wonderful life, Grace." Kitty's voice dropped to a whisper. "I guess I kind of blew it though, didn't I? I guess that's another of life's clichés that I'm learning the hard way." She locked eyes with Grace.

Grace showed bewilderment. "What cliché are you referring to, Katherine?"

"You never know how good you have it, until it's gone." Unshed tears burned the backs of her eyes.

"I'm sorry for your loss," Grace said.

"You want to hear something really sad, Grace?"

"What's that?"

"It wasn't until years later – and I'm talking a *lot* of years later, that I truly let myself love Luke completely."

"Years? I don't understand, dear. How could you marry Luke if you didn't love him? Isn't that what happened with your first marriage?"

"Love was always so risky for me, Grace. I know that I loved Luke on the surface when we married. I felt totally different about Luke than I did about my first husband. But I always withheld a part of myself from him. I could never let him see all of me for who I was. I didn't want to scare him. I'll be the first to admit that I'm not the easiest person in the world to live with."

"How so, Katherine?" Grace's voice was so soothing, it was easy for Kitty to unleash yet more of her hidden secrets.

"Gosh, where do I start? Should I list my shortcomings in order of importance or alphabetically?"

Grace rolled her eyes and waited for Kitty to continue.

"I'm moody and irritable and have so many ups and downs. Half the time I think I'm flat out crazy. I can be temperamental and argumentative. Shall I go on?"

"Really, Katherine, you're not much different than most women. You're being too hard on yourself. You're not so much crazy as perhaps, hormonal. God created women to be emotional and passionate creatures. What does all this have to do with your feelings for Luke?"

"Well, because I'm all these crazy things rolled up into one big mess, I kept waiting for Luke to discover that I was too much for him to handle. I purposely tried to push him away. It was almost like I'd have some sort of fit over something and then stand back and wait to see if he'd still love me afterwards. I'd push him away but he kept pushing back … just loving me through all of my ups and downs. Until one day it dawned on me that Luke was in the marriage for the duration. He wasn't going anywhere. When I finally got that, it was as if this tight binding was finally broken from around my heart. All those bricks in my wall started to crumble one by one. I remember the day I had this life-changing epiphany. It wasn't even anything big. It was over something mundane and inconsequential." Kitty warmed at the sudden memory.

Grace looked thoughtful with a twinkle in her eye as if she too shared the memory. "Just so we're on the same page, Katherine, when exactly did this change occur?"

Kitty bit her lip in concentration. "Hmm, I think it was November 1995 — a few months after my 35th birthday. I had a bit of a mid-life crisis and I kind of did something I'm ashamed to admit. It was completely vain and selfish." Kitty thought out loud for a minute, calculating the years. "Gosh, if that's right, Luke and I had been married nearly 14 years! It's a wonder the man ever stuck by me! I'm a complete moron."

"Why do you think that, Katherine?"

"Because, Grace – it took me 14 years to really allow myself to fall completely in love with my husband. You know – that head-over-heels kind of love people are always singing about in old movies. *Fourteen years!* Oh my goodness, that's got to be some kind of sad entry to somebody's record book. Fourteen years, Grace – to knock down the walls surrounding my heart and finally love my husband with my whole heart."

TWENTY

November 17, 1995

Kitty awoke to intense pain radiating throughout her entire lower body. Grogginess enveloped her making it difficult to roll into a sitting position. She'd been home from the hospital for 24 hours. It felt like she'd spent most of that time going back and forth to the bathroom. The urge to use the bathroom, *again,* was becoming unbearable. She scooted over to the edge of the bed as best she could, although every jerky movement became a new adventure in pain. There was no question she wasn't going to be able to lift herself from the bed without help. She had precious little time to make the journey as the pressure in her bladder increased exponentially.

The doctor assured her the liposuction surgery had gone smoothly and without a hitch. She was a textbook case, he said. Under the fog of anesthesia she vaguely remembered the doctor warning her of some moderate post-operative pain. *Moderate? In a pigs eye!* Kitty mumbled to herself as she grabbed the edge of the bed waiting for her vision to clear from the blinding pain shooting through her limbs. Her pain intensified causing beads of sweat to pop out on her upper lip and forehead. She took several deep breaths to squelch the rising nausea.

In less than 90 minutes, her surgeon had successfully removed what had taken Kitty a lifetime and three pregnancies to acquire. Four liters of body fat had been surgically sucked from her hips, thighs and buttocks in what was becoming one of the fastest growing cosmetic procedures in the country. The good doctor personally guaranteed that Kitty would be up and about in no time and shopping for form fitting jeans in a matter of a few weeks. She swallowed the bile building in her the back of her throat and prayed she'd survive the next few days.

She cleared her throat so she could call out for help. "Hello ... is anybody out there?"

Her throat, still raw from the tube that had been inserted during surgery, caused her words to come out in a hoarse, scratchy whisper. She cleared her throat again and managed a deeper, albeit still very weak, growl.

"Hey anybody. I need help in here!" A few seconds passed and still no response. "Where is everybody?" Searching around for anything within her reach, her fingers latched onto the hard-back book left lying open on the bedside table. It took some doing, but she finally struggled to lift the heavy book over her head and banged it on the wall behind her head. Nothing. She managed to push herself into a sitting position and heaved the book with what little remaining strength she possessed. The book made contact with the lamp on the nightstand sending both crashing to the floor, finally alerting her family to her distress. Luke and her three children came running to her rescue, all colliding in the tight space of the spare bedroom that usually served as the home office, but this week was to be her convalescent room.

"Mom, are you okay?" Eleven-year-old Rebecca asked with genuine concern.

The other two children hung back slightly letting their father pass. Kitty suspected her appearance was scary enough to keep the children at bay and within easy distance of the doorway in the event a sudden exit might become necessary. Kitty knew she must look a sight with her unwashed greasy hair and pale sickly face naked of makeup. Her hair stuck out at odd angles on one side while the other side was plastered to her scalp in an unflattering smashed bed-head lump from lying in one spot for so long. In addition to the post-surgery pain, Kitty winced when touching her scalp, surprised that even her hair hurt.

The last time Luke helped her to the bathroom, Kitty had dared a look in the mirror. The puffiness of her face drew most of the attention away from the dark blotchy circles under her eyes. One look at herself and she was reminded of a phrase her mother often used: *Warmed-over-death.* A brief glimpse of her appearance gave a whole new meaning to the phrase while at the same time giving validity to the way she actually felt.

Luke leaned over her; a look of concern coloring his normally light gray eyes a shade darker.

"What is it, love? What do you need?" He carefully pushed a strand of matted hair out of her eyes.

She managed to croak out her one word request. "Bathroom."

"Again?" He smiled.

She wanted to shake her head yes, but even that slight movement created a fresh wave of nausea.

Luke eased her legs over the side of the bed. She sat for a few seconds waiting for the dizziness to subside.

"C'mon, Baby. Here we go. Stand up now, Sweetheart. I've got you – lean on me." Helping her to her feet, it was more gravity rather than her own strength that caused her to lean into his strong chest for support. "Watch out kids. Coming through. Move out of Mom's way please."

All three children scattered. Kitty was grateful for his steadying arm, but mortified that he insisted on helping her peel the tight spandex garment away so she could relieve herself. The doctor said she needed to wear the tight-fitting garment for six to eight weeks so she better get used to the pain of removing and replacing it on a regular basis.

Shooing Luke from the bathroom, she leaned against the counter waiting for privacy. In her mind, some things were entirely too personal and intimate to be shared, even by spouses. Going to the bathroom by oneself, headed that list!

"Out!" She ordered. He started to argue, but Kitty remained adamant. "Luke, *please*," she pleaded. "I have to draw the line at toilet duties. Just wait for me outside the door and I'll call you if I fall off."

He smiled that wonderfully boyish grin of his. "Hey, I don't want this to come back and haunt me if I don't meet your expectations about fulfilling my promise for all that stuff regarding better or worse or in sickness and in health." He winked at her as he pulled the door closed behind him.

Kitty let her head drop to her chest and sighed in relief having finally made it to the bathroom in the nick of time – and with nary a minute to spare. When she'd finished, she yelled for Luke to come and help her put things in order. Pulling the tight spandex garment back up over her aching body proved much more difficult than pulling it down. Too make matters worse, Kitty was swathed from her ankles to her ribcage in a layer of spongy surgical binding tape. The combination of the tape and the spandex were a necessary precaution to prevent excessive swelling and bruising. Or so she'd been told. The two components together served only to make her feel imprisoned and claustrophobic. As she and Luke struggled together to replace the constricting spandex, Kitty had to constantly dash away the tears that sprang to her eyes resulting from even the slightest pressure on her legs.

Luke, who was bent at the waist working the garment up, stole a peek at Kitty. As the tears spilled from her glassy green eyes, he purposely slowed his movements to help lessen her pain. Once the spandex was mercifully in place, Luke gently pulled her close and whispered words of comfort in her ear.

"I'm so sorry, Baby. I wish there was another way to do this."

Because he towered over her by at least a foot, Kitty was unaware of the pain contorting Luke's face. If she only knew how hard it was for him to mask his own pain at watching her suffer, she might have tried harder to hide her discomfort.

With her strength waning, Luke slowly guided her back to bed. Once she was comfortably situated – or as comfortable as she could get under the circumstances, Luke sat on the edge of the bed with her. He called for Rebecca to bring a fresh pitcher of water and the bottles of antibiotics and pain medication.

Kitty closed her eyes glad to be lying down once again. Luke had offered to sleep on the couch during her recovery period so she could have the king-sized bed to herself but she had declined his offer saying she was satisfied to sleep on the pull out couch in the office instead. The bed was much closer to the ground and a closer proximity to the bathroom since the room was much smaller than the master bedroom. Neither one of them liked sleeping alone, but it was a necessary alternative for at least the first week of her recovery.

Kitty opened her eyes and was embarrassed to find her husband staring at her. As his eyes devoured her, his love and compassion for her was unmistakable. Kitty cried softly.

"What is it, Hon? Are you in pain? Rebecca will be back any minute with your pills." He reached for her hand and brought it to his lips kissing the back of it where a dark bruise showed. He touched the spot where her IV had been. He then turned her hand over and lovingly kissed her palm.

"No, it's not that. You're so good to me." *What did I ever do to deserve such a loving man*, she thought to herself. Her tears flowed freely.

Luke reached over and lightly erased the path of her tears with his thumb. He leaned over and kissed her softly on the mouth.

She tried pushing him away. "Stop it. I look terrible and I smell worse. How can you even want to kiss me when I look this?"

"Like what? You always look beautiful to me," his smiled caressed her.

Kitty closed her eyes against the return of her queasiness. She took a couple of deep breaths in through her nose and blew them out through her mouth.

"Are you feeling sick again?"

Even the slight shaking of her head aggravated the nausea.

Rebecca reentered the room with a plastic pitcher of ice-cold water and two amber colored prescription bottles. Luke measured out water and pills and helped Kitty to lean forward to swallow. She lay back waiting for the pills to weave their magic spell and transport her to the dark abyss of a drug-induced, pain-free *Never Land*.

"The doctor said you might have some residual nausea from the anesthetic. He said that was normal," Luke said, kissing her forehead.

Kitty asked him to help her turn on her side so she could get into a more comfortable sleeping position. He turned her over so she was facing the other direction and ordered all the children from the room. As soon as Kitty was settled, he lay down as carefully as possible in a spoon fashion next to her. He eased his arms over her mid-section and placed his head on the pillow next to hers. He heard Kitty sigh. He snuggled her neck and whispered very quietly in her ear. His words were a prayer for her speedy recovery that tickled the hair around her ear. Luke lay still beside her listening to her breathing slow. He stroked her arm and continued his quiet prayers and words of love until finally, he felt her relax and surrender to sleep.

Two long pain-filled days later, Kitty couldn't wait to be released from her prison of surgical bindings. The morning the tape was to be removed, she would have danced a jig if she'd been at all able. Hunched over at the waist and leaning on the bathroom counter, she pressed her face in a hand towel to keep from crying out in agony as her husband painstakingly unwrapped her like a trussed up mummy. For the past two nights, nightmares had awakened Kitty to the horror of what might lie beneath the hated surgical tape. Her dreams tormented her with visions of grotesque deformed limbs and enormous black and blue bruises lurking underneath waiting to be unleashed. She was beyond anxious to have the tape removed, but fearful all at the same time.

Luke carefully peeled the tape from her swollen body, piece by agonizing piece. Every touch of his fingers, although gentle, made her cry out. Tears coursed down her pale cheeks with every strip removed. If the pain got any more intense, she might need to ask for a leather strap – or a bullet – to bite on! No doubt, this *bright idea* of hers would go down in her book as one of the stupidest things she'd ever done! She really hadn't been prepared for this much pain.

Luke sat on the bathroom floor behind her doing his best to hurry the process along in order to end her suffering.

"I'm sorry I'm hurting you, Sweetie. Maybe you should soak in the tub a while longer to try and loosen the tape some more," he offered sympathetically.

"I don't think it will make it hurt any less," she cried. "I can't stand having this on even one minute longer. It's killing me. Just hurry and get it off!" She was near the point of screaming, but through sheer will and determination, she reined in the urge.

Maybe if she'd been warned of the intense pain involved before-hand, she would have reconsidered having the surgery. *Who was she kidding?* Eliminating her misshapen saddlebag thighs in the span of a few hours compared to months and years at the gym seemed like a far easier solution. She would have scaled a mountain of hot lava barefoot to have a chance to get rid of her hated Charging Rhino Thighs!

At her pre-op consultation two weeks ago, her doctor neglected to mention all of the after-effects that could occur with the minimally invasive liposuction surgery. He focused on the end result, promising her she'd be more than happy with the final outcome. He neglected to mention the claustrophobic discomfort of the surgical tape that would make her want to pull her hair out by the roots at the end of the three-day period. Kitty likened that particular aspect of the recovery to what she imagined a straight jacket would feel like.

The good doctor also failed to mention that the rigid binding tape would squeeze her internal organs so severely she'd most likely suffer from a constant upset stomach. And of course he completely glossed over the fact that the antibiotics necessary to fight infection might quite possibly result in mild to moderate diarrhea. To his credit he did warn her she would need to wear the stretchy spandex undergarment that covered her from her ankles to her breasts for weeks post-operatively. However, he failed to mention that pulling them up and down numerous times throughout the day would most likely cause her such intense pain it would promote frequent displays of psychotic behavior. Kitty couldn't help but wonder why all these little pearls of wisdom were never discussed in glamour magazines and entertainment news programs.

She was relieved however, that as each piece of tape fell to the floor, there was only minimal discoloration of the skin underneath. She glanced up as Luke finished removing a particularly nasty piece of tape from her outer thigh. She saw his reflection in the mirror as he wiped the sweat from his brow and balled up the piece of tape and threw it over his shoulder. His face was so focused in concentration as he performed the task he looked like he was uncovering an ancient treasure rather than his wife's thighs.

As Kitty studied her husband's reflection in the mirror, one thing became abundantly clear to her. She could see her husband in the space between her thighs. While this might not seem like a big deal to most, to Kitty it was huge! After three pregnancies, Kitty's thighs had become so heavy, she often marveled at the fact that she didn't somehow spontaneously combust from the constant friction of her over-sized thighs rubbing together. The fact that she could actually see not only daylight between the space, but her husband seated behind her, meant that the surgery had been successful! Her tears of pain turned to tears of joy.

"Luke! Honey ... I can see your face!" She half laughed, half cried standing up and looking over her shoulder.

Luke stopped what he was doing and looked up at her. "What are you talking about, Kitty?" He dropped his hands to his lap and tilted his head sideways to peer around her leg.

"Baby, I can see you in the space *between* my legs! It's the first time since before Rebecca was born that even a hint of daylight has penetrated the space between my C.R.T.s!" Her excitement grew and she could barely stand still. In spite of the pain, she turned from side-to-side to see herself from all angles. "Luke, the surgery worked! Look at how small my thigh looks without the tape!"

He sat back and examined her almost fully exposed thigh. He was clearly unimpressed by the revelation. "Babe, it looks fine, but then to me – it always did look fine. Now let's get back to business so we can hurry up and get this over and done with. We've still got the other leg to unwrap."

Kitty was disappointed by his reaction. Confused by his response, she bent over and let him continue his painful ministrations. After what seemed like long agonizing hours later, but in reality was only thirty minutes, Luke sat back with a satisfied sigh.

"Done." He stood up, gathering tape remnants as he did so. As he turned to leave the bathroom, Kitty's staying hand stopped him.

"Luke, wait. Don't you want to see how I look? What do you think, Honey? Do I look different ... *better?*" Kitty turned in a clumsy circle. "Well?" She turned hopeful eyes towards him.

"It looks fine. Do you want me to start the shower for you? I imagine after three days without bathing you can't wait to take a long hot shower." He walked over and opened the glass shower door and fidgeted with the hot and cold knobs.

Kitty grabbed her robe off the counter and jammed her arms into it. Tying the sash roughly, she placed her hands on her hips and turned to stare at her husband.

"Luke!" She raised her voice to be heard over the spray of water. "Talk to me. Why won't you look at me? Do I look so horrible that you can't even stand the sight of me?"

He dropped his head momentarily before he turned to confront her. He grabbed a bath towel and threw it over the top of the shower stall. Turning slowly, he measured his words carefully before he spoke.

"I don't think we want to get into this right now, Kitty. Just take your shower and I'll go and get lunch ready for the kids." He turned to leave.

Kitty hugged herself tightly in defense of his sudden cold attitude. "You don't want to get into *what*, Luke? What's wrong with you?"

"What are you expecting me to say, Kitty? You look fine. Okay. I told you that *before* you had the surgery," he said with emphasis. "You haven't heard one thing I've said about your appearance since the day I married you. Why should $5,000.00 worth of plastic surgery make my opinion any more valid," he snapped, and attempted to move past her before she stopped him by grabbing the back of his shirt.

"*What?*" She shoved her greasy hair out of her eyes and shook her head in bafflement. What are you talking about? Why are you so ticked off at me all of a sudden? This better not be about the money thing again! I told you my baby-sitting money that I've been saving for two years was going to cover all the expenses. You said you were okay with that," she snapped in defense.

He turned and glowered at her. "It's not the money!" He barked. "When you agreed to baby-sit those twin minions of Satan's from across the street, I said *fine — if that's what you want to do!* I told you if you really thought you needed to have your body surgically resculpted, I would pay for it. I make enough money that I could have paid for it! You didn't need to bother baby-sitting those three-year-old hellions just because you were too proud to let me pay for this. But you don't get it, Kitty. It's not even about the money!"

"I'm confused, Luke. What are we arguing about, then? Now you're upset because I baby-sat for two years?" Kitty raised her voice to match his.

Luke threw his hands up in frustration. "Agggghhhh! Good Lord, you can be so infuriating sometimes, Kitty O'Connell!"

She stood toe-to-toe with him but had to crane her neck to meet his stare. "Stop yelling at me and tell me why you're so mad at me, Luke."

He placed his hands on his hips towering over her in one big column of agitated fury. "Hmmm ... let's see. Maybe it's because all you've done for the last three days is cry about how much pain you were in and obsess about how you were going to look afterwards. You've barely eaten the last three days because you're afraid of gaining weight now that you've had your 'miracle' surgery. Or maybe I'm just spitting mad because I've spent the better part of the last hour torturing you by peeling off that stupid tape, while I had to sit there and listen to you cry like a baby because every time I touched you it hurt like crazy! Or maybe ..." His anger was fully ignited and he paced the passageway between the bathroom and the bedroom, flailing his arms about. "... maybe I'm so angry at you because no matter how much money you spend on diet products and pills or exercise equipment or surgeries, or how many times I tell you that you look beautiful – your are *never* going to believe what I say. Even with this surgery, Kitty, *you are never going to be happy with the way you look!*" He stormed into the bedroom and grabbed the remote control from the armoire and flopped down on the bed with a huff. He pointed the remote at the television as if he were brandishing a loaded pistol, firing angrily at the TV in rapid succession, ignoring all the programs.

Kitty trailed after him as best as her stiff limbs would allow her. She purposely positioned herself between Luke and the TV interrupting the connection. He dropped the remote on the bed and looked at her accusingly.

She bit her bottom lip and studied her chipped toe polish before speaking. "You don't think that I'm going to be happy with myself once I'm healed?" With her head still bowed, her question was barely more than a whisper.

Luke studied her body language, gauging her mood, becoming irritated that she refused to look at him. "No." He expelled his response with emotion that registered both sadness and disgust. He fell backwards on the bed and rubbed his eyes. He stacked his hands under his head and followed the slow meticulous revolution of the fan blades overhead.

Kitty finally looked up and took two painful strides to the bed. Because of the height of the king-size bed, sitting down was too difficult a task to accomplish so she settled for propping her tender backside against the edge being careful not to lean too heavily with all her weight. She searched Luke's face, feeling his rebuff as he closed his eyes against her probing stare. "Why do you think I won't be happy?"

He opened his eyes and turned his head locking his stare with hers. He sighed again, struggling to put his feelings into words. "Because, you won't let yourself be happy with who you really are and what you look like. You've placed so much importance on your outward appearance that you can't see that it's destroying every-thing that's on the inside of you. This obsession of yours is slowly eating away at you like a cancer and its already killed your joy for life and it's going keep you unhappy with yourself forever."

She felt the weight of his words pressing her heart like a vice, causing her heartbeat to quicken. She neither agreed nor disagreed with him, but adopted a defensive attitude.

"Why do you say that?" She crossed her arms under her breasts and stuck her chin out in mock defiance. "I'm a happy person ... most of the time. Just ask anyone," she argued.

"I didn't say you were an unhappy person, Kitty. I said you are unhappy with yourself. Truth be told – I'd wager that you probably hate yourself most of the time. I think this painful surgery is nothing more than a bandage for what's really wrong." He looked away, staring at the ceiling fan again as Kitty played with the tie on her robe.

As if her tear ducts had suddenly sprung a leak, liquid pooled in her eyes spilling over, running all the way to her chin. She wiped them away with the cuff of her sleeve. The painful truth was a like a direct hit with a sharp arrow aimed for the center of the bulls eye, which in this case, happened to be her heart. Speaking past the lump in her throat was nearly impossible, but she forced the words out that started as little more than a squeak.

"Maybe I do hate myself most of the time. Having three pregnancies so close together added so much extra weight to my body that before the surgery, I could barely stand to look in a mirror. I've been so ashamed of the way I looked for so long. Even though you've never looked at me any differently and have always been so complimentary, I got paranoid and started to worry that you were one of those men that like fat women. What do they call them?"

He shook his head, but said nothing, respecting her need to talk.

"Chubby chasers," she said, answering her own question.

He brought a hand up to hide the smile on his lips. He cleared his throat before speaking. "Kitty, that's ridiculous. I am not a chubby chaser. And for the record I have never looked at you and thought you were fat. I don't know how many other ways I can say it so you'll finally believe me."

"No, you're probably just so used to my bulging butt and tree stump legs that you don't even see them anymore." Her crying became little fits of hiccupping breaths. She continued to be amazed that she could still possess such an endless supply of salty tears. "But I don't understand you, Luke. I'm not blind. I know what I see in the mirror when I look at myself. If I hate the way I look, why shouldn't you?" Her nose was hopelessly red and running in earnest from so much crying. She swiped it with her sleeve again. "In my mind, I thought my having the surgery would not only make me happier with myself, but you would be happier with a more *normal* looking wife." Her sobs were jerky little breaths she could no longer control.

Luke's jaw clenched and unclenched. Kitty saw the vein in the side of his neck beating with his pulse. No doubt his mounting irritation with her and her irrationalities had reached its peak.

He rubbed his forehead and threw both arms across his face blocking out the light and the look on his wife's tormented splotchy face. Kitty suspected he was praying and weighing his words carefully. After a few uncomfortable minutes he pulled his arms away and turned his head in her direction.

"I really hope you didn't have this surgery thinking it was going to make me happy. I already am happy with you. I love you, Kitty. I will always love you. I made a solemn vow not only to you, but to God that I would love you – no matter what. If you gained 150 pounds – I would still love you. If you got into some horrible accident and were horribly disfigured – I would still love you. And even though sometimes you make me so crazy with your unfair assessment of your physical attributes and your obsessions that I really just want to leave … guess what? I won't ever do that because … that's right … I – LOVE – YOU. There is nothing …" he rolled over on his side and propped his head on one elbow. "… and I mean – *nothing* – that will ever make me stop loving you. Are you *ever* going to get that, Kitty?" He sat up and dragged himself to the edge of the bed next to her side. He reached for her hand and interlaced her fingers with his.

She tried to pull her hand away, but he pulled it back, clasping it tightly. "What if you get tired of me?" She hiccupped. "Look what happened with my Dad. He left my mom for another woman. And my ex-husband — he …" she trailed off.

He silenced the remainder of her argument by leaning over and placing his large hands one on either side of her face. He kissed her slowly at first and then unleashed all the pent-up frustration, anger and passion she fueled in him. He deepened the kiss letting his tongue tease the contours of her lips.

Kitty tried to push him away and pulled back from him. "Stop it," she breathed huskily. "I look gross." Her argument as well as her resolve weakened from his deeply sensual kiss and the promise of love that it held. "You …"

Luke cut her off by gently placing his hand over her mouth. When she tried to pull it away, he shook his head "no."

"Kitty – shut up," he ordered without even a hint of harshness. His smile caused the corners of his eyes to crinkle. "Now, I know you're tempted to argue this indefinitely, but you need to know that you are never going to win this one. If you haven't learned anything about me after nearly 14 years of marriage, then hear me now, Baby. I am not your dad. And the fact that you would ever dream of comparing me to your ex, insults my character. I will *never* cheat on you with another woman. EVER."

Kitty tried to look away but he trapped her face in his large palms again forcing her head still.

"God …" he closed his eyes for a millisecond and then opened his smoky gray eyes that burned with his desperate plea. "Please get this, Kitty," he begged. "You are the most beautiful woman in the world to me. Why would I want another woman when God specifically hand picked you for me? I'd be slapping God in the face if I ever stopped loving you. You are my answer to a very specific prayer. If you can't trust that I love you with my whole heart, then – please – trust God. He brought you to me. If you have any more doubts or questions, then you can take it up with Him. I'm done trying to convince you." He gave her a quick kiss before shoving away from her and left the room. He closed the door soundlessly behind him.

Kitty leaned against the side of the bed and cried as her emotional wall collapsed in on itself. She didn't know what she'd ever done to deserve the love of such a wonderfully caring man – a godly man. Her tears became more cleansing than condemning. As they washed her clean, she vowed she would never take Luke's love for granted again.

Her heart swelled and exploded with something so encompassing, she had to cover her chest with both hands. The feelings that gushed from her heart spewed like an erupting volcano and could hardly be contained in the small space provided. For the first time in her marriage, Kitty knew with a certainty that Luke loved her as Christ commanded him to. It was a certainty she would take to her grave and that she would cherish for the rest of her life. The realization that had taken so long to grab hold, finally wrapped itself around her, leaving her shaken and overwhelmed. She pushed away from the bed and made her way to the shower, shaking her head in wonderment.

"Good gosh, Kitty. You are a first class idiot," she mumbled out loud. "What in the world took you so long, you big moron? Thank God Luke has waited all these years for you to finally get it."

She continued to chastise herself as she removed her robe and stepped into the spray of the shower.

TWENTY-ONE

Kitty sat quietly soaking up the sudden silence of the room. She absently rubbed her hands back and forth over her thighs against the numbness she felt.

"Well, that was eye opening, wasn't it?" she finally said.

"Yes. It certainly was." Grace said.

"Watching myself — I can't believe I was so stupid for so long. Holding a part of myself back from Luke the way I did. He is ..." she caught her verbal error and had to choke back her unexpected sadness. "He *was* such an amazing husband. On some level, I think I was always waiting for him to walk out on me the way both my dad and ex-husband did."

"Why would you assume he would leave you?"

"Oh come on, Grace. You've seen the films. My husband is no slouch in the looks department. I hear it all the time from my girlfriends about how gorgeous Luke is. I kept waiting for him to come home and tell me he was leaving me for one of his clients. Anticipating that he would do what most good-looking men usually do – I think I probably pushed him away. I justified it by telling myself that if I checked out emotionally, then it wouldn't hurt so bad when the inevitable happened."

Grace scrunched up her face in disapproval and harrumphed. It was the first unpleasant face she'd made so far. "Nonsense! I think you were merely using that as an excuse. I guess it's lucky for you that your husband turned out to be such a good guy and stuck around. Too bad you had to waste all those years though, isn't it?" Grace spoke the last with a layer of barely disguised sarcasm.

"Ok, so I admit it. I already acknowledged my own stupidity. Why couldn't I simply trust my husband's words and actions from the beginning? He always was so much smarter than me about so many things. He never held any emotions back from me. He loved so completely and simply."

"That's because he grew up surrounded by loving parents who taught him relational foundations and relationship basics."

"Yeah, no dysfunction there. How come he was able to pinpoint what was at the root of my low self-esteem issues so easily? He nailed it when he said I hated myself. I've been here for hours, maybe days ... is it still today, Grace?"

"I thought we already discussed the whole time continuum thing, Katherine."

"Yeah, yeah, whatever. It feels like we've been here forever." Kitty massaged her temples withdrawing inside herself.

"What were you going to say, Katherine?" Grace prodded her to keep her from lapsing into silence and slipping away.

Kitty stood up and paced the aisle. Each time she walked in front of her, Grace would pull her legs under her allowing Kitty to pass.

"Watching my past unfold I've figured a few things out, Grace." Getting a second wind, Kitty lengthened her stride, her steps becoming quicker, almost agitated.

"Do you want to give me a 'for instance'?"

"It's obvious my eating disorder started when my Dad left us. Food was the tool I used to make me feel better about him leaving me. I still do that. I mean I *did* do that right up until the end. Whenever Luke had to leave for a business trip or go golfing on the weekends, whatever – I would start eating, worrying about if he was going to come back. Talk about insecure, huh?"

Grace raised her palms up in surrender. "No argument here."

"When Walter entered the picture I started gaining weight as a protective barrier against his advances. So that makes sense to me now. Causing the car accident was the pinnacle of my desperation that guilted me into becoming a Christian. In the end, that worked out okay though and salvation gave me an anchor to hold onto through the tough times with my first husband." Kitty stopped her self-analysis long enough to turn questioning eyes towards Grace.

Grace nodded letting Kitty know she was on the right track.

"But the one thing I'm still not seeing clearly is why after having a nearly perfect husband and great kids and a pretty wonderful life overall, why did I continue to have such low self-esteem and struggle with self-loathing? Why do – or rather, why did I hate myself so much, Grace?" Kitty's endless supply of tears spouted and ran in twin rivulets down her cheeks. Kitty worried her bottom lip with her teeth trying to figure out the unanswered questions.

Grace stood up and walked over to Kitty. She wrapped her arms around her and hugged her. It was a whole body hug that Kitty felt all the way to her internal organs.

"Katherine, I'm so proud of you for finally making these revelations. Your life and all of your experiences have been fashioned like a puzzle. You still might need a little help to finally put all the pieces together to see the whole picture. I believe there's one more person who may be able to help you with that."

Reaching for Kitty's hand, Grace steered Kitty towards the double doors they'd originally entered from. Kitty froze thinking her moment of truth had at last arrived. Panic flooded her. Her breathing automatically quickened. She pulled up short, halting Grace's steps. Kitty nervously adjusted her workout clothes trying to make them appear like something other than what they were. She pinched her cheeks hoping to add a spot of color to them.

"Oh, Grace. I really don't think I'm ready to meet *Him* yet. I thought I would be by now, but I'm really not." Kitty shook her head in denial, punctuating her barely contained anxiety. "Look at me – I'm not even presentable."

Grace moved behind her and gave her a slight shove towards the door, whispering in her ear. "It's all right, Kitty. It's not *Him* you're going to see." Grace reassured her with a slight pat on the back.

Kitty stood rooted to her spot and turned her head to talk over her shoulder. "Then who?"

"You'll see. It's right through here, out the door — follow the path."

Grace opened the door and pushed Kitty forward. Extending her hand, she pointed to the path. Grace stepped aside to let Kitty pass. Grace smiled at her and hung back. Mercy loped through the door and joined Grace, squatting beside her.

Rather than the corridor they'd passed through upon their initial arrival, Kitty now found herself outside. She had to bring her hands up to shield her eyes against the sudden change of light and the glare of bright sunshine.

Taking a moment to saturate herself in her surroundings, she gasped in surprise by what she saw. Her senses went on immediate overload. It was impossible to know what to focus on first. Everything she looked at, smelled, touched or heard was a sensory surplus. The sky overhead was the most azure blue she'd ever beheld. So blue, it nearly burned her retinas. The air had a wonderful crispness to it and was so clean without the usual thickness of smog and urbanity she'd grown used to her whole life. Inhaling deeply, she filled her lungs and felt revived by the purity of breathing in both air and sky simultaneously.

The pungent smells of springtime in bloom wrapped around her assaulting her nostrils with fragrance and new life. The temperature was perfect, but then it would only stand to reason that Heaven would be climate controlled. The slight breeze in the air tickled her nose with heady aromas. Mingling with the gentle air, Kitty felt she could physically taste the smells of hyacinth, jasmine, roses and new spring grass. She closed her eyes savoring the smells wafting about her.

When she at last opened her eyes, she swayed with dizziness from her heightened senses. She stood in the middle of a lush green field displaying vibrantly colored flowers all competing for her attention. Kitty felt like a woman who'd been denied beauty her entire life. Her soul feasted on the splendor. Her insatiable desire to be nourished by God's majesty and nature's bounty fed her senses and her long-starved spirit. The colors were so rich, Kitty bent over wanting not only to smell each and every bloom, but to touch them as well. Colors of this magnitude could only truly be experienced by drinking in the touch of such beauty with one's fingertips. The intensity of the hues cried out to be captured on canvas by a gifted artist. Kitty imagined even the most brilliant masterpiece would pale in to comparison to the exquisite palette spread before her.

The sound of running water off to her left distracted her before she could finish feasting her eyes on the dazzling blossoms. She stood up and walked towards the sound of the beckoning water. Trees of every variety lined the banks of a pristine stream. She wanted to rush over and dip her hands in the pool for a cool drink. The urge was tempting as was the impulse to remove her shoes and socks and wade in knee deep in the clear spring.

An old-fashioned footbridge spanned the width of the gurgling stream. A lone figure was stationed on the other side. Kitty brought her hands to her eyes using them like invisible binoculars to see who waited beyond the bridge. Dropping her hands, she was unable to distinguish the solitary sentry who waited for her. Kitty twisted her hands in nervousness. Her apprehension made movement difficult. Her feet stepped forward as if of their own accord, dragging the rest of Kitty with them.

Please, Lord, give me strength for whatever is about to happen, she silently prayed.

Drawing nearer, she could tell her visitor was a woman. Her long flowing gown was similar to the one Grace had been wearing. Any remaining color dotting Kitty's cheeks drained as she closed the distance to the bridge. Kitty grabbed the bridge railing for support as a great tsunami of emotions flooded her mind and heart. Recognition dawned and escaped in a strangled cry.

"*Mother?*" Overcome with the tidal wave of memories, Kitty collapsed in a heap, unable to move forward to greet her mother who had been dead for the past two years.

"Surprise." Sophia's tone was light-hearted, testing her opponent. "It's all right, Katherine. Don't be scared."

Yeah, right, she thought. If this isn't scary, I don't know what is.

"Well look at you. You're every bit as pretty as the last time I saw you. I'd forgotten just how beautiful you are."

Kitty shook her head, not sure her hearing hadn't been impaired in some way. The woman standing across the bridge from her may have resembled her mother, but she definitely didn't sound like her,

Kitty argued with herself. She strained her eyes as she surveyed the woman who was indeed Sophia, minus the ravages of time and age, but with a peaceful, more joyous countenance.

Kitty rubbed her eyes to clear her vision worried that maybe she was dreaming. Sophia's face appeared minimally lined, without the harshness it once held. Her hair had lost that dull mousiness of age and was now shiny and bouncy, with only a slight graying. She no longer carried the signs of bitterness that had etched her features with hard lines for most of her life. Sophia looked relaxed, carefree and genuinely happy. Try as she might, Kitty couldn't honestly ever remember seeing her mother look happy.

Using the railing to hoist herself up, Kitty placed one foot on the bridge to cross over.

Sophia halted her with raised palms and a stern warning. "No, Katherine, stop! You can't cross over yet." Sophia grabbed the railing on her side for support.

"Mother?" Kitty stared down into the flowing water searching for something to say to her mother. She dashed away tears, annoyed that they flowed so continuously. She always seemed to have a ready supply just hovering below the surface. No words would come, only tears. Kitty forced a smile to her lips, hoping the mere act of smiling would help ease her tension.

"How are you, Mother?" Kitty asked awkwardly, for a lack of anything more profound to say.

Sophia returned Kitty's smile and brought her hand up to her chest. "Oh, Katherine. I'm wonderful. Nearly perfect, in fact. I imagine you're pretty surprised to see me, of all people, here in this place, huh?" Kitty shook her head numbly. "But to be honest, you're being here surprises me as well."

Anguish clouded Kitty's face, reading between the lines of her mother's statement. *She doesn't think I belong here? But yet she's here!* Kitty became incensed over her mother's misplaced judgment.

"No, no – it's not what you're thinking at all, Katherine. I just meant that, of course you belong here, but I didn't think it was your time yet. You're still so young." Sophia brushed her hair back and shook her head,

Kitty visibly relaxed at her mother's clarification. "Mother, let me come over there to you. I've …" Kitty floundered for the right words. "It's been so long since I've seen you." Kitty faltered as memories assailed her. She could recall perfectly the last time she saw or spoke with her mother. It was on the eve of her mother's surgery for lung cancer.

* * * * *

Kitty had waited for her siblings and their spouses to take their leave before she dared approach her mother. Walter had been sent on some trivial errand to get him out of the room since his inebriated presence upset everyone in the small private room; especially Sophia. Kitty wanted to speak with her mother in private, even sending Luke and her children on their way.

Once the date for Sophia's surgery had been confirmed, Kitty had launched her attack, arguing Sophia's need for salvation. Even facing life-threatening surgery, Sophia adamantly refused to let Kitty pray for her. Because of the pain medication Sophia was taking, she was less argumentative than usual, but still stubborn as all get out.

"Why would God care about me now at this point?" Sophia argued. "I'm not about to change my ways at the 11th hour and become some holy roller and make promises I can't keep. It's too late to be negotiating with God for my soul. I think I missed that boat, Katherine. God's already given up on me and so should you. You're wasting your breath."

Kitty threw caution to the wind and forged ahead.

"Mother, I'm not leaving here until I pray with you. You need to make things right — just in case."

"Just in case what? I die during surgery. Who gives a damn? I don't believe Hell could be any worse than what my life here on earth has already been. Fighting this cancer, living with Walter ... You and your bible thumping husband and kids can just get out of here and leave me in peace."

Pain seared Kitty's heart like a knife wound. She wanted to stay and pray with her mother, but she didn't want to upset her further.

Kitty was genuinely shocked that her mother continued to be filled with such bitterness.

"Well, then ... I guess I'll go. I'll be here in the morning when they take you to surgery." Kitty turned to leave, forcing back the tears that burned her eyes. "Mother, I ... I'm sorry." She wasn't even sure what she was apologizing for. She wanted to tell her mother she loved her, but the words stuck in her throat like she was trying to swallow a wad of cotton. Before she could talk herself out of doing it, Kitty turned back towards the bed and bent over Sophia's shriveled form. She placed her hand on Sophia's chest and whispered a hurried prayer in spite of Sophia's resolute refusal. Sophia went still and said nothing, so Kitty pressed her advantage and whispered her private thoughts to her mother. As she turned to leave the room, Kitty saw the glint of tears on her Mother's pale cheeks. They were Kitty's undoing.

Kitty joined Luke and the kids and the five of them all prayed together for Sophia's well being. It wasn't the same as actually holding Sophia's hand and praying with her, but under the circumstances, it would have to do.

Sophia died the next day during surgery. Kitty was overcome with grief. She carried the burden of remorse around like a heavy backpack weighted down with wet cement. She'd failed in her attempts to lead her mother to the Lord, when her mother had so desperately needed salvation.

* * * * *

The memory of that day still haunted Kitty.

Sophia's voice broke through, drawing her back to the present.

"No, Katherine. You need to stay on your side of the bridge. We'll just talk for a little while, if that's okay. Let me look at you. Turn around." Sophia waved her hands in a circular motion signaling her request.

Kitty obeyed, turning slightly for her mother's perusal.

"Well, you certainly look good, Katherine. Just as pretty as ever, dear." Sophia smiled, lighting her eyes that were more amber than brown to a warm soft glow. The words of praise flowed effortlessly from her lips.

Kitty was taken aback by her mother's casually spoken praise. Kitty couldn't recall her mother ever offering words of kindness before, let alone little terms of endearment.

"Hello. Who the heck are *you* and what in the world have you done with my mother? She's a skinny little Italian fireball about yay-big." Kitty snorted in disbelief as she raised her hand to chin level.

Sophia wrestled with embarrassment. "I know. I'm sorry I was so stingy with my compliments. It's not exactly my style, is it?

"You think?" Kitty answered sarcastically.

Sophia glanced around at the beautiful surroundings and instantly seemed buoyed by the majesty.

"Yeah. I was a pretty lousy mother, huh, kiddo?"

"Yeah, well, I was never tempted to nominate you for any mother of the year award, if that's what you mean." Her words had a nasty bite to them, making Kitty feel instantly contrite. The scent of a heady fragrance floated by her nose, reminding her of her beautiful surroundings. It seemed an act of sacrilege to harbor ill will in a place so lovely as this. She set her bitterness aside and opted for levity, changing the subject. "So … what's new with you, Mother?"

The old Sophia – the one Kitty knew intimately, had little or no sense of humor. This new Sophia threw her head back and roared with laughter – a great big belly laugh that made her shoulders quake. Kitty could count on one hand the number of times she'd heard her mother's laughter. The unexpected response was quite foreign sounding to Kitty's ears.

"Oh, other than being six feet under for the last couple of years, nothing much. How about you? What's new with you?"

They both laughed simultaneously as anger and embarrassment fizzled and fell away.

"Oh well … not much with me either. Although, I'm being fitted for a set of wings and a halo, even as we speak." Kitty laughed so hard, she nearly cried. Their playful banter was such a refreshing change form their formerly stilted dysfunctional relationship, both were reluctant to let it end. But somehow, an unknown urgency pushed its way to the surface. Kitty sensed her window of opportunity for answers would only be open for so long, so she pressed her advantage.

"So – you really think I'm beautiful? How come you never told me that before, or anything even remotely resembling a compliment?" Her words were little more than a whisper as if she were afraid to disturb Sophia's uncharacteristically light-hearted mood. She desperately wanted – no, *needed*, to believe her mother's kind words. She had spent a lifetime waiting for even the slightest scrap of encouragement from the woman, only to be disappointed by her harsh criticisms time and time again.

"I don't honestly know why I was always so miserly with my affections. I'm sorry, dear. I'm afraid it took my unexpected death for me to have the scales removed from my eyes. I wasn't a very nice person in my old life, Katherine." As if sensing Kitty wanted to interrupt, Sophia rushed on, talking more rapidly. "No – no, it's true and I accept that. You don't need to agree or disagree with me. I know what I was like. But for the record, Katherine … I really am sorry."

Sophia looked away and Kitty saw her visibly swallow past the lump in her throat. She quickly recovered and pushed on. "I wish I could go back and do everything differently with you and your brother and sister. I *am … sorry.*" Sophia stopped again, this time searching Kitty's sad, needy eyes.

Unsure whether her mother was waiting for absolution, Kitty's conscience lingered between old hurts and her unfulfilled need for her mother's love. Those two little words, *I'm sorry*, stirred Kitty's simmering emotions.

It started as a small tremor around her fragile heart at first. It was the breaking down of the wall she'd erected in defense of her mother's rejection, until a giant earthquake of forgiveness shook her to her center. Kitty brought both hands up to cover her face and sobbed.

Sophia stood quietly on the other side of the bridge, not talking, merely listening and watching her daughter's suffering. Sophia cried her own tears, only hers were tears of shame, guilt and regret. It was a few moments before either woman spoke. Kitty was the first to break the silence.

She took a deep breath to fortify herself before she spoke. "So, that's it, Mother? That's really all you've got after your two years here?"

Kitty slipped back into her insolent, unforgiving attitude, shocked at herself that it had been so easy a transition from only moments ago. Deep down, she knew she wanted to forgive her mother, and she knew herself well enough to know that forgiveness was the right thing to do. But for some unexplained reason, Kitty needed a couple more laps in the pity pool. Just a few more minutes treading water in the deep end of misery couldn't hurt.

Kitty had worn her anger towards her mother like a heavy winter coat. She'd been wrapped up in it for such a long time she was reluctant to part with it. It had all the feelings of a security blanket. She was terrified she'd be lost without it. But still ... this *was* her mother.

Sophia appeared stricken as if she'd been slapped. She drew her shoulders back a slight degree and stood ready looking like she was willing to accept whatever Kitty dished out.

"You've got every right to be upset with me, Katherine. I know I was a bad mother. There I said it. Is that what you're waiting to hear?" Kitty remained silent, offering only a non-committal shrug. "I'm quite certain I'm one of those women who really should never have had children, but in my day and age, we weren't encouraged to question tradition. In my defense, all I can offer is that it was very hard for me to give something to my children that I myself never possessed. My parents were very strict with me – very undemonstrative with their affections. I never received much love as a child, so naturally I found it hard to give something to others that I knew nothing about. I never heard my parents tell me they loved me – not once in my whole life. I grew up thinking that was what families did. I passed that inadequacy onto my children and for that I'm deeply regretful." Sophia waited for some kind of response from Kitty. Her fleeting glance at Kitty was hopeful.

Kitty hugged herself around the waist, shielding herself from her mother's confession. The lighthearted banter from only moments ago completely forgotten, replaced with a smoldering hostility.

"Why couldn't you have tried to be different then? I grew up thinking you hated me my whole life. You made me hate myself, Mother." Kitty winced at her own words as if they were revealing more than she'd wanted. Thoughts swirled around inside her head, pounding their point home, again and again like an annoying muscle tic that you wished would stop, but won't.

"I thought because you hated me, I was totally undeserving of love. I thought there was something wrong with me because my own mother despised me. My whole life, those thoughts and feelings clung to me like a heavy anchor dragging me down. *What's wrong with me that my own mother – my flesh and blood, can't stand me?* Do you know what that does to a person or how that feels?" Kitty's pain erupted in a new flood of anguished tears.

Sophia dropped her head to her chest before she bravely looked up searching Kitty's face. "Yes, Katherine. I know exactly how that feels. I think I duplicated my relationship with my own parents — my mother especially, with you three children. I felt justified. Anger and resentment were my lifelong constant companions. After a time, I got so used to carrying around all that animosity, that it became a familiar weight on my shoulders. I couldn't let go of my bitterness. Old habits are very hard to break. And, I didn't have the same kind of faith you have. I had no hope." Sophia finished, looking somewhat deflated.

"Without faith it's impossible to please God, so how is it you ended up here, Mother?" Kitty stretched out her arms and turned in a wide circle, reminding her mother of where they were. "I know this isn't Hell. It's too beautiful and perfect to be anything other than a paradise. I've met Grace. She's an angel of God, to be sure. How is it that you didn't go to Hell for all of your bitterness and unforgiveness? Without Christ as your Savior you were doomed to be cast into the lake of fire for all eternity."

Blast it all, she wanted answers, and she wanted them now. Kitty placed her hand upon the railing again and put one step on the first board of the bridge to cross over.

Sophia screamed out a warning. "NO! Not yet, Katherine. Please, don't come any closer!"

TWENTY-TWO

Kitty did as ordered and stepped back, waiting. "Why?"

"I'm here in this place because of you!" Sophia's word became desperate, almost frantic. "You and Luke and your children ... all of you and you're prayers for me! You're all what saved me from an eternity in Hell. I'm here because you never gave up on me! Your faith, your last prayer for me, God's mercy, all combined to save me." Sophia placed her hand over her heart. "When you placed your hand over my heart that last night, heat radiated throughout my body. The fact that you still wanted to pray for me after I'd said such horrible things to you. You're simple prayer melted my heart. And then your words to me ..." Sophia was caught up with her recollections. "Do you remember what you said to me right before you left me?"

Kitty shook her head as a new batch of tears from her never-ending wellspring cascaded down her cheeks. "I said, 'I love you, Momma. Please don't die. Don't leave me yet, I still need you.'" Kitty wiped her tears and runny nose with the bottom of her tee shirt.

Sophia dashed away her own tears. "That's right. You hadn't called me 'momma' since you were a little girl. The desperation in your voice – that really got to me. When you left me that night, I was completely broken. Rock bottom – if you will. I'd spent most of my life convinced I was undeserving of anything good, and then you showed me that you loved me even though I didn't deserve it, and I felt *His* tug. I knew my condition was serious and that the surgery was dangerous. A person can't argue with those kinds of odds, can they? I asked God to watch over me … to forgive me … and take care of me for all eternity. *Your* Savior became *my* Savior that night, Katherine. When I say I'm 'eternally grateful' to you, I sincerely mean it. Thank you for loving me enough to bring me here."

Kitty threw her head back and stared up at the deep blue sky for a few seconds composing her thoughts, cataloging her hurts. Lowering her head, she glanced around scanning the lush green grass beneath her feet, but not really focusing on anything in particular. She followed the flight of a butterfly before it skittered away. She closed her eyes and inhaled deeply the sweet aroma of wildflowers. She kept her eyes closed as she answered her mother.

"Some days – I hated you. But deep down, I loved you as intensely as I hated you. I just wanted you to love me in return." Kitty's eyes opened, locking with her mother's sad dark eyes. "Throughout my life, you were the voice in my head that steered all my relationships like a giant negative compass. All I ever wanted was one word of approval."

Sophia choked on a tortured sob.

"Luke finally convinced me you weren't capable of giving me what I wanted because you simply didn't know how. He was such a smart man." Kitty's eyes softened at the mention of her husband's name.

"Yes, he was. I always liked him. I'm sorry I never told you that." Sophia's apology flowed naturally – a surefire sign that she'd definitely been reborn. Apologies were another first for Sophia.

"Well, I can't take all the credit for marrying such a great guy. It seems as though fate had a hand in our being together. Thank the good Lord for that. I had a very blessed life in spite of your treatment of me, Mother."

Sophia smiled, "I'm glad, Katherine."

"When I prayed with you that last night we were together, I left your room feeling like a total failure – as a daughter, as a Christian. But despite that, I still loved you, Mother. I know that in my own strength I couldn't love you if it weren't for God. He makes all things possible. When I left you that night, I prayed for forgiveness for all my years of bitterness towards you. I didn't want to carry it around with me anymore. I released you to God and asked Him to take away that constant pain of the unfulfilled relationship I had with you. For the last two years I've been tormented by the idea of you going to Hell. I did everything I thought I could do while you were alive to help you find salvation, and yet I was powerless to control your eternity. Ultimately, I knew the decision had to be yours. I couldn't choose salvation for you. You had to choose it for yourself."

Sophia crooked her mouth in a half-smile. "That's some burden you've been carrying around the last couple of years. I wish I could have put your mind at rest. I'm sorry I made your life so hard, Katherine. None of it was your doing. It was all my fault. Even with your father. That was mostly my fault."

"Daddy? What about him?"

"I should never have kept you from having a relationship with him. I was so hurt by his infidelity; I thought it was my right to keep him from you children. He wanted to be the one to raise you three, but I put a stop to it. When I kept you from him, I knew that would hurt him worse than anything. It felt good to hurt him in that way. You always were his favorite, you know?" Sophia's eyes twinkled as if sharing a preciously guarded secret.

"I was? I didn't know that. I mean, I kind of thought that maybe … you always said he didn't want anything to do with us anymore – that he no longer loved us."

"In my bitterness, that's what I needed you to believe. I'm sorry for that. He really was a good man. Still is – I'm sure. I hope you made amends with him and made things right between the two of you while you had the chance." Sophia sighed, rubbing her hands together. "You know, Henry was ten times the man Walter was."

At the mention of her stepfather's name, Kitty grimaced like she suddenly had a bad taste in her mouth. She instantly turned away and became defensive. She hugged herself wanting to trap the pain inside. "I'd rather we not talk about him, Mother." Kitty couldn't even bring herself to say his name out loud.

"Oh, Katherine, please turn around and look at me."

Kitty slowly turned to face her.

"I need to tell you about Walter, but I can't even think of how to explain him. He was … well, Walter was a means to an end. When I demanded custody of you children, I did it for revenge, but I really had no idea how on earth I was ever going to provide for you financially. I considered myself lucky when a man – *any man* – wanted to marry me. With the burden of three children to care for, I jumped at the chance Walter offered me. He was different from your father, but he was a good provider in the beginning, so it was easy to overlook his drinking and other problems." Sophia stopped and waited.

Shame and embarrassment caused her mother's cheeks to redden quite noticeably. Sophia avoided looking Kitty square in the eyes. She felt bad for her mother and her obvious discomfort.

"Did you know, Mother? Did you know what he was *really* like? With me?" Kitty held her breath.

Sophia stared at the ground and was quiet for so long, Kitty wasn't sure if she'd heard her or not. Finally she raised her head and shoved a nervous hand through her slightly graying hair.

"Yes, Katherine. I knew about Walter."

Kitty gasped in shock.

"I had suspicions after our first few years together. You were always very standoffish with Walter. You hated to be left alone with him. It wasn't until years later that I figured it out. After your children were born I pieced it all together. It was your reluctance to let the children come visit us. I knew you let your children go for weekend visits with Luke's parents. I was hurt you never let your children out of your sight when you came to visit at our house. When you and Luke went to Hawaii for your 10th wedding anniversary and you let the children stay with their other grandparents for a week … well, I was hurt. I put two and two together. I knew Walter had a pornography addiction he kept cleverly hidden away. I chose to ignore that side of his personality." Sophia shook her head. Whether at her husband's bad habit or her own denial of it, Kitty couldn't be sure.

"You have to understand, Katherine, that at my age, I was afraid of growing old alone. Walter was the lesser of two evils. Did I already say that? Oh well, no matter," she waved her hand like she was shooing a fly away.

Kitty nearly smiled as she recognized her own mannerisms in her mother.

"Coming from the generation that I did, women didn't divorce *twice*. It just wasn't done. It was completely unthinkable. So I chose to stay with a man I didn't like very much rather than end up as fodder for the gossip-mongers and to avoid growing old all alone." Sophia bit her lip in much the same fashion Kitty did when she was thinking something through.

"But you wasted your whole life with a man you didn't love? For what, Mother? Security? You had me and Wesley and Maria. We would have helped you."

Sophia's false bravado wavered at Kitty's suggestion. "I couldn't expect you three to help me after the way I treated all of you. I didn't deserve your help. In my way of thinking, Walter was a lifetime penance I was forced to serve."

"Penance? For what? What could you possibly have done to deserve a lifetime of misery in a loveless marriage?"

"There are so many things you don't know about me, Katherine. Things I'd be too ashamed to share with you. Let's just say I didn't believe I deserved to be loved and leave it at that."

"Nothing could have been bad enough to bind you to lifelong bitterness and unhappiness? Help me understand … *please*."

Kitty wanted to race across the bridge and hug her mother. Instead, it became a contest of wills to stay put and hold her ground.

"Oh, Katherine," she sighed a resolute sound of defeat. "I didn't … well, I …" she hesitated. "I wasn't what you would call a nice girl when I married your father. I had a bad reputation and a few skeletons in my closet when we married."

"Tell me," Kitty pressed. Her eyes were filled with such unquestioning compassion, that Sophia relented.

"Well, for starters, I had a *Walter* of my own in my past. Only his name was Gio and he was my uncle. I was only 13 when he approached me the first time. He took advantage of me. When I was 15, he got me pregnant. My mother found out and took me to stay with her sister in Chicago until the baby was born. She blamed me — said it was my fault, that I'd seduced my uncle. I was worried that she was right. After the baby was born, I returned to New Jersey and my mother enrolled me in a Catholic school. I never knew what happened to my son. No one told me anything about him. I met your father when I was 17. He was wild and reckless and everything my mother hated. Out of rebellion, I married him as soon as I was 18, much the same way you married your first husband at that age." Sophia's shoulders visibly relaxed after finally revealing her secret.

"Is that it? You were sexually abused as a young girl and then bore a baby out of wedlock. Do you seriously think that was enough to sentence you to a lifetime of living in an emotional prison?" Kitty looked incredulous. "Oh, Mother, God's grace would have set you free. What happened to you was terrible. It's beyond terrible and it never should have happened. But you were a victim. You didn't ask for any of that, regardless of what your mother may have told you. God's mercy could have set you free. You could have had such a different life."

"Perhaps. There was no one for me to turn to, though. I became what my mother accused me of: a *bad girl*. I could have made choices to change my life while I was at Catholic school, but I made a decision to be as rebellious as I could. When I gave away my son – it did something to me. It crippled a part of me. It didn't matter that he was the result of a rape. He was still my baby. Good mothers don't give away their babies. I should have fought to keep him and I didn't. So you see, I really did deserve the life I ended up with, because I made the choice by not fighting for him."

"But you were only 15. You weren't emotionally equipped to make that kind of decision nor to take care of a baby at that age."

Sophia shook her head, refusing Kitty's understanding. "I know that now. But back then ..."

I'm sorry, Mother. I'm not buying it. Okay, being forced to give your baby away – well, I'll give you that. That sucked. But *you* sentenced yourself to a lifetime of hell on earth. You didn't have to carry all that shame and your secrets around your whole life. That's what forgiveness is all about. You were a victim in a nightmare, just as I was a victim of Walter's abuse. But I made the choice to forgive him and move on with my life. You could have done the same instead of letting the bitterness eat away at you the same way the cancer ate away at you at the end of your life. God's grace and His death on the cross were bigger than all of your shame and unforgiveness. You could have lived a life filled with love and peace. I tried to tell you that on more than one occasion, but you called me a religious fanatic. I prayed for you for so many years. My friends, Luke, the kids – we all prayed for you. You didn't have to choose to live that way."

Kitty grieved for all of her mother's disappointments and tragedies and for her sad, wasted life. Just over the ridge beyond her mother, Kitty noticed a bright glow rising up from the horizon.

Sophia turned her head to follow Kitty's stare. She became anxious and spoke more quickly. "Don't you think I know all that now? The good news is that with God, it's never too late. Or at least in my case, it wasn't. He waited for me to say yes to Him before He brought me home. I'm thankful you and your family never stopped praying for me. I owe you everything."

The glow of light drew nearer becoming more intense. Sophia kept looking over her shoulder as if to do so would slow its progress. "Oh, Katherine, there's still so much I wanted to say to you. So many things to talk about and share, but I'm afraid it's very nearly time."

Kitty grew fearful. "Time for what, Mother? What's happening?"

Sophia turned to leave. Kitty screamed. "Momma, don't go! Please stay with me!"

"I'm sorry, my sweet daughter. You are so precious to me! If I've learned anything at all since I've been here, it's a newfound sweetness and joy that can only come from God himself. I can't undo the past, but I can leave you with the love I've found. It's time for me to go, Katherine. I ..." Sophia paused and smiled at her daughter. "I love you, Kitty. I love you so much, baby girl! I always did but could never say it. I'm sorry."

Sophia waved and blew a kiss. To Kitty, her mother had never looked more beautiful. It was a picture Kitty would carry with her forever. Sophia walked away with a skip in her step. She turned, stopping for one final look over her shoulder before she was swallowed up by the bright glow of light.

TWENTY-THREE

Kitty stepped back in terror, searching for a hiding place. Her legs shook so violently she was unable to move much beyond her spot near the bridge. She was terrified by the approaching glow of light.

"Grace," she cried out. "Where are you? I'm scared. I need you." She looked around frantically, searching for something familiar — anything she could hold on to.

Grace was suddenly beside her, wrapping her arm around Kitty's waist in a comforting squeeze. Mercy joined them and sat down on the other side at Kitty's feet.

"See, dear. You are safely nestled between Mercy and Grace."

Kitty looked from one to the other. "I know, Grace. But I'm still afraid. Please don't leave me again!" Kitty pleaded.

Grace hugged her, whispering in her ear. "Remember, Katherine … *God has not given unto you a spirit of fear. But of power and love and of a sound mind.* You'll be fine, I promise. It's time."

Grace kissed her gently, first on one cheek, then the other and moved to cross the bridge. She beckoned Mercy to join her. Kitty felt cemented to her spot, incapable of fleeing, unsure what to do next. She was so focused on wringing her hands she barely took notice of the transformation to her appearance. Glancing down, she was simultaneously dumfounded, yet relieved to see a beautiful gossamer gown had replaced her sweat stained exercise clothes and worn out running shoes. Kitty grabbed the skirt of her ivory gown encrusted with tiny seed pearls, and gave her hips a little swish causing the material to dance around her ankles.

"Oh thank goodness," she sighed in relief. "At least my clothes won't embarrass me. That's one less thing to freak out over."

Grace beckoned Mercy a second time, but the dog refused to obey Grace's command and chose instead to remain at Kitty's side. Kitty knelt down until she was eye level with her furry friend. She rubbed Mercy's velvety soft ears vigorously. She threw her arms around the dog, drawing strength and comfort from her beloved companion. As Kitty stood to her full height, Mercy stood on her hind legs and plopped two overly large paws on Kitty's shoulders. Mercy swabbed Kitty's face with her long pink tongue. Kitty hugged the dog again, kissed her snout and felt her nervous stomach calm somewhat.

Grace crossed over the bridge and as it was with Sophia, she too was swallowed up in the blinding light. Kitty heard muffled voices and gentle laughter and was instantly buoyed by the sound.

"Mercy, come!"

Both Kitty and Mercy turned their heads in unison at Grace's gentle command. Before Mercy crossed the bridge to follow, the wonderful big dog turned and delighted Kitty with a farewell bark and a yip. Kitty could have sworn she heard the words, *don't be afraid*, in Mercy's dismissal, but she might have only imagined it. Anything was possible at this point. She heard a deep voice greeting Mercy, more gentle laughter and Mercy's eager responding bark followed by a couple of playful woofs. The dog's reply lit Kitty's face with a tender smile filling her with hope. It gave her a warm feeling to know that her beloved dog was also loved and appreciated by the Son of God himself.

She took several short breaths to calm her nerves and queasy stomach. In her head she zeroed in on a fragment of Scripture that seemed to come from a forgotten corner of her mind. *Peace I leave with you; my peace I give you. Do not let your hearts be troubled and do not be afraid.*

"Don't be afraid, Kitty. Don't be afraid," she repeated over and over.

In all of her years as a believer, she'd tried to envision her initial reaction to meeting her Savior face-to-face when the appointed time arrived. She and Luke talked at length about how they thought they'd behave in the presence of Jesus. Kitty fantasized that she'd approach eagerly, with just the right amount of trepidation and humility. Luke always joked that he'd be the one who would greet Jesus blubbering like a baby, because "real men have deep feelings too," he'd say. Now that her moment of actual introduction was upon her, Kitty froze. She didn't want to embarrass herself at this auspicious meeting. The last thing she wanted to do was shame her Lord.

Unable to move from her spot and spying no haven to run to, she dropped to her knees and bowed low to the ground in a classic *duck and cover* move. She crouched in a tight ball, her face resting upon her clasped hands. She dared a peek and saw the glow move and stop in the middle of the bridge. Kitty pulled her head in again like a frightened turtle cowering in its shell. *Don't be afraid, Kitty*, she reminded herself for the umpteenth time.

Her brain was a jumble of thoughts. Her mind tumbled with Old Testament Scriptures. She marveled at how easily the words floated back to her. She recalled stories of God leading his people in the desert guiding them by a giant cloud during the day and a pillar of fire at night. *Lord, that little trick would sure come in handy,* she thought. It would certainly cut down on the some of the guesswork of life.

Kitty remembered the story of Moses descending Mt. Sinai after spending 40 days and nights with God, and of how God had talked with him face-to-face like old friends. *Are you my friend, Lord? Am I yours? Oh please ... be my friend.*

Kitty also remembered that peppered throughout the Old Testament were stories of people who were punished by God's wrath as well.

Fear not. Do not be afraid, Kitty.

How was she supposed to feel and act right now? Every part of her body quaked with fright at the unknown. She knew her Bible well enough to know that even though God was slow to anger, He was capable of wiping out entire nations with a mere command.

Fear not Kitty.

He could calm the wind and the rain in an instant or bring the dead back to life with a touch or a whisper. So many contradictions! He was all powerful ... all knowing ... omnipotent ... and yet - He was standing eight feet in front of her!

Fear not.

Kitty was excited and terrified all at the same time. From somewhere a line of Scripture surfaced, but she couldn't recall where she'd read it. *"O give thanks unto the Lord, for His mercy endures forever."* She repeated it slowly in her head. *"O give thanks unto the Lord, for His mercy endures forever."* She said it over and over again, thankful that when she needed it the most, the Word of God was now a light unto her feet.

"Thank you, Lord." Kitty felt a rush of gratitude. "Thank you, Father."

Not daring to look up, she remained crouched on the ground, her tears washing her clasped hands as she repeated the Scripture again and again like a mantra. The words worked their way out of her head and found a voice. Quiet at first, they rose in boldness. The louder Kitty proclaimed the words, *"O give thanks unto the Lord, for His mercy endures forever,"* the more the glowing presence surrounded her. She felt safely cocooned, tucked snuggly in a circle of comfort.

Love and warmth combined for the perfect marriage of God's compassion. It began as a slow metamorphosis, until they filled the air around her and became part of the landscape. The trees, the grass, the bubbling crystal spring, the flowers – everything – all cried out in love for the Savior.

At the name of Jesus, every knee shall bow; every tongue confess, that Jesus Christ is Lord.

She felt a gentle pressure on her shoulder – the heat of the touch pulsated through her body all the way to the soles of her feet. She grew still and waited, holding her breath.

"Katherine, arise." The voice was deep and commanding, yet tender and compassionate.

Kitty pushed herself up on wobbly limbs, but dared not look into His face. Her boldness from only moments ago as she recited Scripture suddenly deserted her, leaving her broken.

"*Look at me, Kitty. I want to see your face,*" He commanded.

Kitty kept her head bowed and let her curtain of wavy hair protect her from his prying eyes. "I can't look at you, Lord. I'm so unworthy," she stammered in a shaky voice.

"*Please, child. Let me see you,*" He said with patient persistence.

"Please, Lord. I'm so ashamed. I'm afraid to look at you and see your disappointment in me. I have been such a failure," Kitty whispered in a rush.

He reached out his long arm and ever so gently placed His hand under her chin, tipping it upward. Kitty's first initial reaction at seeing Jesus face-to-face rendered her mute. All she could think of were the hundreds of pictures she'd seen depicting Jesus' appearance. She realized that none of the pictures or artwork even came close to capturing His true character. He didn't look anything like she'd imagined! He was abundantly better than anything her own imagination or an artists rendering could ever devise.

He was quite simply – *perfect*!

He was all things beautiful she'd ever seen with the naked eye; a newborn baby, the Ocean, the Grand Canyon, vibrant sunrises, glorious sunsets, and a star-filled night sky. He was all that majesty rolled into one magnificent, consummate being. Everyone and everything now paled miserably in comparison to her Lord. He was the embodiment of every extraordinary adjective magnified about a million times over.

Kitty looked into His eyes and felt completely exposed – naked all the way to her center. His eyes pierced her to her very soul. She felt certain He would find her lacking. She held her breath waiting for His judgment. But there was none. Only love.

"*How have you failed me, Kitty?*" He asked.

"In so many ways, Lord. In everything. My list is endless. I haven't been the best wife or mother … or daughter. I've disappointed so many people. I had so much anger and hatred in me for so long while pretending my life was fine, but it wasn't." Kitty discovered that once she found her voice, her confessions poured forth like a levee spilling its banks after a torrential flood.

"I lived a lie for so many years. I was a big fat hypocrite. I didn't love people the way I should have. I didn't appreciate what you died to give me, Lord. I was completely selfish and self-absorbed. I spent more time and energy worrying about me and all of the stupid things going on in my own little world, that I ignored the needs of others. I wanted to be more like you, but I continually fell so short. I'm not perfect. I didn't even come close, Lord. I'm sorry. I'm so, so sorry." Shamed flooded her at her long list of sins.

"Kitty, have you lost your senses? You cannot become perfect by your own human effort – just because you will it. It is impossible for you." He smiled then.

Kitty felt only minor relief over His words. She looked down at her toes that were now exposed in delicate jeweled sandals, before she found the nerve to defend herself.

"Then how could you love me? How could you love any of us if we all fall so short of what we should be? Why would you die for people who constantly disappoint you and hurt you – and reject you?" Kitty asked in confusion.

"Because I AM LOVE, and all that love implies. All that Love was created for – I Am."

The simplicity of His answer gave Kitty a modicum of peace. "But *me*, Lord, I'm a nothing – a nobody. Just an ordinary woman. Why would you care so much for me?"

"Kitty, I was sent into the world so that everyone who believes in me could have eternal life. If you had been the only person standing on Calvary the day I was crucified, I would still have gladly made the sacrifice for you. I love you that much." His response brooked no further discussion or argument.

Kitty cried softly at His words. She'd read the words dozens of time in her Bible, but they sounded so different coming from the mouth of the One who not only had inspired them and lived them, but died for them as well.

"You would?" she asked in utter disbelief.

"Yes, child."

"But, Lord, there's more. You wouldn't say that if you knew everything. There's something you should know. I've only just realized it myself. It's the one thing that you won't be able to forgive me for." She looked away, pain twisting her face.

"Tell me, daughter. What is it that you've left unsaid?"

"I see now what it was that Grace kept insisting I was holding on to. It's a terrible sin that carries with it monumental consequences. I've been so stupid!"

He patiently waited, reached down and clasped her hand in both of His. That slight show of affection infused her with the strength to continue.

"I know, Katherine. I know." When he offered nothing further, Kitty turned her head, searching His eyes. The use of her full name wasn't lost on her, but there was no reprimand in His voice, only kindness.

"You do?"

"Yes, Kitty. I know. But you must confess it – not for my sake, but for yours."

"Oh, Father. Please don't make me say it out loud. It's too awful to speak it," she cried in desperation.

"It's not only yourself that you've hated all these years, is it, my child?"

She looked up and in that instant as she searched His face, she knew that there were no secrets hidden from Him. She shook her head in shame. She swallowed, forcing her voice to be released from behind the giant lump of self-loathing lodged in her throat.

"I blamed ..." she didn't think she could bring herself to admit her confession out loud, even though He already knew what she was going to say. Even though He already knew the ugliness of what was hiding in her heart.

"Aggghhhh! Oh God! I blamed you for not making things right between me and my mom! I blamed you because my own mother didn't love me! I blamed you for what happened to me with Walter! You could have stopped him and you didn't! You let him kill my dog! You're God and you're supposed to be able to do anything, but you didn't protect me! I was a little girl. My dad went away and left me and you didn't bring him back, even though I begged you for years! You didn't fix things and I ... I hated ... you!"

233

The last was said through great heaving spasmodic sobs. She pulled away and turned to run away from Him wanting to cower from her own harsh words and criticisms. She wanted to hide from the guilt she'd been storing inside her since she was a very little girl.

"I'm sorry, Lord. To harbor hatred for God is an unpardonable sin. I don't deserve to be forgiven. I don't deserve to go to Heaven."

He cut her short with his words. *"Kitty, do you really think you've surprised me by revealing your feelings? I've always known your heart and your struggle. Today I offer you the gift of forgiveness. But in order for you to be completely forgiven, you must accept my gift. Can you take this gift I offer you?"*

Too shocked and overwhelmed to speak, she shook her head yes and cried like the lost little girl she'd been for so many years. What she had been waiting for and searching for her whole life was standing right in front of her. He was her Lord – her Savior, and He was the embodiment of total forgiveness.

He closed the distance separating them and did the one thing she'd secretly dreamed of for as long as she could remember. He wrapped His huge loving arms around her, pulled her close and let her cry as she unleashed a lifetime of misery. Kitty sank into His bear hug. She buried her face against His massive chest and squashed her ear against the beating of His heart.

The Heart of God.

She stretched her arms around Him as far as they would reach and let Him swallow her in the solid rock of His comfort. For the first time in her entire life, Kitty felt totally safe and completely protected. She felt utterly loved and accepted. And more importantly, she felt absolute forgiveness. She thought her heart would explode with the intensity of the emotions and the magnitude of total surrender. Kitty cried. And then she cried some more. She cried more tears than she thought were humanly possible. Through all her tears – Jesus held her close. He rubbed her back, whispering words of understanding. Kitty never wanted it to end. It was without measure, the most wonderful moment of her entire existence. *Jesus Christ, God's son loved HER.*

TWENTY-FOUR

Kitty's tears began to subside. Her sobs were replaced with little hiccups of indrawn breaths. She hated to pull away, but unanswered questions burned to be asked. An audience with the Creator was a once in a lifetime opportunity she dared not waste.

Kitty pulled away reluctantly. He brushed her hair back away from her face and gently wiped the trails of remaining tears. He stretched out His hands and took a step back, smiling.

"You've nearly toppled the banks of the stream, Kitty. Look how full it's flowing now." He turned and bid her to take notice of the brook at their feet.

"I don't understand, Lord." Kitty hiccupped.

"Look, child. I have captured your tears and saved them. This is your stream, Kitty." He grasped her hand in His and guided her along the bank of the crystal shimmering water. They walked slowly along the edge of the brook. *"This is a lifetime of your shed tears, Kitty. I have seen every tear that has flowed from your beautiful emerald eyes. I have heard your every prayer … your every worry … every anguished cry has been recorded. I have saved them for you. Dip your hand in the stream of your shed tears, Kitty and be refreshed."*

They stopped and knelt down together in the sweet smelling grass. He cupped His strong hands for her. He scooped a handful of the icy cold water into his scarred carpenter's hands and offered it to her. *"It's okay, child. Drink deeply of the waters of life and love."*

Kitty placed her hands, tiny in comparison to His, around his cupped hands and leaned over. She drank deeply of the iciness of the pristine water. The liquid was so intensely cold it burned her esophagus as it journeyed through her body. Kitty drank her fill, letting the pure water cleanse her soul from the inside out. Finally she sat back on her haunches and wiped the numbness of her chin with the back of her hand.

"That was the best thing I've ever tasted," she said, closing her eyes and relishing the renewal of her spirit.

He stood up and offered His outstretched hand to assist her from her crouch. She looked up and placed her hand in His and hopped to her feet.

"I feel wonderful! Better than wonderful, in fact!" She beamed. "I don't remember ever feeling this happy or peaceful – or whole. Thank you," she whispered shyly.

I'm sorry you couldn't feel this peace sooner, Kitty. It was always yours for the taking. I had so many gifts and blessings available for you from the moment you said 'Yes' to me. I've loved you from the beginning of time."

They turned and slowly retraced their steps to the footbridge.

"I know I've read all of that in your Word, but yet I couldn't believe I was worthy of your promises. I kept thinking I would get there *someday*, but I needed to work harder to make my way there." Kitty let Him guide her slowly, loving the feel of her hand in His.

"There is no fine print in my word, Kitty – no footnotes that excluded you from receiving the fullness of my mercy. You can't earn your way into my favor. You can't buy your way into my graces. You don't get extra credit by reading Scriptures each day or memorizing chapter and verse in my word. My word was meant for your comfort and your direction. An instruction manual for lighting your way. You had all of my promises at your disposal; all of my power was available to you when you entered into a relationship with me. Just by the admission of your sins and your willingness to repent of those sins, I gave you access to all that is mine."

Though the distance they needed to cover to return to the bridge was slight, their slow pace didn't bring them any nearer to their destination. Kitty marveled at this anomaly.

She turned her head to study his face before she voiced her further concerns. "See, that's what I'm talking about. Why would you continue to love me when I was so blind and stupid? I believed with all my heart every bit of your word for everyone that I ever prayed for. But yet, I couldn't make myself understand that your word applied every bit as much to *me* as it did to everyone else. I think because I harbored such blame towards you for the bad things that happened in my life, I felt like I'd crossed a line and wasn't worthy to call you *Lord*. But I knew that I couldn't survive without you. I felt like I had to earn my way back into your favor. I didn't expect to be forgiven like everybody else, because I thought my sin was much worse than everybody else. I suffered in silence with my inner demons. My lifetime of penance ..."

"Your lifetime of penance," He spoke the words at exactly the same moment she did.

Kitty's words trailed off as He spoke them with her. Her mother's words echoed in her mind. Understanding dawned. She was the same as her mother; living with a lifetime of guilt, trying to make up for circumstances that happened during her childhood for things that weren't her fault. The difference being that Sophia made no excuses for herself, while Kitty argued that she had faith and forgiveness, when in fact, she was unable to operate in them.

"I always felt like I was defective – like there was something wrong with me. I was certain I was the only person who ever must have felt the way I did."

"Kitty, I didn't omit something in you that I gave to everyone else. I love you equally as much as I love all of my children. I have never looked at you and thought for a moment that I made a mistake when I created you. Your many gifts and talents have given me such joy." He squeezed her hand in reassurance and graced her with a warm smile.

"Gifts and talents? Hah! That's a good one!" She pulled away from him and turned away slightly, not daring to have him see the doubt written on her face. She hugged her mid-section and continued her slow, unhurried pace. "What are you talking about? I didn't do anything special. I am ... I *was* just a mom and a housewife," she corrected.

"Kitty, you are so much more than that. You have an enormous capacity for love for your husband and children. You have made countless sacrifices in order to provide your family with your attention and caring. You've made your house a safe haven for your husband and children to return home to each day. You've cooked, cleaned, counseled and disciplined. You've raised three godly, respectful children and equipped them with a strong spiritual foundation. Your love for your husband has honored your covenant with Me. Your tireless prayers for others, even strangers, have reached my ear. You have great tenacity and integrity ... I could go on and on if you'd like. **All** *that you've done in my name – has glorified Me."*

They stopped walking and He squared off to look into her eyes. Kitty faltered, shaking her head in doubt and unbelief.

"Yeah, but that's just who I was ... I'm nothing special. I didn't *do* anything for You like teachers or pastors or missionaries do."

Lifting his hand Heavenward, a multi-colored butterfly flittered about and landed on his outstretched tapered index finger. Kitty was shocked to see the raised scars on the insides of His wrists; the scars that were an obvious reminder of all that He had done for her making her acutely aware of her own failures.

"Because this beautiful creation of mine doesn't do anything but flit about, does that mean it has no purpose? That it offers nothing of value to me?"

The fingers on his hands circled one another like climbing rungs on a ladder as the butterfly danced back and forth on his digits. His movements increased in speed and tempo, as the butterfly became a kaleidoscope of brilliant colors dancing back and forth with his perfectly timed movements barely struggling to rest on each finger.

"Because Luke wasn't a pastor or great Bible teacher and simply went to work each day to provide for you and your children, do you think his worth and value is diminished in my eyes?"

Her eyes clouded with emotion at the mention of her husband. "No, of course not. Luke was an amazing husband. He worked hard to take care of us."

"Exactly. His hard work gave me pleasure. This lovely insect was created for my good pleasure. Nothing grand. Nothing special ... I think that's the term you used."

The movements of his hands stopped suddenly. The butterfly remained perched on his finger, which he drew close to his face for further examination. He gently rubbed his lips over the velvety softness of the bright blue wings and then extended his finger to Kitty. She touched her fingertip with His and the butterfly hopped onto her finger. She cupped her other hand around the delicate insect and brought it to her face, amazed that the butterfly did not fly away. Once the insect was close to her cheek, its wings whispered against her skin, making Kitty think of butterfly kisses. She smiled with pure joy, extended her hand and watched the insect flutter away in a flash of brilliant color.

"Not everyone is called to be a great teacher or minister of the gospel. Your husband was called to serve me by being a caring husband and provider. Not all men choose to do what Luke did. Not all women can be the kind of mother you were. Raising children is a ministry in and of itself, you know — especially in the day and age you lived in. Sticking it out rather than shirking responsibility ... that blesses me. You were called to serve me by simply being you, Kitty – wife, mother, mentor, and friend. For this season in your life, you are ... were, fulfilling my purpose and plan for your life. I did not ask you for more."

Kitty was speechless. There were no words to describe her feelings at His recitation of what she considered her "nothing accomplishments."

"But you didn't have to do any of those things to get me to love and accept you. I loved you already, Kitty. Doing all of those things in my name, only made me love you all the more." He drew her into an embrace, speaking clearly in her ear. *"Well done, my good and faithful servant. Well done, Kitty."* Pulling away from her, he kept his hands on her arms.

"Oh — my — goodness!" she sighed in little spurts. "I don't know what to say – *wow*." She covered her mouth in embarrassment. "I'm speechless. I never thought I did anything special. I was just being *me*."

"Yes, Kitty. You did all of that and more. You are my child. My special creation. You were never, just a mom, or just a wife. I grieved each time you belittled yourself because you didn't think

you mattered to me. All the times I heard your cries and your words of self-hatred, I cried with you. I loved you enough to die for you, Kitty. All of your years obsessing about your outer appearance … that's never mattered to me, child. Step back, Kitty and see what I see when I look at you."

He extended his arms and held her at arms length. As she stepped back, Kitty's body glowed with intense heat and light from every orifice. She looked down and couldn't see her arms or legs or any part of her physical body. In the center of her chest where her heart should be, she saw a pulsating orb. The light from her center burned so brightly, it blinded her to all else.

"Whoa! Is that my heart? Is that … *me*?" She was awestruck. "It's amazing! So beautiful! *I'm* beautiful! What a wonder!"

"Yes, Kitty. When I look upon you, I don't see you as you see yourself or even as others see you. I see your magnificent heart and your capacity for love. Even though you think you have fallen short in your love walk I know that you have a deep love for others. How many times have I heard you make the statement 'deep down in my heart of hearts'*? You were talking about your soul, Kitty. And you have a beautiful soul. That is what I see when I look at you – not the color of your skin or the shade of your eyes. I see nothing of your outer appearance. What you weigh or how you dress does not affect the way I feel about you. You assumed the way your parents felt about you, was the way I felt about you. That is a lie. Even if your mother or father abandoned you, I will always hold you close. I am your rock and your refuge. I will never leave you or forsake you. I have always been and ALWAYS will be – everything you will ever need."*

"Oh, Lord. Thank you is such an inadequate word to express my love and gratitude. I have no way to repay you for all that you've blessed me with. I wouldn't even know how to begin."

Suddenly Kitty heard the light strains of music floating on the breeze. She thought it was coming from just over the ridge. He moved around her and she had to turn a tight circle so as not to take her eyes off of him.

His smile lit his eyes and burned into hers. He pulled her close for another embrace. *"You're welcome, Katherine."*

"Seriously, how can I ever repay you? Especially for my mother. I can't believe she's here. You made her whole – and happy. That means more to me than words can even say."

"I know, Kitty. I don't expect you to repay me, so please stop worrying about that. Simply accept my gifts and love me completely. That's all I ask."

He reached for her hand and together they closed the distance to the footbridge. The music swelled around them like a choir of angels all singing together, becoming clearer with every step they took. Beyond the strains of the music, Kitty heard other noises – disturbing and chaotic. The noises frightened her.

"It's decision time, Kitty."

He looked deeply into her eyes. Kitty saw herself mirrored in his gaze and delighted that for that brief instant, her eyes reflected her father's eyes.

"What do you mean, Lord? What decision? Can't we talk for a while longer? I have about a million questions and you're the only one who can answer them," she begged. "I don't mean to sound so pushy, and I'm anxious to get on with the rest of this journey, especially now that some of the scary stuff is over, but just being here with you is so nice." The music and loud noises penetrated her thoughts. "What's beyond the bridge, Lord? Are you keeping all the secrets of the universe on the other side? Is that heaven over there, or is this it? Not that *this* isn't spectacular, mind you. But still ..." In her mind, she thought if she kept him talking and distracted, she wouldn't have to make the big decision he'd mentioned – whatever *that* might be.

"Yes, Kitty. Your eternity lies just over there. But you have to decide here and now, if you are ready for it."

"Well, of course I'm ready. Why wouldn't I be? Let's go." She tried to move around him and pull him with her. She placed one foot on the edge of the bridge. When she did, she felt herself go light-headed and her body swayed as if it had every intention of floating away.

"Wait my child. Are you sure?" He paused in thoughtful silence as the music and the chaotic noise swirled about them making Kitty's

head swim. She heard unfamiliar voices, but then in the midst of the noise, she heard Luke's panicked plea.

"Please! Don't stop! Do something! I can't lose her! She's my whole life! I love her ... Kitty ... Baby, please!" Luke's frantic cries intensified, drowning out the sounds of the music.

Luke's wasn't the only voice floating on the wind.

"Dear Lord, please save my mother! I love her! Please God!" Rebecca's voice rang out and joined the chorus.

"Father God in Heaven ... please – please save my mom!" Matthew's insistence pushed past the melodious words of praise.

Kitty pulled her foot back slowly, listening as her youngest daughter's cries pierced through the fog, stabbing her heart with stinging accuracy.

"In the name of Jesus, please let my momma be okay!" Sarah pleaded rising above the choir of angels.

And then a tiny small voice she didn't recognize, but knew instantly was the voice of her unborn grandchild. A tiny baby boy ... I love you Grandma. I can't wait to meet you!"

Rebecca was going to have a son! That precious baby's voice mingling with the cries of her husband and three children, drowned out all else until Kitty was forced to cover her ears and unleash her own tortured cry.

"Dear, Lord! Please make it stop! I love you so much – I really do! Thank you for everything that you've shown me! But, I love them! I'm sorry – but they need me! And I need them!" Kitty surrendered to a feeling of loss she'd never known before. "I'm sorry!"

"It's okay, Kitty. I understand. But before you go, you must understand what I have given you. Don't waste this experience. Make it your life's purpose to share this knowledge with others and tell them of my love. Tell them I died for them! Always remember, Kitty – I love you too! Go in peace, my daughter. Carry me close to your heart. Your father in heaven loves you!"

Kitty felt her body being propelled through a long dark tunnel. She was traveling headlong and being jettisoned back through a black hole – sucked through a vortex with no beginning and no end. What was her past ... now became her future. Kitty fought it, not understanding any of what was happening.

"Come on, Anderson! Think, man! How long has she been down?"

"Seven minutes, Doctor."

"DO IT! Charging paddles – three hundred! CLEAR!"

The shock of 300 volts of electrical current surged through Kitty's body like a bolt of lightning striking her chest. As the electric heat coursed through her, every fiber of her entire being cried out in rebellion. She gasped suddenly and coughed her alarm as her life breath was physically forced back into her lungs.

"We've got a rhythm! Her stats are coming up!"

A collective sigh of relief coupled with expressions of gratitude rang out amidst the throng of medical personnel, who all continued to work with practiced efficiency and all due diligence. The emergency room exploded with activity as they stabilized Kitty's vital signs, doing their medical best to keep her amongst the land of the living.

"Mrs. O'Connell! Are you with us?" An unidentified voice leaned over her. A myriad of hands poked, prodded and probed her everywhere.

Kitty fought to open her gritty eyes. She turned her head slightly to avoid the bright glare from the overhead lamp and the beam of a pencil thin flashlight waving in front of her eyes.

"Ouch," she croaked in a raspy whisper. "I'm here. Please don't do that shocky thing again," she groaned in obvious pain.

"Welcome back, Mrs. O'Connell! We thought we lost you there for a few minutes. You gave us quite a scare. I'm Dr. Chung. You're in very good hands. We've got someone here who's quite anxious to say hello to you." The doctor stepped back as Luke forced his way to his wife's bedside.

Luke's face loomed above her. His tears rained down and mingled with hers. "Oh, baby, baby, baby! Thank you, God! I thought I'd lost you. I love you, sweetheart. I love you! I love you so much!" He cried and laughed all at the same time, wanting desperately to cover every inch of her face with his kisses, but already a nurse was gently pushing him aside. He drank in every detail of her face, wanting to memorize every contour, every freckle, every fine line. He was grateful beyond words that she'd come back to him. The reality of how close he'd come to losing everything he held dear, nearly paralyzed him.

As efficient nurses hustled and bustled about like ministering angels, Luke was ushered aside and forced to leave the room. Kitty breathed deeply and wept grateful tears as she heard an explosion of her family's joyous shouts outside in the hall where they received news of her condition. With the swinging of the doors, the relieved voices of her family and friends could be heard offering prayers of thanksgiving for her miraculous recovery.

Kitty closed her eyes and wrestled with the lethargy threatening to claim her as if it waited to swaddle her like a warm towel fresh from the dryer. Dying was a physically exhausting ordeal, she thought. She sighed her relief and closed her eyes. As she lay there, she succumbed to her body's demand for rest and the inner peaceful feeling swathing her. But there was something more. Lying there surrounded by strangers, lost in her own feelings of unbelievable gratitude, she felt complete for the first time ever. Her thoughts danced riotously in her mind. *He knows all my faults and weaknesses ... He knows my every sin and shame ... yet – He still loves me! Thank you, Father for seeing me just as I am and loving me anyway and for letting me see myself through your eyes!*

"Oh give thanks unto the Lord for his mercy shall endure forever," she sighed in exhaustion. Kitty smiled and closed her eyes to sleep and dream.

EPILOGUE

One Year Later

"Ladies, ladies! Can I have your attention, please! Wasn't that a wonderful time of praise and worship? I can really feel the Holy Spirit in this place, can't you?" The speaker's words were met with a spontaneous round of applause. "Now ... in keeping with that Spirit, I'd like you to give a warm welcome to Katherine O'Connell. I had the privilege of hearing Katherine speak last month at a Women's Conference in Los Angeles and I think that you'll agree with me when I tell you that she has a remarkable testimony to share with you this evening. Katherine witnessed first hand a life-after-death experience that to my knowledge, has yet to be rivaled."

Collective "oohs" and "awws" could be heard throughout the room.

"Ladies, please help me welcome to the stage, Katherine O'Connell." The room erupted in excited hand clapping.

From her seat, Kitty took several slow calming breaths before she made her way to the stage. *Please be with me, Lord. You know I can't do this without your help. Let my words be your words. Use me to help these women come to know you more intimately than they have ever known you before. In your name I ask this, Amen.*

She finished her silent prayer and joined her hostess on the platform. Shaking the woman's hand, Kitty thanked her politely before taking her spot to the left of the podium. She cleared her throat and pretended to ignore the audience as she adjusted the seams in her black skirt and straightened her white silk blouse. She smoothed her jacket over her slim hips. Scanning the audience, she caught sight of her two daughters and her best friend, Dani and Dani's daughter, Tiffany, all sitting together in the front row. She smiled and winked in their direction before she began.

"Good evening, Ladies. Thank you for inviting me to your Women's conference this evening. I'm honored you asked me here to share my testimony with you."

Kitty relaxed her pose and draped one arm casually across the podium with such natural ease; a stranger might have mistakenly assumed she'd been a public speaker forever. She breathed deeply through her nose, expelling it in stingy little puffs.

"But before I begin, do you mind if I ask you all something?" She straightened her posture and turned from side-to-side and then pivoted around in a tight circle. "Does this skirt make my butt look big?"

The crowd twittered with nervous laughter. "What? Am I the only one who ever worries about the size of her behind?" Kitty looked completely innocent as she bent slightly at the waist, flipped her jacket up over her hips and pulled her skirt taut across her rear end. The crowd exploded with wild laughter and sudden applause.

"Come on, now … as women, if we're being honest, isn't that what we *all* are thinking at some point nearly every single day?" She surveyed her audience and saw women shaking their heads yes and whispering with one another with smirks and giggles. "Maybe the real question I need to ask you all is … does this coffin make my butt look big?" A huge photo of an open, silk-lined mahogany casket appeared on the screens stationed on either side of the stage. Uncomfortable twittering laughter could be heard around the room, until the voices quieted to a near dead silence.

Kitty looked down at the podium for a second and then grew serious. "That's not such a funny question, is it? One year ago I was clinically dead for seven minutes. And I learned more in those seven minutes of death than I learned in my 40+ years of life. One of the things I learned is that when it's time to measure you for a casket, your husband … your children … your family and friends aren't going to care one iota about how big you thought your butt was.

You could have enormous thunder thighs covered with cellulite – or as I like to refer to them, C.R.T.s, which stands for Charging Rhino Thighs, and nobody is going to notice them once they lay you out in that coffin.

"When they dress you in your Sunday best and lay you on those satin pillows, your family isn't going to be worried that they've chosen the wrong outfit to bury you in because the stripes make you look frumpy. No one is going to notice if you're bloated from P.M.S. or if you've just come off a three-day binge of Oreos and Pop-tarts. And you know why they won't care? Because all they're going to care about is that you are … d-e-a-d! Dead and gone!"

Kitty heard contagious murmurs spreading around the room. She gave them a few seconds to quiet before continuing.

"One year ago this week, after a stupid move on my part, I had an unfortunate accident while I was on my treadmill. I stupidly thought I was coordinated enough to eat a lollipop while I was running – running mind you, not just walking on a very fast moving treadmill. I tripped on my shoelace, fell backwards hitting my head on a dumb-bell with such force I bounced forward and jammed the sucker in my throat. And just to make sure I was good and dead, God decided I needed to have a minor heart attack while I was at it. I caution you ladies, do not try this at home. I definitely recommend that you make it a point to never eat while exercising." Nervous laughter floated all around. "I also recommend that if you're going to use a treadmill, take advantage of the safety clip – it's there for your protection. That's why they call it a *safety* clip. Contrary to what you may think, the safety clip is not just for whimps. That little piece of plastic could have saved my life. By the way, that's my consumer endorsement and good deed for the day."

More laughter.

"In addition, I'm here to caution you about your mouths and the sometimes stupid things we say without thinking. Things like … *I'm going to lose this last 10 pounds if it kills me!* Guard your tongues, ladies, because you might get exactly what you wish for."

Kitty noticed a nervous shifting of energy. She knew she'd struck a painful chord, but pressed on anyway.

"Seriously though, I have to confess that I'm not sorry I went through everything that I did. Sadly, it took something as catastrophic as death for me to come face-to-face with all of my obsessive-compulsive behaviors. My death forced me to deal with the years of emotional baggage I'd been carrying around. And it took seven minutes of death for me to realize exactly who I am in Christ."

Kitty paused to control the catch in her throat and the tears that threatened to spill over. "If it weren't for my death last year, I don't know that I would have ever truly understood just how much Jesus Christ loves me, and what He died to give me."

A lone tear escaped and skipped down her cheek. Kitty brushed it away and sought the faces of her daughters and friends, drawing comfort and strength from their smiles and tears. Rebecca and Sarah, Dani and Tiffany all wiped their own tears away. They smiled through their tears and splotchy faces and gave Kitty a thumbs-up and the courage to press on.

"Ladies … I'm here today to share with you the incredible story of my death and my rebirth … all in the hopes of making you realize that the Lord Jesus Christ loves each and every one of you, every bit as much as He loves me. And He loves you no matter how you look on the outside. God doesn't give a hoot about the size of your butt even if it's the size of a small township in Nebraska! He doesn't care if your jeans make you look fat or if you've got muffin tops pushing up and over the top of your bras. He flat out doesn't care!"

Laughter erupted and was followed by thunderous applause.

"Friends, I've seen how the Father looks at me through His eyes, and I am pleased to tell you that He thinks I'm beautiful! And guess what? You're going to love this … He thinks each and every one of you is beautiful as well! *God loves you!*"

Kitty paused for dramatic effect and made eye contact with as many women as possible before continuing. She repeated the phrase and pointed to women scattered all about the room.

"God loves you! And you! And you! I see you way back there by the snack table! God loves you too" Peels of giggles could be heard above the applause as Kitty pointed out women all around the crowded room. "GOD LOVES YOU!" Kitty's heart swelled with love for her heavenly Father at the positive response from the crowd as she spread her arms wide to encompass the group.

"Before I share with you all what death and Heaven are really like, I'd like to take a moment to thank the one who made my being here possible. Would you all mind bowing with me so we could all thank Him together, please."

All around the room, women bowed their heads to join Kitty. Many were unable to accept Kitty's proclamation of God's love. Gentle weeping, loud sniffling and nose blowing abounded throughout the auditorium. Teardrops flowed freely as the gathering of women listened expectantly to Kitty's sincere, heartfelt prayer.

She closed her eyes and blocked out the presence of all the women in the room. She drew in a long cleansing breath and let it out slowly. Kitty conjured up the image that had been burned deep into the core of her soul. The breathtaking image of her loving Savior as she remembered Him. He stood before her, love emanated all about Him, encircling the two of them. He embraced her and encouraged her. As usual, the vision brought with it a flood of tears. The love and gratitude she felt towards her heavenly father flowed from her and touched every person gathered in the meeting hall. Kitty glowed with the memory of his arms around her so that she radiated the love of Christ.

Slowly she began her prayer, gaining strength as her father's Spirit communicated His unconditional love for her.

"Precious Lord ... we want to offer you our thanks! Thank you for your love that you give so freely not only to me, but to all of my sisters gathered here today. We are so grateful that you love each of us the same and that you have no favorites. We are awed that you love us so unconditionally just as we are. Open our hearts to receive the message you have for us tonight – and please, Father, help each and every woman here to see themselves through your loving eyes ..."

*"But the Lord still waits for you to come to him so
He can show his love and compassion.
For the Lord is a faithful God.
Blessed are those who wait for him to help them."
Isaiah 30:18 (NLT)*

SCRIPTURE REFERENCES

The following is a list of referenced Scriptures found in *Her Father's Eyes*. Unless otherwise indicated, all references are taken from the New International Version Study Bible, (Copyright© 1995 by Zondervan Publishing House, Grand Rapids, Michigan 49530, USA)

1. For we must all stand before Christ to be judged. We will each receive whatever we deserve for the good or evil we have done in our bodies. (2 Corinthians 5:10 New Living Translation, Copyright© 1996 by Tyndale House Publishers, Inc., Wheaton, Illinois 60189 USA)

2. Set a guard over my mouth, O Lord, keep watch over the door of my lips. (Psalm 141:3)

3. Therefore we are always confident and know that as long as we are home in the body we are away from the Lord. We live by faith and not by sight. We are confident, I say, and would prefer to be away from the body and at home with the Lord. (2 Corinthians 5:6-8)

4. For he chose us in him before the creation of the world to be holy and blameless in his sight. In love he predestined us to be adopted as his sons through Jesus Christ, in accordance with his pleasure and will – to the praise of his glorious grace, which he has freely given us in the One he loves. (Ephesians 1:4-6)

5. For you created my inmost being; you knit me together in my mother's womb. (Psalm 139:13)

6. And even the very hairs of your head are all numbered. (Matthew 10:30)

7. But do not forget this one thing, dear friends: With the Lord a day is like a thousand years, and a thousand years are like a day. (2 Peter 3:8)

8. You shall not commit adultery. (Exodus 20:14)

9. Jesus looked at them and said, "With man this is impossible, but not with God; all things are possible with God." (Mark 10:27)

10. The Lord is not slow in keeping his promise, as some understand slowness. He is patient with you not wanting anyone to perish, but everyone to come to repentance. (2 Peter 3:9)

11. I tell you that in the same way there will be more rejoicing in heaven over one sinner who repents than over ninety-nine righteous persons who do not need to repent. (Luke 15:7)

12. The Lord is my shepherd; I shall not want. He maketh me to lie down in green pastures: he leadeth me beside the still waters. He restoreth my soul: he leadeth me in the paths of righteousness for his name's sake. Yea, though I walk through the valley of the shadow of death, I will fear no evil: for thou *art* with me; thy rod and thy staff they comfort me. Thou preparest a table before me in the presence of mine enemies: thou anointest my head with oil; my; cup runneth over. Surely goodness and mercy shall follow me all the days of my life: and I will dwell in the house of the Lord forever. (Psalm 23:1-6 King James Version, Copyright© 1988 Holman Bible Publishers, Nashville, Tennessee 37234 USA)

13. However, do not rejoice that the spirits submit to you, but rejoice that your names are written in heaven. (Luke 10:20)

14. If anyone's name was not found written in the book of life, he was thrown into the lake of fire. (Revelation 20:15)

15. If we confess our sins, he is faithful and just and will forgive us our sins and purify us from all unrighteousness. (1 John 1:9)

16. "For if you forgive men when they sin against you, your heavenly Father will also forgive you. But if you do not forgive men their sins, your Father will not forgive your sins. (Matthew 6:14-15)

17. Husbands, love your wives, just as Christ loved the church and gave himself up for her to make her holy, cleansing her by the

washing with water through the word, and to present her to himself as a radiant church, without stain or wrinkle or any other blemish, but holy and blameless. In this same way, husbands ought to love their wives as their own bodies. He who loves his wife loves himself. (Ephesians 5:25-28)

18. And without faith it is impossible to please God, because anyone who comes to him must believe that he exists and that he rewards those who earnestly seek him. (Hebrews 11:6)

19. For God has not given us a spirit of fear and timidity, but of power, love, and self-discipline. (2 Timothy 1:7 NLT)

20. The fear of the Lord is the beginning of wisdom; all who follow his precepts have good understanding. To him belongs eternal praise. (Psalm 111:10)

21. For the Lord is good and his love endures forever; his faithfulness continues through all generations. (Psalm 100:5)

22. Your word is a lamp to my feet and a light for my path. (Psalm 119:105)

23. Therefore God exalted him to the highest place and gave him the name that is above every name, that at the name of Jesus every knee should bow, in heaven and on earth and under the earth, and every tongue confess that Jesus Christ is Lord, to the glory of God the Father. (Philippians 2:9-11)

24. "Peace I leave with you; my peace I give you. I do not give to you as the world gives. Do not let your hearts be troubled and do not be afraid." (John 14:27)

25. By day the Lord went ahead of them in a pillar of cloud to guide them on their way and by night in a pillar of fire to give them light, so that they could travel by day or night. (Exodus 13:21)

26. When Moses came down from Mount Sinai with the two tables of the Testimony in his hands, he was not aware that his face was radiant because he had spoken with the Lord. (Exodus 34:29)

27. Have you lost your senses? After starting your Christian lives in the Spirit, why are you now trying to become perfect by your own human effort? (Galatians 3:3 NLT)

28. "For God so loved the world that he gave his one and only Son, that whoever believes in him shall not perish but have eternal

life. For God did not send his Son into the world to condemn the world, but to save the world through him." (John 3:16-17)

29. You keep track of all my sorrows. You have collected all my tears in your bottle. You have recorded each one in your book. (Psalm 56:8 NLT)

30. The Lord hears his people when they call to him for help. He rescues them from all their troubles. The Lord is close to the brokenhearted; he rescues those who are crushed in spirit. (Psalm 34:17-18 NLT)

31. "His master replied, Well done, good and faithful servant! You have been faithful with a few things; I will put you in charge of many things. Come and share your master's happiness!" (Matthew 25:21)

32. But the Lord still waits for you to come to him so he can show his love and compassion. For the Lord is a faithful God. Blessed are those who wait for him to help them. (Isaiah 30:18 NLT)

Breinigsville, PA USA
03 November 2009
226945BV00001B/58/P